Message to My Butterfly

By

Gabriela Sbarcea

For Cheryl with love.
...Sbarcea
New York
12/17/2013

Message to My Butterfly

Delizon books and other media products are available at special quantity discounts, for use as premiums and sales promotion, or in corporate training programs. For more information, please send your email to the Director of Sales, sales@delizonpublishers.com, contact your local bookstore or write to our Europe Office:

Delizon Publications,

19 rue des Alliés,

64000 Pau, France

Cover design by

Delizon International Book Publishers

www.delizonpublishers.com

Europe . Africa . North America . Asia

Love is passion, endurance, perseverance and madness.

It knows no boundaries and no humiliation.

Dedication

To Titus Tomescu,
one of the greatest sculptors of all time -
my inspiration to write this novel and
my parents for giving me life.

To D. J. Herda, one of the most brilliant authors
of all time, my editor and guiding light to
making my manuscript publishable,
and seeing this book in print.

Opening Statement

Why do the greatest love stories sculpted in time need to be polished by tragedy? Romeo and Juliet, Tristan and Isolde, Achilles of Troy and Helen, and many others were offered as the sacrificial lambs on the altar of love. Is it human nature or character infused with glory equaling sadism, morphing the most sublime feeling between people into extreme pain to make it worthy of a great legend and veneration of generations to follow?

My questions are rhetorical, I realize that my dear readers. Yet, if the cover of this book, or some rumor about it, somehow compelled you to give it a chance imagine that the humble and stale routine of an everyday existence is closer to heaven and hell than we ever expect. You alone will decide on whether or not to view this story as an example of things never to do, at least not if you want your most tender life sentiments returned. Or perhaps you will find this a maddening love story, a story of acceptance and abandonment, defying all traditional and contemporary laws of courtship. Or perhaps anything else you would like to make of it. I, for one, can only relate it as it happened, the naked truth, painful, glorious and illuminating, standing on its own.

Chapter I
About The Past

Foaming Black Sea waves
And old romantic songs
Seagulls floating high
Defined my rustic home

Wind gusts on wheat fields
Giant sunflower seeds
Wild berries and red grapes
My childhood nourishments

Streets paved with rock
Churches veiled in dust
Fences rotted by rust
Enclosed my mere past

     I was born on and raised along the shores of the Black Sea, in Constanta, Romania. I was blessed, as my parents liked to remind me, from the moment I made an appearance in this world. Their financial position was above the norm for that time and place, and it improved significantly as I grew up. I needed nothing and I could ask for everything from my dad and have it all provided promptly - aside from the motorcycle I pleaded for when I was sixteen. My mother would have no part of that, for safety reasons, she said.

Of course, everything came with a price tag: I was supposed to maintain straight-A grades in school and then go on to college. It seemed at the time a reasonable enough basis for a parents/child relationship.

My parents were hard-working and simple people, deprived of a college education by the politics that plagued Eastern Europe after the Second World War. All they wished for was that their children make it through life more easily than they had, independently, with college degrees and the ability to fend for themselves, all by means of their own hard work and perseverance.

After my first year in the university with a journalism major, I decided to follow my heart and my love at the time. He was a Romanian boy, also born in Constanta. His family had immigrated to Chicago in his teenage years. His rebel personality drove him to run away from home at nineteen and return to where he was born to "find himself." His spirit incited something within me, and we fell in love soon after we met. He was handsome in appearance and quite intelligent, a virtual walking encyclopedia of geography and history.

I felt trapped by my family as a teenager, suffocated by their rudimentary and conventional old-world judgments. I aspired to something greater than their level of prejudice and education. Although my parents were fantastic in seeing to it that I had everything I wanted and needed, I was imprisoned by their narrow ways of thinking.

I was desperate to discover who I was. I found refuge from the pressures of a stagnating mentality and the superficiality of my own generation in reading the classics. I soon adopted the philosophies of Plato, Aristotle, Kant, Schopenhauer, Nietze, Eliade, and Cioran. I questioned things about life and dug for answers around me and within myself. Philosophy became the mental cove where I found a harbor from the tumultuous nervousness of my teenage years. A philosophy major, on the other hand, would hardly ensure my financial independence. Reality conflicted with my avid need for freedom; so, I decided instead to study journalism for all its practicality in terms of finding a job once I was graduated.

My destiny decided to bring along my path this seductive, unique, and bright Romanian boy with an American accent speaking our native tongue better than most of our colleagues in school in my first writing class. My dad had insisted that I take private English classes in high school. He considered it to be the key to my future and sensed it was my passion - I read books in English as I was growing up and practiced for hours writing the words I had heard in American movies with white chalk on our dark green front porch.

So my new love and I dated for seven months and got married despite our parents' objections, more his than mine; mine knew that I would simply overrule their protests, just as I had when I turned eighteen. At that age, an uncontrollable rage boiled through my system. It was the spring of my life ... I yearned to explode out of the protective shell of my childhood. My dad tormented me with a dinnertime routine: "If you don't get accepted into the university, you will end up plowing the fields for a living." When I turned eighteen, I ran away from home to hide in a monastery near Cluj, a city on the other side of the country that housed the most reputable of all Romanian universities. I'll do it, but I'll do it *my* way.

My escape was less than a stunning success. My parents found me within 24 hours and brought me back home with the promise that they would never again try to impose any of their demands upon me. At least I won *that* round!

My new husband and I tied the knot and enjoyed a two-week honeymoon in the beautiful Carpathian mountains before he informed me that his parents needed him suddenly back in the states. I still recall the moment when we said goodbye at the airport. It was Machiavelianly painful. We suffered for three months like dogs, simply like dogs, in the middle of the Arctic with no shelter. My parents constantly infused in me the notion that he would never come back to get me, that it was all a game designed to draw me into social shame and disgrace forever—imagine a newlywed bride whose husband had already left her! His parents secretly hoped we would break up in the process. After all, we were too young to be married.

My husband did come back. He came back to claim his young wife in the fall of that year.

One of the last things my father told me before I took off for the United States that cold September day was, "Once you achieve all your educational goals, you are to return home and pursue a respectable career in Romania. Your roots are where you were born, next to your family."

I nodded my head absently and looked deep into the ground as these last words echoed in through my brain. *Where your roots are.* I uttered my tacit agreement … all I saw was a fog over my future as I wondered if I could ever honor his wish.

My husband and I found our way to Chicago where we enrolled in Loyola University. We took full-time jobs to pay for our own expenses and part of the tuition. Luckily, our good grades earned us scholarships through our first two years, and then the public accounting firm for which we worked sorting mail paid most of our remaining tuition until we were graduated. We functioned as one another's life support system until one day when my husband began to feel the pressure of our new and overwhelmingly committed relationship. He cheated on me two years into our marriage with a Hungarian girl. The pain was excruciating, but I somehow managed to live through it and forgive him. We worked our way through college, helping each other with our

4

assignments, putting in interminable hours of overtime to pay for our escalating expenses.

He had another brief adventure with an Italian girl while in our third year of college. I found some emails between them on his computer. I made a pact with him: if he did it a third time, I would move out pronto, with no questions asked. He seemed to understand that I was serious. We somehow managed to conduct a reasonably normal life for the next two years.

He did it a third time the fall of our graduation year. This time he went off with an Iowa farm raised girl. I couldn't for the life of me see what he found in her that was so attractive. She was plain, had bad teeth, and was all in all nothing like the girls in whom he occasionally had expressed a casual interest. Looking back, perhaps it was the novelty of finding and bedding someone—*anyone*—new. We had been working by then 16-hour days at the same public accounting firm. My schedule left little time to attend to my husband's needs - cooking, cleaning, and of course sex. I became less than a perfect young wife. For that, perhaps, I was to blame.

The third time is the charm, they say. I'd had enough. I could no longer juggle life attempting to be an exemplary young wife with a demanding job and a two-timing husband. Garnished by lengthy fights and unresolved arguments, my marriage became too much to endure: I was a divorcee by the time I reached my mid-twenties.

Defeated. Abandoned. A failure, yet somehow re-lieved. I travelled as often as I could in order to avoid running into him as much as possible. I moved into a small studio in Chicago's near north side and changed jobs to avoid the grueling office gossip. Would these storm winds help me sail in a new direction? Did I no longer belong in Chicago, in America, in life? The solitude growing within me was overbearing. No family around; the two friends I made in between my hectic work and school schedules weren't exactly what I'd call "reliable." It was impossible to give in to my parents' request to return home to Romania without feeling like a complete societal dejection, just as my quest for financial independence was beginning to blossom. Aside from that, I could not fully dismiss my pride.

And my parents - I hardly had the heart to call and tell them about my divorce. I concealed from them as much as I could about my struggles to keep my marriage together. Still, they read between the lines. My mother said to me once over the phone, barely containing her sobbing, that they had visited my grandmother the day before. When my mom revealed the sad news to her, she replied instantly: "Go bring the girl home. How can you leave her there alone, so far from her family?"

My parents knew better than to attempt to follow my grandmother's advice. Though they did not come personally, they sent in a delegate on a scouting mission that winter - my older sisters on a "visit".

Fortunately, my new job kept me living out of my suitcase and I had very little time to spend in my box-like studio. My travels were pure therapy a healing time and, simultaneously, an opportunity to discover the world around me, a big new world that included me, alone, at its center.

That year, I flew between the US, Asia, South America, and Europe so often that I accumulated jet lag just as effortlessly as I collected frequent flyer miles. Not that the numbness was a bad thing. It did help take my mind off my ex and our failed marriage.

My extensive business trips did not take from me the pain and loneliness I carried around within. I found myself crying all alone in fancy hotel rooms and later that evening dining with co-workers in glamorous locations. I took lots of photographs in an attempt to make head or tail of who I was, what I wanted from life, and where I wanted to go from there. I desired no more love; I had had enough of that.

Instead, I needed a safe harbor, a perfect shell offering me peace and security, time to nurture my love for my family, and time to focus on the other aspects of my life. I needed to move on, distance myself from a painful relationship and time to heal and grow past it ... all of it.

And then something extraordinary happened. Four months after my divorce, I met Peter, a Ukrainian who presented himself as the perfect emotionless (and, thus, safe) man. Peter brought all my shuttered pieces together, bound them so well into a new me and gave me the self-confidence that I had lost during my marriage. I found the will to live again and tackle the world once more, one day at a time. I grew closer to Peter and slowly came to trust again. Did we have a future together? As frightening a thought as that was to me when he proposed four years later, somehow it seemed right. He kneeled in front of me in Paris, on a bridge close to the Eiffel Tower, and slipped that magnificent engagement ring onto my finger. His confidence in us, in our future together, was contagious.

We set a date for the ceremony. The closer the day came, the happier I grew. I took great pleasure in the wedding planning process, finding a reception place and the perfect dress. The day of our wedding approached. I found myself questioning why I was rushing into a permanent relationship. It was all so contradictory to logic. It made no sense at all. Something was awfully wrong. I couldn't put my finger on it, yet it was obvious. Even my friends to whom I confessed my conflicting feelings could make no more sense of it than I could myself. I began to wonder why life suddenly become so fluid.

It dawned on me - there was no one reason, there was no one answer. There was a whole barrage of reasons.

I had felt cozy and secure with our connection, so much so that I lost any trace of creativity infusing my mind and senses before Peter. With him, I developed a different kind of love, the one you grow into because the person is exceptionally good to you in numerous ways.

Yet, our relationship lacked the level of insane and intoxicating passion, adoration, and abandon I needed to feel every second of my existence—vibrant, transcendental, and ethereal. I wasn't too keen to learn Ukrainian. I despised his kind yet backward family, his reluctance to move to Romania or even Western Europe until we retired, his overconfidence bordering on cockiness in knowing that I would be there for him no matter what. Our blind, unquestioning trust in one another lead to him taking me for granted.

Most of all, though, the thing that concerned me most was Peter's steadfast refusal to move back to Europe. I planned on returning to my native land, where I belong. I argued the point with Peter after only a week of dating, and a couple of times after that. In between his tears, I agreed to back off, allow some time to pass, and see how things developed.

We set a date for our wedding and I tackled the subject again. We went round and round for the next six months. All I was able to secure from him was a promise to return to Europe once we retired, whenever that might be. My heart sank within me at the thought. I became sadder by the moment. My home, my family, all I had loved and left behind, would eventually grow old and cold, and my sisters would grow farther away and more foreign to me with the passage of time.

All these things weighed upon my mind as our wedding day approached. Something else struck me. Why was I *really* getting married to this man? Was I that desperate to be coupled with someone and fit into the "normal" pattern tailored by society, friends, and family, to overlook all of the things that aggravated me about my fiancé, choosing instead to concentrate on those few good qualities he possessed?

8

Was I that insecure, that needy? There wasn't enough of a bond between us to make a second marriage work.

One crucial element, only one missing: a man to make my heart tremor with excitement every time he looked at me, as much for the rest of our lives as the first time we met. There must be someone out there who could do that for me, I rationalized. Despite all my disappointments and a failed first marriage, there must be *someone.* David Thoreau's principle echoed in my head - there had to be more to life than what I had been inoculated to believe, even for a woman raised in a strictly traditional Eastern European environment: "Go confidently in the direction of your dreams. Live the life you have imagined."

No. This marriage was not to be. It *could* not be. Once I reached that conclusion, I quickly reached another. I had to take some time off from dating. Two bad relationships. Eleven years of my life gone. I was not willing to make the same mistake a third time. I simply couldn't. I couldn't stand the pain.

Chapter II
New Year's Eve

My mind shall never part with you
It's trapped by our first gaze at one another
The year was new ... the beginning of our own eternity

We embraced each other
When millions of miles of seconds stood between us
Our lips met apart
As we roamed through different worlds

Our palms clenched in the fist of passion
While you walked in sunrise and I in sunset
Days beneath our toes cemented our love in time

All that was old, was washed away
It was the birth of our happiness
The absolute imperative of life for one another

On New Year's Eve 2009, I expected another cold and eventless evening to play out its role in my mundane life as an accountant/financial advisor/auditor. Still plagued by the recent breakup with my Ukrainian fiancée. November and December spent in agony, mainly alone, grieving over a breakup ultimately in both sides' best interests. That, however, did not lessen the guilt of destroying a young man's life so much as veering my life's course onto a path to the unknown simply in order to follow my dreams.

My friend, Olivia, insisted I not spend New Year's alone. Her friend, Radu, invited us to a house party at the last moment. A cover-charge affair thrown by a Romanian man ... hmm, slightly unusual. Quite a few other Romanian people were there. Since I was eager to get more involved in Romanian circles here in the States, it sounded perfect. While mingling with the Ukrainian community for four long years, I missed my home, my culture, and all that was good and bad about it. I was part of the American-Slavic lifestyle resembling old communist Russia, unpolished and un-evolved beyond World War II, for far longer than I could bear.

It is a common mistake for Romanians to be thrown into the same pot with the rest of the Russian-based eastern European cultures. Although Romania is surrounded by Slavic states, its origins are largely Latin since it was a part of the Roman Empire that left its significant footprint not only on the Romanian language but also on its overall culture, people, and mentality. My upbringing and education emphasized the French, Italian, English, and Germanic languages over the Slavic ones until Slavic words sounded harsh to my ears. As harsh as the Slavic customs and traditions seem in the modern western world.

None of this entered into my decision to ring in the New Year at the home of some perfect stranger, of course, except that I was pretty sure I didn't want to spend another night partying with still more old-world Soviet transplants and all those stuffy socialists. That might have meant the possibility of running into my ex-fiancée and his compatriot friends and possibly joining them skiing in Galena, up in northern Illinois. I often wondered why he had been so reluctant to step outside of his restrictive Ukrainian-Russian circle of friends. He spent over ten years in the states, yet his American-born friends could be counted on one hand.

11

Nevertheless, our relationship was gradually fading into history. I thought it best to allow it to continue along its way.

Another New Year's Eve possibility was to go to a small house party organized by an ex-coworker, Anthony. We'd spent way too many late hours and weekends working and traveling together. At least we were on the company's expense account. Come to think of it, that was scant consolation for our lack of personal time and a life spent in the office and on airplanes.

Yet, not even that possibility piqued my interest so much as Olivia's suggestion - a private Romanian party. This one was the most viable and held the potential for being the easiest to duck out on in case the evening turned out to be a total disaster.

Back then, I was living in Chicago's Lincoln Park area, across from the park, one of the most popular and trendier neighborhoods in the city. For good reason. Those who know Chicago understand; for the others, you must believe me. The vicinity is wild with life, stacked with chic bars and clubs, shops, and restaurants, and saturated with museums. It's conveniently located near the Lincoln Park Zoo, a botanical garden and greenhouse, and the sprawling Lake Michigan beachfront. Young families and singles fresh out of college make up a good portion of its demographics. When they climb to the next stage of their lives, most of the Lincoln Park "yappies" migrate to the Chicago suburbs to join the ranks of other more mature and better established Midwesterners.

Suddenly the alarming sound of my new text phone punctured my thoughts. I pulled it out and checked my messages. There was a new one from Olivia.

Olivia - Are you ready, lady? I am about to exit Lake Shore Drive. I'll be by your building in 10 minutes. Be downstairs pronto. We're late as it is. This place is far out in the suburbs.

Olivia had a habit of texting people instead of calling them. In fact many of my friends did. I was not completely opposed to texting. Being somewhat old-fashioned, I still found communicating verbally to be more effective than by typing words onto a screen, especially when it came to social functions. I discouraged my friends from texting me by calling them back whenever they did. Most of them got the hint soon enough. Olivia obviously did not. I called her back and told her I'd be ready when she arrived.

Olivia assigned me the task of printing out directions to our destination. *Might as well save a tree,* I thought, and I emailed them to my blackberry. I was certain we would not lose our way since most of the itinerary consisted of driving along Irving Park Road, a main east-west thoroughfare running parallel to Lake Shore Drive. My blackberry ran out of battery while we were deeply immersed in a long and complex conversation about our love lives. We missed our exit and ended up on the south side of Chicago, the exact opposite of where we were supposed to be.

"Can you believe it?" Olivia said. "We're on the wrong side of town!"

"Serves you right," I told her. "Spend more time watching the signs and less time arguing with me!"

"Charge your blackberry since you didn't print out the directions! Dam, I wish I had a GPS." She laughed out loud. I laughed out loud. What else could we do? Two damsels in distress – utterly lost on the South Side of Chicago with no idea of where to go next or how to get to our destination.

Olivia turned the Beemer around, and we headed the car north. After what seemed an eternity, we finally arrived just shy of eleven, an hour before the big New Year's Eve countdown. Not that either one of us was expecting all that

13

much. We were both pretty dispirited about life in general and men in particular, and our expectations for the party were anything but glowing.

They didn't improve much as we climbed out of the car and hiked up the steps to the large, imposing house looming over us. Parked cars littered the front lawn, crowded in one next to another. A tall, bald man who looked like a bodyguard or a gargoyle from an old French cathedral opened the door. The man smoked like a locomotive, and in between watching him puff, I couldn't help but wonder what kind of homeowner would let a couple dozen tons of hardened steel and rubber chew up his front yard, even in the dead of winter. Come spring, it was going to be quite a mess!

After Quasimodo directed us into the house, I stopped short, frozen in place. People swarmed everywhere, their voices laughing and shouting and babbling incoherently. Somebody shrieked; somebody cheered. Cups of wine decorated the room like ornaments on a Christmas tree. Smoke hung in the air like a giant forest fire. A typically Romanian interior loomed over us, masculine and threatening, like the insides of some old forbidden castle. Someone had thrown together several tables to hold the liquor, ashtrays, and several large platters of assorted food. An unmistakable aura of excitement washed over me. Something extraordinary was going to happen in this very extraordinary place that night; I felt it—something far beyond the mere counting down of the old year melding into the new. I felt it within moments of entering the room, as though I were witnessing the metamorphosis of my own humble existence.

My friend Dan and his girlfriend, Maia, sat at a table close to the entrance, near the lobby fireplace. I stopped by and greeted them, shared the usual cutesy hugs and greetings, and set my purse and vintage fur wrap on one of the nearby chairs. Olivia and I made our way through the crowd to the kitchen, looking for a place to get a drink to help take the edge off. We kept our voices low to avoid being over-heard - half the people there were speaking Romanian and the other half, English, or both. Someone was sure to overhear whatever we said. I was notorious for saying the wrong thing at precisely the wrong time when I should have kept my thoughts safely locked inside my head. I rarely spared anyone my pure and honest opinions on topics that ranged from fashion and art to history, politics, and just about anything else anyone could think of.

We looked around, stopped to sample a few food dishes, and quenched our thirst with our drinks. An incredibly wide array of authentic Romanian dishes loomed before us. There was carnati (smoked sausages), cheese pie (which is not to be confused with cheesecake!), shnitzel (similar to the German version), musaka, cozonac (sweet bread with raisins and nuts), and, of course, sarmale (stuffed cabbage), the most traditional of all Romanian dishes, the mainstay of every Romanian holiday and special event since the begin-ning of time - baptisms, birthdays, weddings, even funerals. Still other delicacies called out: fruits and cheeses, salads, seafood, and a few other goodies I can't even recall. Things that never tasted so good as when someone else prepared them, not because I'm a bad cook or anything like that. After all, a young girl's learning to cook is a critical part of her preparation for marriage, especially in the Old World.

Olivia went straight to the bar and ordered a tequila with cranberry and orange juice. I did the same. She worked as a bartender, and I always trusted her tastes in drinks, although not necessarily in men. We most certainly had different affinities in *that* area.

We took a quick tour of the rest of the house. The liv-ing room looked more like a club than a home. Olivia introduced me to her friend, Sandu, and a couple of other people. Codrin, a pleasant enough middle-aged man, short

15

and stocky, with a cheerful demeanor, came up and introduced himself. I asked him if he knew the host. "Yes, of course, it is Tudor, Tudor Popescu. Would you like to meet him?"

His open enthusiasm stamped a strong impression on me; I just had to know more about this mysterious host.

"In time," I said. "The evening is still young. There's plenty of opportunity for introductions later." I motioned with my head across the room. "This house is fascinating. The décor, the Romanian elements, the people, the atmosphere. They're all so *tantalizing.*"

Codrin smiled. "Oh, I have to introduce you to him then, he is a very, umm..." he paused, as if searching for exactly the right word, "*tantalizing* individual." His eyes sprayed the room before stopping suddenly. "There. Look. There he is, right there, by the curtains, in the living room."

I peeked in the direction of his stubby little finger and sighted the back of a rather short man in his early forties, with dark curly rebel hair, wide black suspenders over a crisp white shirt, and black pants. When he turned around, I noticed that the first three buttons of his shirt were undone, unveiling part of a Titan's chest.

Hmmm, I thought. *What a first impression! I MUST meet him.* The *need,* as if I couldn't possibly wait another minute, another hour. Yet, that might not be proper.

"Great," I told Codrin. "Whenever. Now or later, I'm sure that..."

Before I could finish, the man disappeared into a sea of bodies in search of his host and friend.

I took the time to drink in more of the atmosphere. I was floating somewhere in a fairytale: *Alice in Wonderland?* It all seemed so strange, fabulous, rough, cozy, charged with a surreal energy. It penetrated every particle of my being. As I searched the room for my new acquaintance, my eyes fell upon a collection of Romanian pots, hand-carved wooden spoons, and an antique charcoal iron blended with straws suspended above the kitchen island. Brightly, wildly colored butterflies and insects were pinned to Styrofoam panels on the living room walls, similar to what I had seen as a child in the Grigore Antipa Nature Museum in Bucharest. A sudden wave of nostalgia swept over me, washed me back to Bucharest's Romanian Village Museum, back so many years to my childhood. I was near my grandmother's house in a far-from-civilized world, a little village within the county of Tulcea.

And then someone tittered excitedly near my left ear *...Life calling Adelle, come in please. Can you read me?* echoed in my mind. I was back at the party, back among a set of boar tusks, various travel souvenirs, a sculpture representing a large crucifix of Christ, pictures of family and friends, original drawings and paintings hanging on the walls in no particular pattern or order. Books of all types and subjects, in English, Romanian, and French (as well as a few foreign-language travel dictionaries) sat piled atop one another against the walls and on the tables, sporting a thin layer of dust. Some of the decorations were obviously expensive, possibly priceless, while others held little or no value except, perhaps, to their owner, who undoubtedly viewed them with immeasurable sentimental value.

Symbolism? A personal signature? A clue into who Tudor was and what he stood for?

I looked around for more. A rather large and relatively empty living room had been transformed into a hip, contemporary lounge, with sheer fabric hanging from the ceilings, dancing in the breeze and pulsing to the colored lights. The place was simply the most magnificently disordered assemblage of romantic elements I had ever seen. That bizarre world of Alice's Wonderland absolutely intoxicated me. This man's sophisticated and complex mind, his charismatic character, and his unbending personality had helped create a whimsical, charming, fabulous, fun material universe all unto itself.

Suddenly, I fell into a trance as I fantasized about the man responsible for that magnetic disarray of things as if high on some mysterious drug, unknown yet to humankind. There was no hope - I adored him even before I'd met him. His persona was overpowering, greater than anything I'd ever known before. It was all over that house - him, single, bachelor, as evident as a mountain rising from the middle of the ocean. It was clear by looking around: No woman had ever been allowed into his life long enough to add a gentile feminine touch to *this* décor. The house was Tudor, pure and elegant, breathing through the walls and through every object, randomly drawn together into a beautifully ordered chaos. I was in love with it and with the man who had skillfully pieced it all together. Could that be? No, it couldn't possibly. I felt suddenly feared that when I woke up, all of this would be nothing more than another one of my castles in the air. Was this man real, or was he only a character in a novel by Eliade or Cioran, one I must have read once in my teenage years and now, triggered by this fantastic place, slowly transformed its fantasy world into reality? An average existence, mediocrity, was not enough to satisfy me. I needed more out of life. Half-measures were far worse than no measures at all. Tudor's home had awakened within me a desire to learn more, to explore, to discover what kind of man stood behind the creation of such a spectacular domicile.

Olivia and one of her friends appeared at my side and began making small talk. I tried not to seem bored and actually focused on the conversation for a couple of minutes. When I heard Codrin's voice behind me, I leapt for joy. It was about time I met the man I'd been trying to imagine since I had walked into that house.

He grabbed me by my right arm and said, "I would

like to introduce Tudor to you." I turned around with my drink in my left hand and faced the man of my fantasies. There he stood. He was average-looking and rather shorter than I had originally thought. But as soon as my eyes met his, fell on them for but a fraction of a second, I was terrified. I turned away. It was that or fall into his aura permanently, forever. I *had* to turn away, and I searched frantically for Oliva and her friend or anyone to come to my rescue, to say something to me, to distract me from him. If only for a second or two while I composed myself. But it was too late. Codrin continued. "Tudor this is Adelle; Adelle this is Tudor and his girlfriend, Cristina."

His girlfriend?

I turned back to face him, gathered myself together, and replied, "Good evening! What a pleasure it is to meet you."

He bowed his head graciously.

"And I'd like to thank you," I continued, "for this wonderful party. It's absolutely perfect, so many people from home. Just amazing!"

Ouch! I thought. Had I overdone it? That last comment seemed a bit strained. Would he think me peasant-like, some silly little girl just off the boat from some small village in Romania who'd never seen anything of the sort before? *Damn! What a ninny!*

To my surprise, he said simply, "Sure, my pleasure."

No doubt about it. I was definitely over-thinking things.

"I know what," Codrin said. "Let's take a picture for the record," and I was relieved because my mind had gone completely blank, and if I'd had to mastermind another remark to keep the conversation going, I would have died, as simple as that. I was beyond the use of mere words.

I made my excuses and turned back toward the crowd to find Olivia, tactfully, I'd hoped. But my heart was pounding, and I couldn't explain why. After all, I was still trying to settle my feelings for my ex-fiancé, and Tudor already had a girlfriend. I was batting 0 for 2 with two men out in the bottom of the ninth. What was I thinking?

I fought as hard as I could not to get too close to him, nor to let him get too close to me. I isolated myself in the far right corner of the living room where the dance floor and DJ were busy entertaining the guests with lively Romanian, Western European, and American tunes, both old and new, music blended skillfully to entertain a variety of ages and accommodate everyone there. And then suddenly I saw Tudor dancing in a circle of friends quite near me. I tried desperately to squelch the rush of emotions. Was he dancing so close to attract my attention? Had he chosen to do so to entice me to join in?

My purse suddenly vibrated and a tingling noise came falling out. *A message!* I had forgotten all about my phone! I collected myself and pulled the blackberry out of my evening purse. The "brick" took up more than half the space, leaving just enough for a tube of lipstick. I checked my new text message.

Mihaela - Happy early New Year!!!! Good fortune and good health! I know it's not quite midnight in Chicago yet, but I wanted to make sure you got this before the clock chimes in the New Year. We miss you so, so much; we love you and we wish you were here, with us, home. Mom and dad are already asleep, but they asked me to send you their greetings.

My eyes glazed over. My middle sister, Mihaela, had visited me not long ago. She spoke and wrote perfect English.

I quickly texted her back.

Adelle - Happy New Year to all of you! I know I am eight hours late, but the lines were busy when I tried calling earlier. Oh ... Mitziii ... you have no idea how much I wish I were home now! Kiss mom and dad and, certainly, Vio! I will call home in the morning. I'm at a party now.

My hands were shaking and tears pooled in the corners of my eyes as I typed. *I'm OK, I'm OK, I'm OK!* If only I could split myself in two! A massive crack was forming in my heart, growing larger by the minute, dividing who I was from who I was to become. Where I was from where I wanted to be in life.

Another message popped on my screen as I pressed the button to send my reply. I suddenly felt like the most popular girl of the year.

Peter - Hey, love! I've been trying to call you. It's midnight! HAPPY NEW YEAR! *Znovom Rocum*, as they say in your future language! All your Ukkie friends here say hi. How is the Romanian party?

Texting. *Wow!* I was overwhelmed. My thumbs flew around the keyboard.

Adelle - Fabulous. Thank you. Happy New Year to you too, and say hello to everyone. I'll talk to you when you're back in town. There's too much noise here. I can't call you right now.

Noise there was, that was a fact. Was there enough of it for me not to be able to call back the man whom I was supposed to marry by the end of February? The man whose engagement ring I hadn't been able to return yet because he refused to accept it? That... I wasn't so sure of. But he certainly seemed to be sure of the idea that Ukrainian was

21

still my "future language" for some reason!

I needed another drink.

I made my way through the kitchen and up to the bar. Olivia was nowhere to be found. A picture on the wall with Tudor on a boat holding two giant fish, one in each hand, caught my eye for a few moments. *Hmmm...the man likes to fish, and not for just anything.*

When I turned my head to walk away, I saw him standing in the corner of the kitchen, close to the bar, surrounded by a group of friends, his girlfriend hanging on his arm like a charm on a bracelet. I found myself captured by his bewitching stare. *He is fast, I must admit! He was dancing only a minute ago.* I wondered if my expression had betrayed my thoughts.

I considered the idea of turning around and walking back out, but I didn't. I told myself I wanted another tequila and orange with cranberry juice, but I wasn't sure *what* I wanted until Tudor turned toward me, and our eyes connected yet again. Every atom in my body exploded. My skin tingled, my hair ached. He stared back at me from across the room, surrounded by strangers, at the arm of the Romanian girl he appeared so detached from, and in this house where I felt more at ease than in any other place I'd ever been in the eleven years I'd been away from home. *Oh, why? Why can't I just run away???*

I turned my back to him and tried to re-channel my thoughts toward my ex-fiancée, from whom I seemed to be drifting further apart by the second. There was blankness within me for him, nothingness...no sorrow, no pity, no remorse, no hate, no love, not even affection. It had all become as intangible as the air between us in the last months while we struggled to keep our relationship together. Our last arguments before he'd left for his skiing trip dried any trace of fluid that might have nourished us. I'd left my Tiffany's engagement ring in its blue box on my nightstand that evening. What we had was dead with no chance of rebirth. It was time for a new chapter in my life, with all the novelty life brings.

I breathed in deeply. Tudor's home was a place of wonder, majesty, awe, framed by a novel, surreal, ethereal air.

I directed my sight to the abnormally large birdcage in the foyer: was I so fascinated by it because it contained what my life would have been had I married Peter? Or was it just a perspective of what my future held in relationship to Tudor?

I shook away my thoughts as a strange, tall, mediocre looking man, a typical Romanian, came up and asked me to dance. I wasn't in the mood to dance, and I certainly wasn't anxious for more house-party chit-chat, so I respectfully declined when Tudor walked suddenly by, pausing just long enough to stare into my eyes for what seemed an eternity. We were both hopelessly attracted to one another. That was clear.

My past was irrelevant all of a sudden, and my future was something I wanted to explore to its darkest corners and its deepest core. The quest for substance bubbled within me, and I was ready to explore every nook and cranny.

I peeled myself off from the awkward situation with the stranger and began searching for Olivia. It was time to leave. I was overwhelmed, and I wasn't sure what to do next.

I checked the clock and was surprised to find it was after three. The tension between Tudor and I mounted by the second. A second longer in that place, I'd lose control.

I found Olivia and convinced her it was time to leave. We grabbed our coats, and we started for the door. Tudor spied us and worked his way to my side. His eyes once again pinned me to the spot, stared through me, my legs beginning to quiver. Then, just as suddenly as he had come, he turned and drifted off, his hands in his pockets, his head held high. That look! My God! Would I ever be able to rid myself of this sudden need I felt to be his? To revel in the feelings he brought to me, deep down within my soul?

We met Codrin by the door as we were leaving, and he held it open for us.

"I hope you had a good time," he said.

"We had a great time," Olivia replied.

"It was really nice," I said, my eyes trailing off for one more look at the man who had somehow, in some small way, managed to steal my heart in a sudden stroke of lightning. "Thanks so much for your hospitality. And please thank Tudor."

He was going to talk to Tudor about getting together for a cup of coffee sometime, but my mind was whirring and I heard only small bits and pieces. I remembered giving him my telephone number earlier. I was sure he would call within the next few days.

As for Tudor...well, only time would tell. The catalyst for the change I had willed for myself had been set in motion. Now, only time would tell.

Chapter III
Facebook

Beyond the realm of reason
Emotions constructed chaos
Just like an abstract painting
Splashes of colors on a blank canvas

Patterns ... there were none
Red round drops next to green and blue shapes
There was no need for order
To compose the superlative beauty of love

After many months of persuasion, a friend finally convinced me to open an account on Facebook, a social media Website that had gained world-wide popularity overnight. Facebook was created by a college kid who became one of the youngest self-made millionaires in history. Soon enough I started spending way more time than I should have on the site; it was truly enticing. It was addictive, a delightful contemporary evil, altering social interaction radically forever. It spread like a highly contagious disease, a waste of time taking over busy lives in the era of advanced technology and reduced human contact.

Although I was sure I wouldn't find Tudor on the site, I decided to search for him just the same. And guess what? I found his name and profile just like that. The picture didn't look at all like him, but I sent him a "friend" request anyway. If it wasn't him, I figured he'd ignore it. A couple hours later, he posted a message on my wall: "It was so nice meeting you. I asked Codrin if we could all go for coffee this weekend. I hope you can make it..."

He liked me, after all, and wanted to see me again. I wondered if he wanted to see me as much as I wanted to see him. Silly schoolgirl meanderings. I had to be cautious - many of my friends on Facebook hadn't heard of my split with my fiancée, and somebody posting messages on my wall could raise the risk of soiling my reputation. I wasn't prepared to face *that* just yet.

I was tempted to respond to Tudor's post with a post of my own on *his* wall. A red flag to signal the world how taken I was with him? Instead I sent him a private message. He was Romanian, and because I wasn't sure when he came here or whether or not he was born here, I thought it was safe to message him in English. My command of Romanian deteriorated over the past few years, and although I still spoke English with a Romanian accent, I was determined to adopt my new language and culture as quickly as possible. I mean, when in Rome, do as the Romans do, right?

Tudor responded to my message in English, and I was grateful. The chain of messages between us, two minds bound instantly by an unknown, unseen force, are humbly recorded in the epistle below, allowed to speak for themselves.

January 2, 2009

Adelle - Sure, would love to go for coffee - only that I live in Lincoln Park and don't quite drive, so when you are in the city, give me a buzz.

Tudor - Lincoln Park? Even better. Where about? I will call you over the weekend.

You are amazing, I hope you know that. My date sensed you as a threat instantly and I was smitten with you in the same amount of time... Look forward to seeing you again!

Adelle - Now, now ... you are making me blush. I just thought you are a fascinating character just by looking at the pictures and things on your walls. I did a fair amount of travel around the world myself. I hope I did not create any problems; I had no intention of the sort. My deepest apologies for that.

I live at Armitage and Clark.

Kind regards,

P.S. Also thought you are intriguing and remarkable at the same time.

January 3, 2009

Tudor - Thank you, you are flattering. Coming from you it's equally so. You exude distinction and magnetism beyond words. You didn't create any trouble, nothing that I wouldn't welcome, that is. You have a look in your eyes that's irresistible. I just couldn't pry myself away from it. I'm sorry if I seemed persistent.

Armitage and Clark? That's a great neighborhood. Maybe we can meet a bit west of there, at Cafe Morena, on Halsted. Let me know when is a good day for you.

I'm glad you came to the party... really glad! Here's my number as well. Just let me know when you're free and I'll make the time.

XO

January 4, 2009

Adelle - I see that some of our first impressions are mutual.

I've been living by the lake ever since I came here, eleven years ago, and Lincoln Park is like my home now ... well, I should say my home away from home. The lake reminds me of the Black Sea. I grew up practically on its shore and when I miss it, I spend time on the balcony, I go for a run or get on a plane and go home.

Codrin called yesterday, briefly, and mentioned the three of us could meet for coffee today around one. I am not sure what happened, but since it is passed one, I suppose this may not work today as I have early dinner plans.

I will ring you next week, maybe we can do dinner at Cafe Morena sometime during the week or next weekend.

Kind regards,

A

Tudor - I heard you grew up in Eforie Sud. Nice. I used to spend summers there as a kid. I like the sea as well. I love Miami, or Cozumel. I enjoy snorkeling and scuba diving. Do you?

I'm sorry lunch plans didn't work out today. Actually, I'm feeling a bit weird myself. I just split up with Cristina, the girl I was with at the party. She stormed out of my house, because she was under the impression that I didn't post enough pictures of her and I on this site. She was right. Maybe, subconsciously, I didn't. Maybe, as charming as she is, we don't have enough in common to make it last. Perhaps it was genuine jealousy, who's to say? Maybe my paranoia about the fact that her interest in me is solely based on getting her papers in this country has a lot to do with it ... a lot of maybes, too many...

Yes, let me know when you have time for a coffee. Let me recover from this rebound. It's weird, when you're in a relationship, even though the feeling on both sides is that it's headed for a dead end, you still suffer when it's over. The attachment, I guess....

Enjoy your day!

Adelle - Hmm ... I haven't ventured out yet to scuba or snorkel ... great fear of sharks. Miami was like my second home for a couple of years when I travelled there for work and fun so I would say that it is great, but I would trade it in for the quiet and white sands of Destin, mainland FL by the Golf, anytime.

I am sorry to hear about Cristina. She seemed to be a nice girl. Relationships are difficult and sometimes no matter how much time and effort you invest in them the "happy ever after" is not guaranteed. As a friend, if you would be a woman, I would recommend watching *Sex and the City* re-runs on TBS every evening ... but I am not quite sure what works for men ... I would say maybe Sartre's novel *The Age of Reason.*

I am going through a long and painful breakup also ... and I am not sure how and when I will make it final. I, officially broke off my year-long engagement to a wonderful Ukrainian man, recently, ... purely for cultural differences and because I wanted to find a way to live both here and home since all of my family is still there and refuse to come here to the states. My parents are the only Romanians I know with green cards who come here only to visit once a year and can't wait to go back home after one week.

For about four years and a half I spent so much time into a world that became more foreign in time than my first instincts perceived it. Since he is a great character and we've had nothing less than a blast together, I was hoping we could work out our differences in time and he would eventually accept my need to be home as much as here, learn some Romanian, etc. His family is here and he is very much attached to it. Yet, we are struggling because we both admit to these differences and at the same time, are bound by some trait of feelings that for now, at least, refuse to die off as easily as we expected. Although we both know this is not going anywhere in the long run and we would both be happier to be with people who are closer or at least neutral to our own cultural backgrounds.

I have some Romanian friends, very few, so one of my own mistakes I recognize is that I haven't been more involved in Romanian circles. This New Year's, your house full of people from home, was the breath of fresh air I needed ... I felt closer to home once again ... not trapped in a world I half dreaded and blocked off for the dear sake of someone I cared about.

In the meantime, my friends have been more of a life support system, especially in the past couple of months ... meeting new people has also been a great deal of help. Every person is like a book ... sometimes being able to read between those lines helps you make sense of your own.

Coffee as friends would be lovely. I hope you feel better soon.

A

Tudor -

Sorry to hear about your situation, as well. I honestly don't know of any truly happy people. If that is the case, then they share some major grief for a common tragedy. God has a sick sense of humor...

I'm glad you felt at home. It is the only group of Romanians I could have had over this New Year's Eve. I know Romanians coming from all walks of life, some high-class intellectuals who rarely associate with the "commoners" and some low-life Romanians whom I've since screened out of my circles of friends. On occasion, people from each group intersect, and then you see them together at my house. I've managed to bring them all together at times, and when the music is on and when the basic instincts of hunger and thirst are quenched, barriers disappear and they all forget who they are for a moment (unless they start talking about religion or politics!). I like to attract people with open minds, people who can make an abstraction of their ethnicity and social status and talk about ideas and ideals beyond our mundane

30

confinements. For that, however, we must have smaller parties.

We go back to Romania as tourists, because no matter how much we'd like to live there, we realize we have evolved at a higher pace here, and while Coca-Cola commercials and everything that the capitalist surface has tempted the world with has been adopted by the mother country expediently, the deeper core that formed this country was misunderstood. America took 200 years to get where it is and Romanians don't understand that. You cannot make a good book analysis if you only look at the cover and read the title page.

But... we'll talk more when I see you. I hope you like coffee...

XOX
Tudor
PS. How did you hear of the party, from who?

I never answered Tudor's last Facebook message. Enough was said to confirm that our feelings for one another were aligned perfectly ...we were already in a mist resembling something beyond simple attraction and didn't know it, or if we did, our rationale rejected it. We were both mature enough to understand that for something of this magnitude to be less than an illusion would be almost irrational. Could it be real? Possibly. Was it likely? Hardly. Yet, we lived every second of it. Every emotion cut through us with the speed of light and the depth of the universe alone.

Chapter IV
Our First Date

We sit in a café across the narrow table
Our sinuous chatter mutes the rest
Your right hand gently holds my left
Our tired eyes wonder away at time.

Words sink into a random pattern
Ideas last a moment on our minds
They rush from one end to the other
Drain through our conversation fast

Tudor and I had each other's phone numbers. Our text messaging turned into frenzy like never before.

January 4, 2009
Tudor - Hi Adelle, I'm now in Wrigleyville. Are you close? Are you free?
Adelle – (A couple of hours later) I am still at dinner and it's getting a little late. Can we meet some other time?
Tudor – Sure.

January 6, 2009
Adelle - Hi! The last few days have been a little crazy – trying to catch up with friends after the holidays is always a little challenging. I, again, have plans for the rest of the week after work, but this evening opened up. If you'll be

around the area for any reason, I will be home around six, we could catch up. I hope you have a wonderful week.

Tudor – Sure, give me a call. I have to be around Foster and Lincoln around four.

Adelle – I should be home no later than five thirty or six. I'll send you a text when I get home.

Tudor – OK

Tudor – (Later that afternoon) I may not be able to make it tonight. I'll let you know around five.

Adelle – No problem.

Tudor – (About an hour later) I can't make it today. I forgot I have to do something at five in Schaumburg. I'll never make it back in time. I want to relax around you, not look at my watch.

Adelle - I see … we'll catch up some other time. I noticed your sculpting talent in some of the pictures on Facebook. It's fantastic! I would love to see some of your work one day. We'll be in touch.

Tudor – Thanks. I look forward to the physical semantics of that expression.

The timing was all wrong and I wasn't ready to deal with such a bold, aggressive and incredibly tempting assault from a man I hardly knew. By looking at his Facebook profile I learned that he was twelve years my senior … interesting. He never tried to conceal that fact by hiding his birth year, as most people do on their profiles.

I made a status update on Facebook: "Patience and passion … the sculpture of life. Patience is the medium and passion the substance of it."

Tudor posted a comment on my status: "Yes … patience and passion, I see both in your eyes." He added "I am jealous!" to one of my portrait pictures with my ex-fiancée. I still kept our pictures in my profile. I hadn't yet found the time or motivation to remove them.

I replied privately in a Facebook message.

Adelle - A beautiful-looking sculpture has many flaws. Pictures are no less than that. Thank you, nonetheless. I am humbled by your words.

Tudor - Which words? In connection to what?

Adelle – Pictures.

Tudor - I see. Yes, I have yet to discover your flaws. I will happily explore every inch...

Adelle - *Bonne nuit, monsieur!*

It was late on Saturday, January 10, when we talked on the phone for the first time. His voice was masculine, yet candid and reassuring. My heart raced. We agreed he'd pick me up at seven that evening.

Tudor arrived at my doorsteps at seven sharp. I descended the stairs and leaned down to peek in at the driver. His features were not yet well imprinted in my memory, and his Facebook photos made his image even more confusing. When I glanced at the man in the car, yet a third portrait of him sitting behind the wheel struck me: prematurely aged, tired and stressed out.

I sensed his uneasiness even more stinging than mine. The ball was in my court. Despite my nervousness, I allowed him to choose the place. We drove to Elephant's, a café new to me somewhere far out west of town on Belmont, an obscure area of the city. He talked a lot, rather unusual for a man.

Tudor was a brilliant artist who managed to sell his work and was able to make a small fortune from the talent in his own hands. But his personal finances lacked discipline. He invested most of his capital in real estate and new construction, even though the market had been depressed for months. He abandoned his sculpting in order to develop new residential construction. He'd made some bad financial decisions, which only made his overall financial situation

34

worse. He talked about his finances openly, suggesting perhaps a need for advice since I'd told him I worked in finances. He asked financial questions I refrained from answering knowing I couldn't possibly be of much help without diving into his situation deeper. My accountant's natural skepticism held me back, even though he sounded sincere. But what if he weren't? What if he were merely posing these questions to test my level of professionalism or my empathy with him?

We finally parked. He got out first, opened my door, and took me by the hand, guiding me around several puddles of slushy brown snow. We walked up to the café, and he opened the door to a heavily Eastern European atmosphere, a place I was sure that most recently immigrated Romanians would find perfectly homelike and comfortable. A few people smoked, even though smoking in public had been banned for years.

As we walked in, I felt a million night-creature eyes turned toward us as if we had been in the deepest woods. I felt a bit uncomfortable, as if the center of all attention, so I asked Tudor if we could take a table upstairs. Before long, the eyes had all but turned away and the waitress arrived to take our order. She was young, most likely Romanian, and she greeted Tudor as you would an old customer. Yet this girl did it with a pleasant, slightly inappropriate welcome smile and insecure voice. The girl looked straight into his eyes, fidgeting awkwardly with her pad as she took our drinks order. He returned her smile - his mouth upturned at the corner as if the two shared an inside joke or story. He chuckled without even realizing it when he pulled his eyes from the girl's and directed them toward the table, avoiding my curious gaze. Why ask questions that yield potentially hurtful answers? I hardly knew the man. His past was his business and I had no right to impose my curiosity where it wouldn't be welcomed. Who doesn't have a past, anyway?

And then he surrendered to my curiosity.

"That was Joanna, an ex of mine. We dated for a couple of weeks, but it didn't work out in the end. She is too young and I lost interest in her rather quickly. Our conversations were limited to cartoons and … and I think that was about it. She is also here illegally, looking for someone to marry for her papers."

I frowned, unsure of whether or not to offer a comment. Finally, I said, "I understand. Unfortunately that's the case with many people who come here illegally, Romanian or not. A sad fact"

Hmmm … ex Number Two was after him for papers. I was fortunate enough not to have had to deal with such a situation myself, although I wondered if I could do what she was doing, what so many other illegals had done. People can gain legal status through less drastic means, such as work visas and true-love marriages, however, too many have to resort to fake marriages. A single Romanian man, a US citizen since teenage years, was probably an easy target for these women.

Tudor and I put that aside, and we went on to chat for hours, each of us absorbed into our own space with four invisible walls around us. Everyone else suddenly disappeared. We were alone, together, in a newfound world, ours alone.

I laid both my hands on the table and he suddenly and quite gently took my left hand into his own and began reading my palm. He said I was going to marry for love and have two kids, one of them a boy. Tudor's touch raised a storm of emotions within me. I sensed his power over me from the very start. He was omnipotent, invincible—or so he seemed. He awakened senses within me long since dead. Butterflies exploded in my stomach … my flesh pounded to the rhythm of my heart. My cheeks and ears turned red, smoldering to the point of embarrassment. Tudor's hands shivered. Was it nervousness, insecurity, excitement ... or all three? His hands trembled and his body quivered. The waves of his emotions were even greater than mine.

Deep into our conversation, he extended his left arm across the narrow table, his strong hand reaching behind my hair and drawing my head near his. Our eyes locked. His lips touched mine in our first soft kiss. They opened and closed again as though gasping for air. His touch was warm and reassuring, strong, yet incredibly sensual. He held me prisoner by the back of my neck while he hungrily explored my mouth, conquering me as a general might conquer the vanquished in the greatest war ever fought. The feeling— exquisite, unforgettable—was carved into my mind forever, just as surely as the greatest sculpture ever made. I was powerless in his hold and abandoned to his arms every single barrier I had built for myself in preparation for our first meeting. I surrendered to his divine power right then and there without ever once stopping to question it.

Later that night Tudor sent me a text as soon as he got back to his car: "You are simply mind-blowing."

On Sunday morning I awoke with my head spinning, still thinking about the events of the night before. They seemed as if in a dream. My heart beat faster and the adrenaline rushed through me at the mere memory of what had transpired. Tudor. Whoever would have imagined! Suddenly nothing else seemed to matter. Nothing else seemed necessary. Was I complete?

I received a message from him later that morning: "Do you want to go out or stay in and have sex for the rest of the day?"

As tempting as the thought was, I wanted a real first date. The past evening hadn't quite qualified. It all happened so fast. I needed to know if my feelings—*our* feelings—were real. I needed to know that they were based upon something more substantial than infatuation - a schoolgirl crush on the man of her dreams. Was it the mystery, the splendor and insanity of it all that swept me away so quickly? Or was he really a force so much larger than he and I together, larger than the universe itself?

I suggested we go to The Art Institute. Judging by his Facebook pictures, he sculpted in a manner similar to that of the great Renaissance artists. I craved his thoughts on the museum's masterpieces.

He picked me up around three on Sunday afternoon. He was quite chivalrous, opening the car door for me and even bowing his head slightly as he closed the door behind me. We, European women, live for that kind of good old manners.

The thick grey clouds of a typical Chicago winter afternoon hung low on the horizon. A light dusting of snow settled against the windshield was cold; my red coat was too thin to stand up against the merciless January winds blowing in from the North. I shivered and my hands sunk deep into my coat pockets. I guessed it was from the cold, but who could tell? Tudor turned to me gently, smiling. It was the same smile he found looking back at him. It was a smile that said we found one another. And we were happy.

The Art Institute was fairly busy that day. Those mournful winter Sundays don't allow many options for Chicagoans looking to escape the monotony of television and life at home; so, they jump in their cars and head for the city and lake shore's attractions like lemmings to the sea. For the Art Institute, the History Museum or the Museum of Science and Industry or the Adler Planetarium, the theater, the opera, the ballet, the Chicago symphony —anywhere to forget the everyday routine of their lives.

I took hold of Tudor's hand, and as we breezed through the drawing gallery, he explained how a sculptor first sketches his concept in the initial phase of preparing for his work. He spoke quite naturally of the lines, shadows and subjects within the drawings and told me a little about the various popular artistic movements throughout the history of art. I asked him what his favorite subject was to sculpt. He looked at me matter-of-factly. "Why, the human body, of course."

He led me like an art instructor through the strokes of the greatest artists: Renoir, Degas, Monet. He seemed to come to life as he spoke. It was obvious that he loved art more than anything else in his life. Well, I hoped, not *anything* else.

When we entered the Renaissance exhibit, Tudor absolutely glowed. The energy emanating from him explained why he sculpted the way he did. He blended remarkably with that world. His vast knowledge of the era, along with his manner and attention to the smallest of details, seemed to fit in with the greatest masterpieces of all times. When we finally made our way through that gallery, I felt as though I had finally seen the Art Institute for the very first time. I had been there dozens of times in the past. Never before, though, on the arm of someone so knowledgeable and steeped in the very art of life. The paintings I had seen a hundred times before I was seeing for the very first time— and the drawings and sculptures, as well.

Leonardo Da Vinci walked me through the Renaissance, bringing to life paintings, drawings, and sculptures hundreds of years old as Tudor explained them to me. Their complexity of shape, shade, color and depth of detail seemed so natural when described by his carefully chosen words. The sophisticated artistic concepts Tudor eloquently expressed echoed in my mind for days, weeks and months, and each time they revealed to me an entirely new aspect of life. The galleries were his home.

We stopped by the stairwell only long enough to kiss lightly, lovingly, longingly, before retrieving our coats from the cloakroom. Outside, the gloom had turned to darkness, and a million twinkling city lights turned the night into day before our very eyes.

"What do you have a taste for?" Tudor asked. His question came like a splash of cold water awakening me from a dream. I felt no more hunger and thirst; my brain functions and senses had been intoxicated by our last hours together. Was he asking to what solar system I wanted him to take me to continue our voyage to infinity?

"Why is there need for nutrition when there is art?" I replied.

Tudor's look made me burst into laughter.

"Ah ... you see ... aside from our brains and imagination, our bodies need food and water as well," he finally replied. "In fact, judging by the looks of you, a giant burger and some fries would do you well. Do you fancy eating once in a while, or simply feed off of air and water? You can't possibly weigh more than a hundred pounds with winter clothes on."

"Yes ... fine ... I am an easy target for underweight jokes. But I do eat, I promise you. And just to prove it, you can take me across the street. I hear there's a great place called Tenton's that has fantastic burgers. I'll let you buy me one. But for demonstration purposes only!"

"Very well then ... shall we? You'd better eat the whole thing, though, or else you may end up walking home." He smiled. And all throughout dinner, I ached to see Tudor's home again. Would I find it so completely captivating as I had the first time I saw it? I wondered. I wondered, too, about the works I'd seen in the photographs when I Googled his name. There were pictures of works he had sold, sketches of some planned projects and a crucifix that was part of a limited edition series he had up for sale. They were all I could think about—those and the absolutely marvelous collection of porcelain dolls he was renowned for, reflections of a sweet, playful and innocent side of his character.

The sculpture featured on his webpage was a hollow terracotta man struggling to undress his skin and reveal his true self. That one work alone forced my mind to compress, contract, and expand at the same time, all the while challenging me for the meaning of life - naked, exposed, painful, and extraordinary all at the same time. It signified what I was looking for in myself, the very core of my beliefs; a self-scrubbed symbol of the impurities of existence and routine which appeared to protect it, when in fact it constructed a crust between its purity and the mask it wears, shaped by time and shaded by life's experiences. It moved me more than any other sculpture I had ever seen. What was in his mind when he created it?

We drove back to Tudor's home after dinner. He parked the car in the garage and, as if on cue, and opened the door for me. Before I knew it, we were locked in one another's arms again. We stumbled through the kitchen and the living room, kissing, squeezing, fondling one another before we finally managed to find our way to his master bedroom.

"Where are the lights," I asked as he nibbled on my lower lip.

"They're not necessary," he replied. "I can see all I need in the radiance of your eyes."

He was right. We didn't need lights. The heat of our bodies designed an unmistakable map of all we wanted to know. We were in each other's arms.

Tudor transported me back in time, back to the golden era of the mid-1800s. His confident and yet meticulously sensual touch was the same one I had envisaged growing up in Romania, reading my beloved classical literature and watching those magnificent old period films.

Tudor was out of our world. Who was he? Were he and his corky, amusing, unusual home real? Or were they simply a product of my own fantasies? I feared I might have disconnected with reality completely. What if one day I hit the pavement of reality too hard and it all turned out to be a fluke?

He intimidated me.

He enticed me.

He inured me.

I *had* to have more.

"What are you thinking about?" he asked as he stepped into his trousers and pulled his shirt up around his shoulders. I let out a short giggle. I pulled myself up to my elbows and lay across the bed mere inches from his touch. "What is it?" he asked again, his own smile radiant.

"I was thinking about how wonderful I feel."

He paused, slipped his arms into his sleeves, and began fastening the buttons down the front. "You *should* feel wonderful," he said. "You deserve to feel wonderful. You deserve to feel everything that is good and beautiful in life."

I crawled out of bed, nuzzled up to him, and looked into his eyes. They were smiling eyes, strong and confident. I wondered where he had acquired such strength, such power.

"May I see your studio?"

He paused, and for a brief moment I thought I had stepped beyond some rigid, unseen line. Had I violated his artistic integrity? Broken with protocol?

"Of course," he said finally. "I don't ever want to keep *anything* from you."

He handed me my skirt and bra and set my stockings on the edge of the bed next to my sweater, and he disappeared into the bathroom.

42

Gabriela Sbarcea

His studio was on our way out of the house, in a back room just behind the garage. It was small, smaller than I had imagined, a place filled with sculptures and unfinished projects, including a nearly life-sized figure of Demi Moore and, of course, the hollow man undressing from his skin. In my wildest imagination I never thought I would find myself in the studio of an illustrious artist just after we made love. I floated on beatitude, and at my side stood GOD.

"These are fantastic," I said, marveling at his creations.

I had an inexplicable desire to be one of them, one of his works, to be molded by his fingers, to be shaped by his hands. If I could only be a simple ball of clay he would pick out of a large mass of viscous material and warm in his palms for a few moments before placing me on his work table to imprint his ideas within me, to create a sculpture to inspire each human being to achieve happiness in his own way!

I wanted to get close to the sculptures, to be one of them and understand the mind that molded their shapes, the feelings - his heart. I could spend countless hours contemplating their lines, following them beyond the physical realm. My imagination became a river with no beginning and no end. Their smooth, rushed, sudden curves and turns transformed chaos into order, an implied order, one hidden from the common eye.

"Adelle ... Adelle, hey? Are you listening?" His words brought me back down to earth.

"Oh, yes. I am sorry. It's getting late. You should take me home. I think I was born dreaming and when I wake up once in a while the cold reality sets in ... figuratively, but in actuality as well. I wonder if it's snowing out yet. It was below zero when we got here. It can't be that much colder now, can it?"

"No worries." Tudor whispered as he clasped my left hand tenderly and pulled me in his comforting embrace. "I'll make sure you are always warm."

I leaned my head on his right shoulder and closed my eyes. *My God! Where am I and who is this man? Is he purely an angel, or is he the evil fallen angel?* I thought to myself.

He took me home that evening and we hardly ever spoke on the phone after that. Before him, I doubt that I had sent eight or ten text messages all year. After, all of that changed. I became a text-aholic. Compulsory texting to one another … as if good old telephone conversations had gone out with the horse and buggy or been outlawed by the phone police and messaging replaced all other forms of communication. Our texts often achieved lengths far beyond their original purpose. It was no longer just a mono-syllabic way of communicating a simple idea quickly, as texts were originally intended. He changed the way I communicated, not only with him, but also with my other friends who could barely believe I had finally dragged myself into the twenty-first century!

I could no longer exist without my phone. It was a chip implanted into my life by the times, by the flow of society I could no longer swim against. Human interaction in relationships had changed so much since I last dated in the real world.

Going back to the safety of the past was no longer an option. The present was disquieting and the future, more compelling than frightening. I was far from being wise; I fought my way through my first year of my thirties, had definitely abandoned my twenties and had no desire yet to compromise what my future would bring pressured by expectations for a woman my age in a modern, yet still heavily conservative American society.

Most of the women with whom I worked in finance and accounting were married, with a kid on the way, if not a second, a considerably large engagement ring on their fingers, riding the CTA buss or Metra trains to their downtown Chicago offices. They all pursued a "stable" future life, that same notion that made my skin crawl. That wasn't me. That wasn't what I was all about, not yet anyway. I had a life to live, an adventure to experience, risks to take ... my sails were ready to go open, regardless of the strength of the wind or lack thereof: they would open. I wasn't like other women my age. I wanted my own future, my own sculpture, my own destiny, sublime in its entirety, whatever it would bring. That way of thinking was the very essence of my beginnings in life.

Why fear what we do not know, what we do not understand, what is written for us when it will play out whether we want it to or not?

But was I ready for it?

Chapter V
Come to Me, Now!

My reason left me long ago
The night your eyes dawned life on me
Or was it eternity you gently led me to?
I walked behind you blindfolded
Stepping on newly broken glass

My days in the office were simply dull; my eyes were pointed more and more often at my blackberry set on "silent" out of courtesy to my co-workers. A "new message" light was my only motivation for the day.

That evening, I got off the bus at the Armitage and Stockton station, my mind running through an all-too familiar script of what I was to do later, and here it played out again:

January 12, 2009
Tudor – Wanna go skiing next Sunday? Close here, Devil's Head. For the day only.
Adelle – Sure. I have Monday off to rest. Bank holiday.
Tudor – Cool. Maybe we can even stay overnight.
Adelle – Let's see how the weather is then.
Tudor – OK. Right.
Adelle – It would be lovely if we do though.
Tudor – I know.

January 13, 2009

Tudor – I want to be inside you now!

Adelle - You are breaking my already low level of concentration. My thoughts are drawn with the force of gravity in the same direction.

Tudor – Sorry for the interruption. Carry on. We'll see each other over the weekend.

Adelle – Perfect.

January 14, 2009

Adelle - Come over to Eurocircle on Friday and pretend you hardly know me. I will do the same.

Tudor – Why pretend? Does it turn you on to pretend we're on a perpetual first date?

Adelle – Well … perhaps … it would be exciting. Never mind if the idea is a little wacky. I will respect your take on this.

Tudor – How is this? I come and pretend I don't know you at all and keep it that way for the rest of the night?

Adelle – OK … no … some people know we know each other. We would carry on conversations and hang with others as if we're just acquaintances. I never tried this so it'd be good to see if it works. Then we can arrange to either discretely take off together or meet up some place, yours or mine.

Tudor – Relax. No need to worry and pretend. I'M NOT AN ACTOR. I will not show up around you again. How's that for a release from my embarrassment? Good luck with people who have no bad reputation. I'm out. This is ridiculous.

Adelle - That's not what I meant! We can go together. I just thought it would be fun.

Tudor – No. You go and have fun! I'm sick of psychotic relationships. Just when I thought I finally met someone normal ... people wonder why I am so fucked up.

Adelle – I no longer care for my reputation. It was a purely idiotic idea and I said I respect your take on it. If you care and I am not just another woman to you, don't throw this to waste.

Adelle – (About an hour later and no response from Tudor) Prove to me, if you care, that the rumors about you were wrong. If you show up on Friday, and actually care to be there with me, then I am yours. If you don't, you make me believe they were true which is not what I want to think of you.

Adelle – (Still no answer many long minutes later) Tudor, what do you want of me? I asked you to have patience with me ... I need time to be myself again and at the same time I could not ignore what is forming between us. I just need time ...

Tudor – Take all the time you need. When you are free from your past, let me know. Until then, I won't stick around.

Adelle – I just haven't had the chance yet to tell all my friends that I've been single for the past month. I lost two of them only yesterday when they heard the news. I want to try to return the engagement ring again, just to be sure he's not still hoping we'll get back together. Hopefully it will all be over in a few days... and then the minutes, the days, and everything else that follows will be ours to enjoy as we please. I have been thinking of you every moment of every day since Saturday. I also hate acting ... I just wanted to see you before Sunday.

Tudor – Maybe I'll stop by Eurocircle on Friday, but no promises.

January 15, 2009

Adelle – I can't stop thinking about you … the unforgettable delight last weekend … my arms, my skin, my lips still remember you as if we were together just moments ago.

Tudor – Right. Just cool off! If I see you tomorrow, I'll just say hi and bye, don't get worked up too much. Besides, Rita and Neli might be there. By the way, where will this thing be?

Adelle – The place is Underwater on Clark and Wacker. Tudor, if you're going to be rude, then it's better to let be what was so far. I want to keep a good memory of it … I refuse to devote time and feelings to rudeness or go far deeper into a relationship that got abruptly stopped in this manner when it started at so high a level. Don't ever think it's okay to respond to my words with "cool off" again. Adieu!

Tudor – Listen, you are very strange, you know that? You are the one who requested I cool off and act like we don't know each other in public. Now you, in the other extreme, ooze over how great our first dates were. Make up your mind! Either, or! I tell you I'll play your absurd game at this event and now I'm the rude one. You know what, fine! You don't want me there, just say so! What's with this belated teenager game? This is crazy. Have fun. I'M NOT COMING, GODAMN IT!

Adelle – You are something of a character yourself, Mr.! The words "cool off" in my book mean bugger off, you're not welcome, fuck off to say it more directly. I am easily offended by such words. I am not used to hearing them other than in an offensive context. You need to calm down a bit, as I said before … I feel like I'm in the position of having to tame the most magnificent wild beast that I have ever met and I am madly attracted to. I did not ask that you "cool off" toward me. If you do show up and care not to play the game, I will do the same. Tudor … we need to get on the same frequency somehow.

Adelle – I am not sure how you were used to treating women before, but, I can only say that I thrive on reason, understanding, and respect for those around me.

Tudor – I have to take a nap. I will talk to you later.

Tudor – (A few hours later) 9086 N. CLARK TOMORROW. I'll be there, like anyone else. Just say hi, that's all.

Adelle – OK

Friday, January 16, 2009

Adelle – Bonjour! I placed an order on your website a couple of days ago. Do you still check that?

Tudor – What website? It's been deactivated.

Adelle – I will forward you the PayPal receipt. That should be connected to a bank account I suppose. The site looks active but it needs some work. I basically ordered your Crucifix.

Tudor – Sorry, Sandu must have activated it again. I will check it. You are nuts. I'll give you one for free. You of all people don't have to pay for a thing.

Adelle – I believe in you and your work is phenomenal for this day and age. It is work and it has value and I don't mind buying it, you just have to autograph it for me. One day it will be worth a lot more than I paid for it, I trust that.

Tudor – You're optimistic. Thanks. Actually I just got a call from the old company to work with them again. I have to meet them in an hour to talk terms. See you tonight then. Thanks, again, I'll autograph whatever you want. I wanna make a sculpture that you pose for. As soon as next week.

Adelle – That's great news!!! See you later!

Tudor – (Later that day) what time are you gonna be there tonight?

Adelle – Hmm … I am having a friend over at around nine. That means we'll take off from my place around ten and be there in twenty minutes to half an hour. Do you want to stop by also?

Tudor – I'll meet you there.

Adelle – ok.

Adelle – (A few hours later) I am ready to embrace my future – yesterday was painful but necessary. The ring is gone and I had to apply a less graceful technique to ensure his hopes are no longer there, but nothing else worked. That was the hardest part. I am over this now. You have my undivided attention.

Adelle – (Nearly three hours later after not a single word from Tudor) If you are here say hi or we are thinking of going someplace else – my friend wants to go to a club.

Tudor – OK, go. I never came. Now my ex is arguing with me. Damn it!

Adelle – I understand.

Adelle – Over and out.

Tudor – For now. I want to be inside you! I'm so tired of cheats and idiots and liars.

Adelle – I want the same … I am here wondering what is the meaning of life. I am so into you … I have never experienced anything of this sort before … why are you not where I am?

Tudor – I'll tell you when I see you.

January 17

Adelle – (Same night, only past midnight) We are spending the rest of the evening in Le Passage by Oak Street.

Tudor – I guess your phone will not work there. I'm sure the temptations will abound. No need phone anymore.

Adelle – Yeah, but none of them is you.

Tudor –With your sexual appetite, will it make a difference?

Adelle – I believe in loyalty as long as it is reciprocal.

Tudor – OK. Sure.

Adelle – You know you have me.

Tudor – One never has anyone. We are all free at all times. A ring and a contract are meaningless these days. I am going to sleep. I am exhausted of playing with myself.

Adelle – A ring means nothing – the meeting of the minds does. The music here is awesome ... but you are missing it.

Tudor – Have fun. I'm sure you will ... GOOD NIGHT!

Adelle –You know my address. I will be home in about an hour.

Tudor – I'll be in dreamland then. And, by the way, you need to get a car.

Adelle – I will.

I wanted to be next to him instead of out partying, I wanted to be in his bed. Tudor's master bedroom had a heavy, mysterious, yet irresistibly inviting charm. The bed was huge, the biggest I had ever seen, taking up a good third of the room. One nightstand was placed on the right side of the bed, with some books thrown carelessly all over it, along with an alarm clock and a few miscellaneous papers. The round table by the windows did not match the rest of the furniture and was used only as a depository for some other books. A thin layer of dust covered everything.

I wanted him pushing me gently on top of the musty sheets carrying the fragrance of some other women. He had an undaunted hold of my hands and mind; he was not the type to bother changing the sheets after each new encounter. Most women were probably aware they were not the first ones to entertain him after a brief self-induced abstinence, but also that he dated more than one at a time. Their presence was nearly perceptible from the peculiar and impossibly to ignore scent of the sheets. All his women fell for him in one way or another, to one extent or another. He was an important pawn on their life's chess tables as well, in a painful yet significant way.

I was visibly detached from reality and overwhelmed by my thoughts; my friends made sure I got home safe a couple hours later. I undressed, threw my clothes all over the floor and slid under the covers, wearing only my underwear. My skin burned with desire for him; the soft white cotton fabric cooled it off ... and then I sled gently into my dreams.

The phone on my nightstand was set to loud, just in case he decided to text me before morning. His message woke me up:

Tudor – (About 2 in the afternoon) Come to Elephant's, now.

Adelle – Good day to you too! OK – well – I need some time to get ready and jump into a cab and I am not quite sure where this place is. What is the address?

Tudor – 87 W. Belmont.

Adelle – I should be there in about an hour.

Tudor – Too late. Make it in half an hour.

Adelle – I'll try.

When I finally arrived, I saw Tudor a little nervous and unsure of how to address me. His wide smile, intense kiss and quick welcoming embrace unleashed an avid need for more of his passionate embrace.

He introduced me to his best friend, Luke.

I sat next to Tudor in the same leather padded booth where he had taken me for our first date. Within minutes my poor ears turned purple from all the salty talk to which they were exposed. I kept up with the conversation as best I could by throwing in a remark once in a while, trying not to feel insulted, although the two men seemed more in a race or contest of some sort: Who can tell the dirtiest jokes? They cracked each other up and it amused me after a while. Their peculiar and funny interaction made me feel at home.

Luke left two hours later and called Tudor as soon as he was out of the café. His friend and his wife, Anna, were the jury for Tudor's new conquests. Tudor related enthusiastically his friend's extremely positive first impression of me, word by word. Did I pass the best-friend test with flying colors?

Tudor's energy pervaded me: he had so much of it; he was like a ball of flamboyant light … a sun in a deep distant galaxy, so close it threatened to ignite me.

We planned on spending a couple of hours at my apartment and then we'd pack-up and go to his house for the remainder of the weekend. He was commissioned to finish some sculptures by the start of the following week. It was all equal for me - I had a bank holiday on Monday and a long weekend at his house. Even without the skiing, it was still a wonderful prospect.

We shed our clothes and melted under passion's fire. But something suddenly went wrong. He said I intimidated him and there was some sort of negative energy he sensed coming from me. It was only sex … how could a man of his statute in life, so much more accomplished than I was, twelve years my senior, with an established reputation as a pathological skirt hunter, come up with such an excuse??? I … intimidated *him*??? I hushed him, kissed him softly on the left corner of his mouth, and showed him I was still the irresistible young girl he had originally met and won. His blissful smile was my ultimate reward.

I asked him if he had read the Romanian novel by Mihai Drumes, *Love Letter*, a Romanian high school lecture classic. The main personage in that book wanted her new marriage to the love of her life to be constantly fresh. Having separate bedrooms and seeing each other only occasionally did the trick.

Tudor agreed immediately and said he too thought spending too much time together with a woman was tacky. He added at the end: "Give me some time to miss you". I declared rather happy: "Well … I am glad we both agree on that."

There was a small risk of unplanned pregnancy since we had used no protection. We debated the cumbersome subject quite openly. He remarked he would marry me in a heartbeat if that were the case, with no questions asked. Right … and I was to believe him because that is exactly what a man of his repute would say to any girl he had just laid. It was a good test of character. I nodded and kept my thoughts to myself.

My phone went off, thank God! It was Olivia asking if I wanted to go out with her. I declined respectfully due to present company and our plans. Tudor overheard the conversation. As soon as I hang up he suggested that I join my friend; he had work to finish that night. He was an artist. I understood clearly how he needed time and space away from the real world in order to create such marvelous works of art. Half-heartedly I agreed to go on with the girls-night-out evening, although my heart ached to be next to him, observing him as he sculpted.

Tudor – (About 11:20 that evening) I want more!
Adelle - Me too!
Tudor – I need to be inside you now! I only got an appetizer.
Adelle – Nice choice of words. Olivia said to tell you hi!

Tudor – Say hi to her too. Tell her she's very nice. I like her.

Tudor – Thanks! I love everything about you.

Olivia and I went to a lounge in the new posh North Avenue and Damen Street area that evening. The place was packed with twenty-somethings. I suddenly felt like forty-plus and a visitor in a world I should have been over by my late twenties. Olivia was twenty-six, and most of my other friends were all in their thirties, especially my American friends. These girls were either already settled into their own families or on their way to be so, either with kids already or pregnant. They had already stopped working to raise their families, or were working part time in order to spend more time at home. And what was *I*????

I wanted to be at Tudor's house reading a book as he worked on his sculptures. I looked around in resignation. The racy music assaulted these thirty-year-old ears as I sipped on a glass of Cabernet pondering the meaning of life, yet again.

What would come of it all? What would come of Tudor and me? We were growing closer, I was sure of that. We were beginning to bond, to meld into one another's lives. I could feel it.

But, I wondered, *could* he?

Chapter VI
The First Good-Bye

You disarmed me like the fire melts ice
A glacial lake immersed in sun blaze

We are tangled up into the absurd
A game you chose to play me in

If your stare was a pretense
I forgive you for trying to lie

Our love and passion are a paradigm
Life became death, a blissful agony

Skiing made winter my top season. I'd missed the slopes buried in other concerns and with neither the time nor the inclination to plan a ski trip that winter - at least not until I met Tudor. Luke and Tudor arranged a weekend trip to Wisconsin. It was a three-day Martin Luther King national holiday weekend, and the banks were all closed on Monday. Even if we left on Sunday, two days and one night would be plenty of time for our first trip together. Baby steps.

I woke up earlier than usual that Sunday morning. I was anxious to continue the packing I'd begun the night before. I had to be ready when Luke and Anna stopped by my place to pick me up on their way to Tudor's. They lived in my area; Tudor was in the western suburbs, on the way to Wisconsin.

I gazed through my large windows facing the lake. A bright and freezing Sunday morning shone over Lincoln Park. The light reflected in the frosty framed mirror of Lake Michigan. I wondered how cold it was. Venturing onto the balcony to check was out of question; I was too snug in my warm, comfy pajamas. MTV Hits channel blasted away while I carried on my weekend morning ritual.

Fortunately for me, my life has a definite and undeniably bright spot in it, one that barks, fetches toys and shadows me around the apartment at every step: Luca, my three-pound Yorkie. She has often been compared to a shoe (since she's no bigger than an average man's foot) and of course to a squirrel or a hairy rat. She isn't particularly pleased with my travels and often shows her rebellion in two ways. As I'm packing, she pulls my things out of my bags and runs victory laps around the apartment until I corner her beneath my couch or bed. When I'm gone, she uses her soft-hearted host's carpets, beds and sofas for her toilet. Never mind that she is perfectly trained and never has an "accident" when I'm home. She knows exactly what she's doing.

I finished packing after a few minutes and ran quickly through the apartment, dusting. I chased the dog around the island bar for a few minutes, which she always found amusing. She loved chasing me and, of course, the reverse was just as much fun. I checked my messages continually to make sure the red message light wasn't blinking.

An hour or so later, I panicked ... what was he up to now? Was he really so tired from working late that he forgot to wake up, forgot to set the alarm, knowing we were to go skiing that day and had a four-hour drive up to Devil's Head?

By the time I finished running the polishing cloth through my condo again, it was nearly eleven. That meant skiing was definitely out, but why wasn't he showing any sign of life??? Finally, the message light started to blink.

January 18, 2009

Tudor – I guess skiing is out for today. We'll leave it for next weekend. I am too busy working anyway. Luke didn't call so far.

Adelle – That's a good idea. I may be able to get my skis in the meanwhile.

Tudor – Right. You probably partied too hard last night also. He's probably having coffee with you now … enjoy!

Adelle – What are you talking about? I was just cleaning my place … something I was supposed to do yesterday afternoon. I was up at eight – we came back at one in the morning. And I haven't had coffee yet because I was waiting to have it with you on our way up north! You need to learn to trust me somehow.

Tudor – I'm just kidding. You know that. Don't take it personally. I don't trust any woman.

Adelle - I guess I need to learn more about you too. I might change your notion of trust in women … but that only comes in time. We'll talk later.

Tudor – Enjoy your cleaning. I was up at five. My stupid canaries take the place of a rooster. I had to clean too. Sheets, used tampons, wine glasses, you know … all the proof from last night …

Adelle – Got it!

Tudor – Just kidding. I went to sleep right before your last message last night.

Adelle – Later!!! When you are done with work!

Tudor – Will not be done soon. I don't wanna leave my house today. I'm in a good mood to work.

Adelle – Fine by me.

59

Tudor – (Later that evening) I guess nobody missed me today.

Adelle – I know you need peace and quiet to work.

Tudor – Thanks for the consideration. You're right about not being interrupted when I work, although I'd like to find at least a text message from you. It's somewhat comforting. By the way, the ski trip might happen tomorrow, according to Luke. I'll let you know. His wife was sick today.

Adelle – OK. Text me when you are ready to go to bed. I'm running to the gym for now.

Tudor – His wife might still be sick tomorrow.

Adelle – I hope she will be well soon. Health is most important.

Tudor – We'll see. She's fine. Just a nasty cold, like half the population now. Have fun at the gym.

Adelle – (Close to midnight) – Still up?

Tudor – No. I'm still working. Will be till four in the morning probably. Xox!

Adelle – When you put your head on the pillow and close your eyes, imagine I come by for a second, and gently kiss your forehead and your cheeks and the corner of your mouth and say sweet dreams my darling!

Tudor – That would get me started. I wouldn't sleep till we collapsed with exhaustion.

Adelle – hmmm …

January 19, 2009

Adelle – Good morning! Rise and shine, sleepyhead. Are you up? Is Luke's wife alright?

Tudor – (Many hours later) Good afternoon. I was up until five thirty. Then I took a nap until eleven, I just woke up again. Luke's wife must be ok. Luke hasn't called the whole day.

Adelle – That's good news.

Tudor – What are you doing?

60

Adelle – Grocery shopping close by … and wanted to take Luca out so just a perfect excuse to see the sun a little.

Tudor – Good for you. Sorry we got stood up two days in a row. Had I not had so much to do myself, I would have said yes to skiing anyway. Next weekend for sure.

Tudor – Promise.

Adelle – No worries – Saturday afternoon was fabulous so that makes up for the rest. Plus you get your work done. I need to get new skis anyway … somehow they got lost … hard to believe they weren't in fact thrown away by his dad. But anyway …

Tudor – There are a few photos of the two of you on Facebook. He's obviously in love with you. I wouldn't be surprised if his dad threw all your things out.

Adelle - Time solves everything … I guess I deserve this as far as they are concerned.

Tudor – Yes, time wipes memories clean. If I don't see you soon, I'll forget what you look like.

Adelle - I don't mind surprises. I might look for a car in the spring, but I need some advice with that, unless you move close by in the meantime.

Adelle – By the way – my Italian friends from Milan are coming in town for work and we are planning to go to dinner with them on Thursday, at the Autograph Room. I would love to introduce you to them if you would like.

Adelle – (Long pause) Guess not. I think we both hate fences just as much. We are wild mustangs.

Tudor – Sure, although Thursday is the wine tasting at the French place and it's also Luke's birthday. I was hoping we can go to that too. How will this work?

Tudor – I'd like to surprise you with a visit. Maybe tomorrow, which is obviously not a surprise. I have to know you are home.

Adelle – Hmm … Thursday sounds busy. We'll figure something out – let's talk when you come over tomorrow. Do you like sushi? I'll get home around 6 from work.

Tudor – Yeah, these damned fences! I know you don't wanna be fenced, much less harnessed. I see it in your eyes. I don't like girls who cling to me either, but I want to love and know that I'm loved back. And I'd love to be able to trust a girl. I'm afraid of you, honestly. I can't let go and relax around you. There's a coolness I feel coming from you. Maybe I'm just paranoid with all the stuff happening to you and me lately.

Tudor – Tomorrow. Sushi sounds good.

Adelle - Yes you are! Then we should spend some more time getting to know each other … just talking … I am intimidated by you also … but exponentially more attracted to you so I am sure we'll get over this initial awkwardness. I guess we are both too taken by these overwhelming feelings and refuse to admit them because we don't want to get hurt. Sushi tomorrow it is.

Tudor – OK, I'll see you at six.

Adelle – (Later that evening)

"The future and the past,

Are two sides of the same page;

One sees the beginning

Only by reading both sides"

Wrote Eminescu (the greatest Romanian poet).

Adelle – Tomorrow is not here soon enough.

Tudor – I agree. Don't make me fall for you if you're not sure, speaking of Eminescu … seeing the end by looking in the past.

Adelle – See the beginning by looking in the past … that's how I read it. We've both learned so much and been hurt already … all I want is peace, quiet, trust and ardent love that's been returned … I don't know how you feel until you tell me; all I want is to drown myself in your eyes and lose myself in your embrace …

Adelle – And now my cheeks are burning for heaven's sake!!! OK … information overload.

Tudor – You're good. Very good. I like this. Don't stop. Sorry I can't respond promptly. I'm working with my headphones on and want to concentrate. I check my messages every once in a while.

Tudor sent a photo of the sculpture he was working on and the following words – "This is the fourth 3D sketch and I'm getting horny doing St. Mary. I'm thinking of you while sculpting her."

Adelle – My ears are getting red! Your work is far better than Rodin's! When you fall asleep, a gentle kiss on your nose and your right palm.

Tudor – Thanks. I'll take the kiss on my right palm and use it as a lubricant for a night cap.

My long weekend was over and I had only seen him on Saturday. It was a waste of free time which we could have used to indulge ourselves by spending it all day in bed and waking only long enough to nurture our bodies with whatever my fridge contained. His work was a perfect excuse though. I would never challenge his work schedule no matter how great my insatiated compulsion to have him next to me every minute.

January 20, 2009

Tudor – As much as I long to see you today, I can't. We'll have to postpone one more day. I haven't finished my work last night and have to work through tonight. I'm sorry. Part of the reason why I didn't finish my work is because I had an incident last night right after you wrote to me last.

63

My ex showed up at my door. When I opened the door she came in wanting to "talk". I had to call the police to remove her from my house. She was drunk and they told her to take a cab home, or else they'd give her a Driving-Under-Influence. They took her to the station and later she must have taken the car, because it was gone at 4 in the morning. Now she's sending me all kinds of nasty messages. She is insane. I wanted to kick her ass in the snow myself, but then the police would have taken me in instead. I'm exhausted and needless to say I slept with one eye open.

Adelle - People do insane things when you break up with them ... sometimes out of their characters.

Tudor – I went out for a couple of hours. I had to meet with Vlad. Now I'm back home and setting up to sculpt.

Adelle – (Later that evening) I need to be out of town the weekend of February 28 ... for a few days or a week even. I am thinking Cabo. Interested, or should I book it to go on my own?

Adelle – (About an hour later) Ok ... never mind – you don't need to answer that kind of question. It's just an FYI then ... I need to be away from the city that weekend for a few days.

Tudor – I'd go. Sure. Cabo sounds good. Let's talk tomorrow.

Adelle – I am falling asleep. Try and think of a happy place when you go to sleep ... where you'd be happy no matter what. I have a surprise for you tomorrow.

Adelle – (After an hour of no response) – Hey – everything ok? Just say yes or no.

I couldn't breathe. It hurt. Everything hurt. Even my mind. How was it possible? Why did he call off and rescheduled our dates again and again and again with absolutely no consideration for my feelings? He stretched my emotions to the max. How much further could I go before I'd break down in tiny pieces?

I checked my phone every few minutes. Every other junk email or friends' texts came through just fine ... all but his.

Well-to-do men were not my cup of cake. The thought of being with one gave me a sense of self-belittlement. Wealth buys power over people and material things. I did not want to be part of any category of things that wealthy people could control in any form or manner. I distrusted these men. Their freedom and flexibility of life was built on my lack of it. They had it because I could not, because I worked for them in exchange for a modest lifestyle. I wasn't well off enough to free up time to think and do better for myself.

I sensed the player in Tudor the moment I met him, the very second he laid eyes on me. Something else struck me about the same time: his immeasurable artistic talent and skill, the beauty of his intellect, his charitable character, his ability to keep every cell of my body constantly charged whenever around him. His magnetism was evidenced clearly in his work; aside from his collectable dolls, the other pieces I saw in his studio belonged in the Louvre, in the same rank with every remarkable artist throughout history.

A couple of our mutual friends made reference to random philanthropic acts Tudor did for people. He loaned money to people who needed it, without expecting it back; he put his name on the line to help new immigrants build credit; he stopped in the middle of the road to help a woman change a flat tire. He threw parties where he invited just about everyone he knew and asked his friends to bring other friends. He nearly always paid for dinners with friends. Moreover, he did it with a smile ... no matter how large the bill was.

Tudor took care of two stray cats, a canary with a broken leg, fed the family of raccoons by his house, and always had food out for the squirrels and birds. He loved gardening, but after a few years of trying to protect his tomato plants and other vegetables from the wild deer visitors, he acknowledged that it was their territory more than his, allowed them to come in peace, and admired them from his kitchen window over breakfast and a cup of coffee. He saw them as nature's gift to people.

January 21, 2009

Adelle – (4 a.m.) Tudor, you are worrying me. I just want to know that you are OK after your story yesterday. I can't get any sleep. If I misinterpreted our relationship, all you have to do is say so. I invest time and feelings only when they are appreciated … were my instincts flawed?

Tudor – (6:27 a.m.) I just woke up, since eight thirty last night. I had so many nightmares. I am glad I'm up. Damn. Can't even rest in my sleep.

Adelle – You need a vacation!

Adelle – I am taking the day off from work … too sleepy … I probably got an hour or less of sleep last night.

Tudor – Sorry. OK, sleep. I sent you an invitation on Facebook for tonight if you're interested. If not, let me know what your preference is.

Adelle – (Several hours later after waking up) My company's stock is up 25 percent today … it never moved that much in one day. They are having the earnings released today. Anyway … in a much better disposition now – I just woke up. Six sounds great … and you can bring any kind of sushi you like. I'll have some white wine, beer and we can do some mixed drinks.

Tudor – sell sell sell!

Adelle – I work for them … it's been dragged down by the environment but never as low as the huge financial

institutions in the past year. It is one of the most conservative financial institutions, I dare say *the* most, these days.
Anything could happen of course, but they have a great
reputation for good reason. They dropped only about 30
percent in the worst months last year … most of the larger
banks lost an average of 80 percent, including Goldman.

Tudor – (Around 4 that afternoon) – Adelle, you're
gonna hate me, but I don't think it'll work out between us.
Sorry, I'm just getting a bad vibe.

His last message popped up on my blackberry when I
was walking back home from the corner drugstore where I
picked up a few last minute knick-knacks to make the
evening perfect. I loved to decorate, paying attention to
every last detail, crowning everything with my own personal
touch… not too cluttered, with dark reddish tints, romantic,
old and contemporary at the same time to create the illusion
of a French lady's boudoir. The choice of food and wine is
always quintessential to complete the picture.

When I saw his message, I was stunned. It hovered
over me the entire morning like a fog of death. I caught a
drift of his plans before he ever intended to put them into
action. When we were together, everything seemed fine.
When we were apart, the fears and doubts crept in, a thief in
the night.

Tudor met with one of our mutual Ukrainian friends
for dinner to inquire about my past, especially about my
engagement to Peter. He found out no more than I had
already told him.

My emotions for this man and my own history of relationships prevented me from accepting so cavalier a
dismissal, even after only a month of dating. We couldn't
simply call a halt to it all over a silly text message, not in my
life anyway. It all seemed so stupid and immature!!!

Rivers of tears washed down my face, out of anger braided by trust in my instincts. I had to be more than just another one of his silly little games. I *had* to be!

I never wanted any other man in my life as much as I wanted him, wanted him next to me, forever. I couldn't let go, not yet.

Adelle - OK. Here's what I think. I think you need to spend time with people to know them. Texting is not how you build a relationship. You have until six today to change your mind. What are you afraid of? I may have behaved a little weird because I've been with two guys in the past twelve years of my life. I don't know how to date.

Adelle – (A few hours later) Almost six … Good bye Tudor! You were my perfect rebound to the real world. Your kiss, your touch and your stare have been etched in my memory forever, though brief, unique, profound and ethereal.

Tudor – I'd better leave, before that image of me gets tainted. The other prognosis is having you return my engagement ring as soon as I fall for your mermaid song.

Adelle – Our "friends" really helped. I wanted to tell you this tonight and I mean every letter of the words that follow: I have never said or felt this before. I consciously tried putting off that engagement as much as I could. He was not the one for me. When my eyes met yours on New Year's Eve, my heart stopped … and as much as I held the "player" type in low regard until recently … I simply melted in your arms, your kiss left me irrational.

Tudor – I wish I could believe you. I don't believe anyone anymore and everyone I meet has a hidden agenda.

Adelle – Trust is a time value, but without time you can never find it. I never asked you to trust me immediately. I asked for time for *both* of us to learn how to trust each other. So, don't fall for me, if that makes you feel better. Get to know me first as I want to know you. We can't erase our pasts. Are you going to crush our relationship by throwing what we feel for each other into the deepest ocean bottom? Why?

Adelle – You kept me on hold from one text message to the next. I don't know how to answer you anymore because I fear you'd be doing the exact thing you did earlier today. My agenda is peace and quiet, intense and honest love, as I have already told you – or texted you, rather. I want to be with and marry the love of my life, someone whom I can trust, will trust me back, have a beautiful family and be able to focus on something creative, something that I love to do for a change as opposed to merely worrying about a lack of trust, or cheating, or any other sort of nonsense.

Tudor – You are good, very articulate and convincing. I'll think about it.

Tudor – (A couple of hours later) I think we are both on a rebound and need some time alone to flush out all the prejudices and bad history out of our systems, before we go into overload. I think we jumped into this too soon. I know the temptation was there and still is. Let's take it easy for a while. I don't know what to suggest. I don't want to stifle your freedom. Despite what you tell me, I see in your eyes a thirst for going out and meeting new people. Please do, I cannot stop you, nor do I want to. Go have fun. If a month from now you miss me, you know where to find me.

Adelle – I understand your point about both of us needing to heal emotionally. As for the thirst for meeting people, it's just meeting people socially, not men in particular. When I met you, I was not, by any means, looking for a relationship. Far from it! What I saw in your eyes was beyond anything I could explain to myself or anyone else. I felt it piercing my every sense with a needle of fire. I don't need time to admit to what I feel for you … but if you want me to take it, I will respect your wish. Try not to slam on the brakes again. See it for what it is and feels. Let me know

69

when you are ready to start living up to and enjoying our feelings for one another.

Tudor – Tomorrow night I'll be at Tornado Bar for the wine tasting. It's also Luke's birthday. If you'll be there, that would be great.

Adelle – Alright. I'll see you there.

Adelle – (later that evening – 11:00 pm) – I miss you!

Tudor – I don't believe you.

Adelle – What would make you believe me? Can you come over?

Tudor – I wish! I'm submitting the package to the copyright office and putting all the photos together.

Adelle – When will you be done? By the way, there is a post office open nonstop downtown if you want to ship it tonight.

Tudor – Thanks. No, I'll have to send it tomorrow morning. I need about an hour.

Adelle – I came over last Saturday to Elephant's – can you just drive here? I don't care … no matter how late it is.

Tudor – I could. But aren't you free tomorrow night? Are your guests sleeping over?

Adelle – They are staying in Tinley Park close to work and driving back after dinner because they have an early flight on Friday.

Adelle – On your way?

I often wondered if he was raised by a pack of wolves or if maybe he'd spent too much time surrounded by the wrong company.

January 22, 2009

A knock at the door awakened me from my haze around midnight. Tudor took me in his arms and kissed me frantically. I felt as if I was dreaming. His hands moved slowly and confidently all over my back and through my hair, drawing me closer to him. We took a deep breath and paused, searching one another's eyes; a smile of pure bliss and happiness lightened both our faces. We continued undressing on our way to my bedroom. Lost in a passion stronger than we could bear, with Frank Sinatra playing in the background, we transgressed into dimensions far away, within the limitless unconsciousness of our being.

We smiled knowingly in the darkened room, where only the vague city lights flickered softly through the sheer gold curtains. He moved his thick and chubby fingers up and down the curves of my naked body. Somehow his hands reminded me of home. My parents had the same type of hands – short fingers, bulky and natural for hard working people. I could feel the sculptor in him through his fingers' slow and skillful motion, just as he molded a clay sculpture. I was still somewhat shy when touching him. What if he simply disappeared? What if I was never going to see him again??? What if next time he sent me another message, one for which I had no appropriate answer to draw him back? I quieted my thoughts and savored that very second; we were suspended in eternity together.

"Let's get married", he said suddenly.

"Well, I already have a $5,000 deposit with Ritz Carlton expiring this year and a very expensive designer gown sitting at Macy's bridal salon, abandoned for now."

He drew up wedding plans for us a wedding in Romania and one here. He asked me how much family I had who would attend the wedding. He remarked that Constanta was a beautiful city on the shores of the Black Sea. His family from Timisoara could travel there for the event.

My thoughts were spinning around my head. How could he move from never wanting to see me again to proposing marriage to me, all in a single day? Maybe he was right … maybe he actually meant what he'd said. Perhaps there are other people like us, perhaps there are situations so

71

perfect. You simply meet the person you are meant to be with the rest of your life, they feel the same about you, and everything else just clicks without any of the usual dating or getting-to-know-one-another nonsense. Tudor's hazel eyes sparkled. They seemed supernatural under the city lights reflection. He gazed at me the same way he did the night we met. It was as if he was trying to make sure he still had a spell on me, to make sure I am not escaping his hold by any means. He leaned over me, gently kissing my forehead, cheeks, nose .... ah ... his lips softly covered mine. I stopped thinking. I existed in his arms, under his weight and a rush of bliss took over me. I felt it in the core of my heart ... no one would ever get any deeper than that.

Tudor seemed preoccupied the following morning. I didn't have the heart to tell him I'd had a nightmare that night. I was aware of his financial problems, but never imagined a man in his forties could lack control of his personal finances so, especially given his reputation as a business-savvy entrepreneur throughout the Romanian community.

What was bothering him? He shouldn't be worrying about investments or real estate or other ways to make money. Those were merely disruptions from what he loved to do, what defined him, what I revered most about him. His hands were gold; his artistic talent was his most precious possession. I often wondered if he was aware of it.

He drove me to the office that morning. The work-day was long and I felt sickly. My gynecologist had recommended some contraception pills about a week before. They turned my system upside down. I felt nauseous, with hot flashes and headaches.

My health and disposition improved slightly by the beginning of that evening. I went to Eurocircle, a well-known social club for networking immigrants, generally

Europeans but also some South Americans, Asians, and others, including Americans. The French wine tasting was unique for two reasons: one, I was to spend the evening with some of my friends for the first time in over four years; and two, Tudor and Luke were celebrating Luke's birthday, and I was going to present Tudor to my Italian friends.

I met Tony and Valentina outside the John Hancock tower before seven. They were juggling shopping bags and carried the biggest Italian smiles I had seen in years. I missed them, Valentina especially. She was one of my dearest friends. But we lived too many miles apart. Had she lived nearer, we would have been like sisters. She was sweet, fun, gorgeous, unique, bright and had that Italian libertine mentality about dating and relationships that I glorified and envied, although my strict Romanian upbringing made me incapable of ever putting it into practice. Her haircut made her look punkish. She radiated a special flair that called out young, playfully chic, stylish, contemporary.

The clear, crisp winter outside the restaurant window left me warm inside. I'd nearly forgotten about Tudor. And then my phone began to vibrate. I checked for a message.

I tried calling him, but as usual, he didn't pick up, no matter the situation or whether we were on good or bad terms. It was as if he just dreaded talking on the phone, period. I didn't understand.

The bar was no more than a tiny room jammed with tables. There was a large L-shaped couch and a lounge style table at the far end of the bar where Tudor sat next to Luke and a couple of ladies. His face lit up as soon as he saw me. He came up to us and kissed me for several sublimely long seconds, and we made the appropriate introductions.

I wore a pencil gray skirt and a buttoned down shirt. Three of my buttons decided to open up while I was in the cab, and there I was, with my bra and boobs hanging out as I was being introduced to Anna, Luke's wife. Tudor let me know he'd noticed, too. "So, what were you exactly doing in the cab with your Italian friend?"

A good looking tall and blonde young lad, pushy to the point of obnoxious, offered to buy me a drink when I went to the bar. I turned him down, but he refused to give up. I allowed him to help me carry one of the three drinks for my friends back to the table. Tudor saw us as the guy carried my glass of red wine. He seemed a little flustered and said, "I can't leave you alone for five seconds and you already have company." When the poor boy saw me with Tudor, he quickly backed away and out of sight.

My friends, still suffering from jetlag, went back to their hotel after a couple of hours. We lingered around the small dance floor for another hour or so. Both Tudor and Luke were disappointed in my dancing: I was never very good. Romanian men feel that women should be great dancers. I had my parents to thank for that shortcoming. They were less concerned about such frivolous things than they were about providing the bare necessities of life.

As the evening drew to an end, Tudor returned with me to my apartment. We climbed aboard the elevator headed toward the nineteenth floor. Our lips locked savagely and our hands exploded in a furious assault on our clothes. We stumbled out and down the hall and I barely managed to get the door open before he lifted me over the threshold and onto the kitchen countertop where he deftly removed the rest of my clothing while I unbuttoned his shirt, my fingers playing with the hair on his muscular, wide chest.

Suddenly his phone went off. He yanked it out of his pants pocket, read the message, and announced, "It's Rita. She wants me to go over to her house for something". He kissed me one more time saying: "No way." I could barely contain my shock. Shock, fear, anger—I'm not sure what I felt. My heart ached at the word, "Rita." Rita was the girl from Constanta he once told me he'd had a fling with, the one who moved all the way from Dubai to be with him. He also said he'd never thought of her as anything more than a friend. Rather plain-looking, but with a good body for a woman her age. I remembered avoiding her irritating questions as soon as I'd walked into his New Year's party. "Are you single?" She was obviously bent upon protecting a territory over which she clearly had no control.

I needed to put her out of my mind.

"Are you okay?"

I looked at him, saw the lust in his eyes, as he followed mine down his chest to his belly and beyond. He swept me into the bedroom.

It was after three in the morning when Tudor finally rolled over onto his side and gasped. "My God."

I shook my head. "You are incredible."

Then, out of nowhere he said: "What if we have a baby together?"

I'd been moving my fingers lazily across his chest when the words hit me. I lifted my head to look into his eyes, as much as I could see of them in the darkness, punctuated only periodically by the flickering city lights outside my bedroom window. "You must be kidding."

"No. I am serious about this. Then I would surely marry you. We'd go to Mexico for our honeymoon and swing to the tunes of love in a hammock for a few weeks." Tudor winked triumphantly.

"I don't believe you. And aside from that, even if I were to get pregnant, I would never make the man responsible for my own mistake. You'd be under no obligation whatsoever. It's one of my principles; I'm assuming full responsibility."

"Why say such things? You know ... I would be proud to have you as my wife. My mother would love you.

You two have a lot in common. Actually, my aunt, her sister, would be quite fond of you as well."

I looked him over, checked out the expression on his face, studied him for several seconds.

"You are kind, really. I can see that. But I just broke up my engagement and you just got out of a relationship. The timing isn't exactly perfect."

"I had my house on the market for a while and an eye on a property here in Lincoln Park for quite some time. I would be close by, only a few blocks away. This is the life I've always wanted, not the suburbs filled with so much calm making me contemplate death more than life."

I couldn't believe my ears. Was I hearing him right? Or had I drifted up to heaven? Would a man who just met a woman have such consideration for her, or was he simply testing my naivety?

The alarm clock went off only three hours later. Exhausted, yet happy, we greeted each other. After some light kissing and nibbling and a breakfast of toast and orange juice, Tudor drove me to work; he lowered his window asking for a last kiss to see him through the day.

January 23, 2009

Adelle – (On the bus home that evening) *Bonsoir mon amour! Ca va? Je suis tres fatigue et veux dormir un peu. Et toi?*

Tudor – Accident. Waiting for the police.

Adelle – What? Are you OK? Where are you? Do you want me to take a cab there?

Tudor – No. It's OK. I have to call the insurance company.

Adelle – What happened?

Tudor – A stupid yappie who wasn't paying attention ran into me as I crossed an intersection. She only hit the rear end of my car, fortunately.

Chapter VII
The Second Goodbye

I should like to think people still have a soul
And a tear in a corner of an eye still washes off
Bitterness in another one's intent

Does anyone still have a human heart
Trembling upon another's silent cry for love?
Or do all erode away at the callous shore of indifference
Just like violent waves in a hurricane?

Does every person left on earth lurk in cynicism
And lies struggling for selfish happiness?

Or is there one, just one, remaining
Who wears the clothing of the rest, and yet, inside
He gave himself to me ... just like I to him
On an arctic New Year's night?

    I was anxious to post on Facebook the pictures we had taken two nights earlier. Tudor filled me with pride - he was a reputable artist and I was his new love. Yet, I feared gossip from my ex-fiancée' friends. I had grown close to many of them in the time we'd spent together and vice-versa.
    Tudor and I, on the other hand, had few mutual friends, so I wasn't worried about anyone gossiping, should

he decide to post them. Tudor implied that posting our pictures on Facebook was off limits, at least for now.

I carried on the rest of my Saturday in peace and quiet and did my hair and nails expecting a big evening. A premonition crept up on me suddenly, but I pushed it aside.

He played the role too well and sent me another good-bye message. I felt like a novice with his games weighing heavily on me. I didn't see the point. Why play with what you have? Why risk losing something you care about when it could vanish faster than it appeared in the first place? What was the point of his sentimental gambling? "Don't give up, just don't give up!" I screamed in my head. "You don't abandon a problem just because you have to think through it, *suffer* through it to find an answer! You stick things out and *work* through it!"

Saturday night alone … hmmmm … well, well … did my Tudor have other plans? What were my options? Play Sherlock Holmes or go along with his far-fetched stories and see where it got me. I fought hard not to overthink the situation. Maybe the mind of an artist *is* slightly more complex than a commoner's and his intent was not a bad one. At least I hoped to God!

I gradually become more and more in love with a man I could not understand, one who possessed demonic powers over me. Every text message was a literary/psychological/philosophical classroom assignment designed to trigger a response. If I followed up, would I lose myself in him? Would I denigrate the values I grew up with and those I learned on my own? Tudor won battle after battle over my heart … but could I allow him to win the war over my mind?

January 25, 2009
Adelle – Hey! I just had a thought … keep your house for another few years. If you can make the payments,

try and refinance. Here's why: you are already famous for your dolls, and some of the other work, with the right PR, you make a good gallery exhibit. Plus the market is likely to recover, and when you sell it, you can advertise it as the house of a famous artist which will bring a whole different crowd interested in buying it. Rent it for a while if you really want to be away from it and live in the city, and rent a loft here also. Just an idea.

Tudor – Idealistic, not realistic.

Adelle – I know ... but I like to think that thriving to make our ideals part of our reality sooner or later pays off; that's the essence of life itself. Why else would you want to be alive tomorrow if not working towards fulfilling your ideals one day? There are always various ways of achieving our dreams ...you know...by using some additional percentage of our brain once in a while.

Tudor – All true.

Tudor – Right ... what a joke. Famous shitty doll artist.

Adelle – What are you talking about? You needed to put your foot through the door somehow to make a name for yourself and also be able to make a living through your talents. You can sculpt what you want now, in addition to the dolls, which by the way, are incredible in their own respect and provide you with the means to achieve your ends. Do you think I ever wanted to be an accountant? In fact I detested the idea. I am decent at math but I hate it. But I'll do anything to be financially independent, period. I worked hard to have a quiet decent paying eight-to-five job to have more free time and start focusing on other aspects of my life. This is only the beginning for you ... and so it is for me ...

Adelle - When you start like this ... once you get where you wanted in life, you can look back and have the greatest satisfaction ever. You've done it all on your own. Life is short ... when you die, you want to have a smile on your face and be able to say that, although it was not a perfect journey, you are proud of it ... it's yours. You left the world a little better place than you found it. Eternal optimist ... helps me put myself back on my feet when everything else crashes around me.

Tudor – Jesus. Your messages are five pages at a time and not in sequence. It's hard to juggle to see which one fits at the end of what.

Adelle – Alright. Sorry about that.

Tudor – I don't know why my phone does that. When I send something out it's all on the same page, no matter how long.

Adelle – It's normal – they are not meant for epistles as long as mine. I get yours in fragments also.

Tudor – Sorry. I'll keep them short.

Adelle – I don't mind them, silly!!! I am glad I have an unlimited messaging plan. I can make sense of yours.

I wondered if he misread what I meant yet again ... or simply chose to interpret it subjectively, without giving me any benefit of the doubt, and without trying to see things from my perspective. It was the male ego, and the fact that he was so much older than I, which erected the Great Wall of China between us.

Adelle – (Later that day) What do you think of going bowling?

Tudor – It's ok but not today. I HAVE TO GO TO A FAMILY DINNER.

Adelle – Enjoy! You are lucky to have them so close.

Tudor – Not always. It's obligation.

Adelle - A great thing to have nonetheless. I pay a dear price for my independence, come to think of it.

Tudor – A lot of girls are like you, independent, and lonely, looking for consolation in bars and on dating sites.

Gabriela Sbarcea

Kind of sad. It all becomes a way of life, to where you don't get attached to anyone anymore. You want separate bedrooms and separate lives, with the occasional one night stands. Always surrounded by friends with similar lives who encourage you to stay single and party until you're too old to reproduce. It's actually nature's way of keeping the population in check. Egotistical people should die alone.

Adelle – That is harsh, Mr. Popescu! And you couldn't be any more wrong about me. I told you I wanted to be with and marry the love of my life and have a beautiful family that includes at least a couple of kids. That man will be happy because I refuse to suffocate anyone. I want to be my own person, not lose my identity. And I want to make my man understand that I'm not an accessory to his life. I want a family and kids! I just always wanted to start from nothing and get someplace through my own hard work and brains and not by relying on the financial help of others!

Adelle – By the way, I didn't meet either of my two Ex's or you in a bar! You can feel what I want … Why do you keep pushing away from me? I WANT TO MAKE YOU HAPPY because I believe in you. And I would never take such words from anyone else. Don't let your fears destroy this!

Adelle – You also mentioned the separate bedrooms as something that appeals to you. If that's not what you want, just say it. I trust my instincts on this … I know this could be one of the greatest things that ever happened to us if we open up to one another, spend time together and get to know each other. I am *not* your other women and you are not like any other man I have ever met!

Tudor – NAH, you want me *because* I keep pulling away. If I were to love you and be close to you, you'd run scared, not to be suffocated.

Adelle – I have never wanted anyone to be close to me as much I do you! How can you say that? How many times do I have to tell you? You make me crazy with talk like that. You already stole my heart on New Year's Eve. It's not easy to admit. I am yours already!!!

Tudor – That's lovely. So much passion! I am touched. How come I don't feel the same? Strange. I can't love anymore.

Adelle – You are not the man you pretend to be when you meet new women. You are not that cold and heartless. I saw in you the profound love you are capable of giving, and I refuse to allow it to escape from the marble crust you've sculpted around yourself for protection. You feel it ... your mind has hardened you against it because others have abused it and mistreated you so. All I need from you is for you to spend time together with me, to unlock that pure feeling, again, and rekindle the bliss I know we can have for one another. Can you still feel love, true love?

Tudor – I cannot trust anybody anymore ... not even myself. I need some time to clear my mind and purify my body. I have to take some time off to do it. I am polluted.

Adelle – You ignite fire in me. You merely need someone to devote her life to your happiness. I want to be next to you and help you see life again as it can be and see yourself for that matter as the greatest thing of value you possess. I will respect your wish ... but I want you to be assured that I am here every second of every day wanting to spend it with you. You've helped me, just by allowing me to meet with you. You helped to bring sense to my life again and I want you to know that it's only because of you.

Tudor – Thanks. Let's play it by the ear and slow.

Adelle – Alright.

What was Tudor to me, anyway? I mean, really? A lover, a boyfriend, or perhaps something undefined yet? The toil of uncertainty, the complexity of emotions I underwent every time we were together?

I set my phone aside and turned the TV on, surfing the channels and spacing out. A random TV commercial caught my eye - a glass being filled with Cognac. The vivid colors, sharp shapes, and beautiful graphics of the image left me hypnotized. I felt my thoughts drifting away. And then, suddenly, all that was human and inherently evil, all of Tudor's actions, became mute. They no longer affected me. I was alone and at peace, with only joy, contentment, and plenitude to keep me company.

But that lasted for only a few brief seconds. When I came back to earth, I regained my balance, I was back in my apartment. It had been an illuminating moment. And it left me with a little more confidence in myself. I breached a psychological barrier ... "I can do this," I said to myself. "I *know* I can!"

Chapter VIII
Our Dreams

A mind has a shape
Our thoughts bounce on its walls
In angles guided by this shape
The question is: what shapes it?
What changes our minds?

He altered mine
It was square before I met him
And it became wholly round
Was it my love for him?
Or was it our love for one another
Etching in each other's thoughts?

My office was located twenty-five minutes by bus from where I lived. The bank I worked for was a respectable financial institution, managing the *crème-de-la-crème* of personal and institutional wealth, one of the few banks surviving almost intact the latest economic crisis. I was proud to work for them throughout those precarious times, such an elitist and conservative institution. Their name was all over the news as a reputable, stable and trustworthy bank and trustee while everything else was crushed to pieces by investors, media and the recession. I was grateful to have a job, of course, considering that people had gotten laid off left and right, unable to pay their bills and mortgages any longer. Desperation and fear of a coming depression lurked at every corner, from one end of the city to the other. You could see it on people's faces on the bus. You could feel it through the walls of an office or at home or even in the public buildings.

Property values dropped. The housing bubble burst as predicted by some economists for a few years. The days of flipping primary residences and investment properties and running with your profit to the bank were over. A majority of homeowners suffered the consequences; even those innocent first-time buyers with perfect credit scores and their twenty-percent down payments.

Throughout the last decade there was a lingering trend to offshore jobs in less developed countries in order to control costs and temporarily improve corporate financial statements here at home. It seemed like a win-win situation for Corporate America: Executives avoided taking responsibility for the big picture while pocketing billions on quarter-to-quarter synthetically inflated profits. CEOs and CFOs moved from company to company with giant incomes, running them into bankruptcy or splintering them into pieces to be bought by private equity firm vultures in real-life Monopoly games, and then retiring early. They used part of their new found wealth to lobby politicians and established low tax brackets for the higher classes through many ways, one of them being dividend income.

The recession came as no surprise. It was rougher for most than any had been since the Great Depression of the Twenties.

Tudor had a prominent and remarkable quality of character: when he put his mind to it (not to mention his hands!), this man could turn dust into gold.

After graduating from college, he worked for a publishing house, copy editing and drawing illustrations for children's books. That inspired him to begin sculpting dolls, porcelain dolls that quickly caught on in popularity with a large Midwestern manufacturer and distributor. His dolls were delicate and had those classic sweet lively features, drawing attention to themselves fast and selling even faster.

Tudor also channeled some of his creative energy into business. The real estate market was booming at the time, with prices peaking in 2006 and 2007. He invested much of the proceeds from his art into residential and commercial real estate, buying some properties outright and mortgaging others. Things went well, indeed very well, at least for a while. And then the bubble burst. Swirled up into the vortex of the marketing tornado just like many other investors, his money remained locked into real estate assets well into 2009. Tudor followed his business instincts and the advice he received from his new real estate venture friends. His assets quickly declined in value. He couldn't sell them. Nothing was selling anymore. Foreclosures loomed everywhere. Renters fell behind in their monthly payments. And he fell behind on his own home mortgage while trying to save his investments.

Pressed by his financial troubles, he curtailed his sculpting and put all his energies into his remaining realty properties. But his expenses far exceeded his income, and he was no longer able to meet his monthly financial obligations. The stress and worries turned him into a permanently grumpy beast, snorting fire from his nose everywhere around him. He found a temporary relief in gambling hearts.

A social butterfly by nature, Tudor organized and attended many parties and social events within the Romanian community, quickly building a reputation as a ladies man, a real-life Casanova. People soon forgot that he was an artist. His reputation as a woman chaser proceeded him, and many women who had heard of his exploits steered clear of him. That of course merely turned him on all the more; instead of backing off, he chased them using even more persuasive techniques until he captured them. Once his hunger was satisfied, he moved on to his next prey with no more remorse than a tiger that has eaten its fill of wildebeest and moved on to something else. Some of his female conquests looked to him as a source of money, but he knew how to use them for what he wanted and managed to escape intact. He just wasn't ready to be saddled.

January 26, 2009

Adelle - *Bonjour mon amour*! I am taking my lunch break and wanted to see how you are. I had a good dream last night.

Tudor – I hope it was wet

Adelle - Not that kind of dream. It involved a lot of green fresh grass, leaves and you running, and a gorgeous tree in a plain field … it felt good when I woke up. It's a great one to have …according to my dream dictionary. Did you dream of anything?

Tudor – Mine was a good one too. I was planting a vineyard on the top of a hill. It was all very green also. There was a house in the background and the sun was shining on the horizon. It was right after rain. A blanket of clouds was still covering the sky, but it was warm.

Adelle – This is amazing! Something good is going to happen … I can't imagine what it is. I wish I could be in your arms right now … or close by so I can see your smile.

Adelle – When are we going to melt into each other's embrace again?

Tudor – Anytime.

Adelle – Coordinates?

Tudor – During the week, if you can last that long.

Adelle – I shall do my best but it's not easy!!!

Tudor – Wednesday night?

Adelle – Super. If the poles change in the meanwhile, feel free to make it sooner.

Tudor – OK.

Adelle - (later that eve) – Do you miss me?

Tudor - Yes, and I am so horny now!

Adelle – So am I.

Tudor – Damn! I am working on my mom's book. I wanna finish it this week. I can't distract myself. So Wednesday is OK with you?

Adelle – Sure

Our auspicious dreams on the same night were a sign. I viewed Freud's theory on dreams as the ultimate authority. I had inherited an old Romanian explanation of their meanings from my mom and grandmother. I looked the dreams up in a dictionary and on the Internet. The green grass, the clear skies, the running and planting of a grape-vine in a vineyard - all had a propitious significance.

January 28, 2009

Tudor – I am depressed and sad.

Adelle – I was planning on a little surprise for your birthday.

Tudor – What, a baby? I need to look up a birth cal-endar.

.

How do I answer this? Did he really want a baby? Even if by accident I should get pregnant and decide to have the baby, was he going to be a good father? How about me? How was I going to explain such a thing to my family, my friends? To society? Was I strong enough to go through with something as life-changing as parenting? What if he was just saying these things to test me, to see if I was as naïve as I seemed by not rejecting the notion out of hand?

These questions kept popping into my brain all after-noon, alternating with the euphoria I felt at the images of vibrant green grass, translucent through the rampant sun light, with drops of rain hanging still by their tips, causing them to bend gracefully to compose the perfect harmony of a spring morning landscape high up in the mountains.

I spent the rest of that evening singing and dancing to Tony Bennett. I climbed on the arm rest of my living room couch by the windows, holding a glass of Cabernet in one hand, and gazed through my sheer window covers at Lincoln Park Zoo, along Lake Shore Drive, across the city lights, through tears of happiness. This world, this life had just become my paradise, even with all its imperfections, despite all its barriers. I was at peace.

I had many more dreams to bring to reality one day aside from those I had already realized. My condominium was one of them: ever since I was a little girl I wanted to buy my own chic and cozy place and decorate it according to my own tastes to reflect my character. I pictured myself a business woman, traveling around the world, living independently for a while, until I found the *one*, a man who'd sweep me off my feet, my prince charming, the love of my life who would climb mountains to retrieve me if I'd dare run away and who would do anything for me just as I would for him ... the unconditional perfect love. Who knows ... maybe someday I may be blessed to find it.

The time had finally come for me to expose my talents as a cook for Tudor. Let him see the traditional "housewifie" side of me, which I often shied away from exposing. Although I hated cooking in general, when I did get into the kitchen, most people raved about the results. A gift horse should not be looked in the mouth.

As the hour drew near, I prepared the ingredients for Tudor's favorite meal: filet mignon with deep-fried baby red potatoes and salad. He arrived right on time, and when I opened the door, our kiss ignited a tsunami of feelings that swept us far beyond the boundaries of reality. I was so wrapped in his love that I nearly forgot the steaks on the grill. The kitchen smelled more like a Montana forest fire than a Chicago dinner. I blushed. He smiled. Burning a meal was hardly the way for a Romanian woman to capture her man's heart!

"I caught it just in time," I said. The outside was a little crisp, but the inside was still pink.

His eyes burned through me as I went about finishing up the meal. We chatted about little things, the weather, the stock market. He seemed genuinely impressed that a woman could talk intelligently on matters of finance and investments.

When everything was finally ready, I asked him to join me at the table. He pulled out my chair and kissed me on the back of the neck as I slid in. He made a few cute remarks about my cooking skills, threw out a couple of jokes about how our sex drive had nearly forced us to eat out that evening.

"That wouldn't have been the worst thing in the world," I said, smiling at him coyly. He raised his glass, and I joined him in a toast, his eyes never leaving mine. When he returned the glass to the table, he shook his head.

"What is it?" I asked.

"You would amaze the world's best French chef," he said. I felt myself blush. "I'm serious. He wouldn't know whether to ridicule you or hold you in the highest regard for what you've put together here tonight. This is an amazing collection. Your own? Do you ever follow a recipe?" He grinned, his steely eyes narrowing.

"No. I never do." I said, feeling suddenly embarrassed. And then it struck me: *Why?* I turned to face him, my stare suddenly challenging his. "Why would I? Why should I? Isn't life a lot more exciting, more adventurous, without all the rules? And isn't it the same with food?"

"Absolutely. Fine, I'll grant you that."

"Do you think I should have followed a recipe?"

90

He swallowed his food and shook his head. "You don't need a recipe if you can cook like this. It's fantastic!"

We went on through the meal like that, with Tudor sparring constantly and me standing toe-to-toe with him, challenging his every thrust and parry. And when the meal was finally finished and he placed his napkin on the table, he said softly, "You are amazing. You're one-of-a-kind. In fact," he added, draining his glass of the last of the wine, "I'm not entirely sure what to do with you the rest of the evening. Hmmm ... let me think."

He slid his chair back, rose, and walked around my side of the bar, lifting me off my chair and leaning me up against the fridge. He pressed his chest against mine and kissed me, lightly, then more firmly, and finally quite hard. He kissed me yet again. He covered my quivering lips with kisses.

"You are amazing, and you know it," his lips uttered after they had finally released mine, staining them dark purple-cherry in color and leaving me gasping for air.

"Ah ... I see," I replied. "You must mean you are ready for dessert! I have it in the freezer. Although I must admit: you are hot, hot, hot, *monsieur*. In fact you almost won the game." I wiggled free of him and opened the freezer door with my left hand, removed the tray with my right, and gazed back at him before leading him once more to his seat.

We poked at our frozen desserts and continued our verbal sparring throughout the rest of the meal, Tudor talking about the problems of nationalism and how so many first generation immigrants to the states have such a difficult time assimilating. He had an answer for everything ... even for my darkest fears. I never dared debate the subject with anyone other than my father over dinner one time when I was home for a visit. I couldn't help thinking that Tudor would get along well with my father.

91

He said something to me, and I barely heard. My mind raced, my heart exploded within my chest. I looked into his eyes and saw that his mind was racing, too. *To hell with immigration and nationalism* I thought, and I learned closer to him, begging for a kiss.

Within seconds, we were grappling with one another again. And then the inevitable happened: a pleasant enough discussion had turned into a wild race to undress. Our lips locked as our tongues met gently, seductively. My hands slipped beneath his shirt, feeling the hardness of his bare skin and taut muscles; his hands slipped up behind my sweater and down my back, down into my jeans. Our passions only intensified. The dance of love had begun. It was intoxicating. It was delicious. It was destiny.

We somehow moved from the sitting room into the bedroom. What was it, I wondered, that had infiltrated our senses even deeper than the time before and the one before that and onward into infinity? I had nothing but my cotton ivory sheet wrapped around me. I was pressed against the most amazing man I had ever met. *What could shatter this immeasurable happiness?* I wondered.

Absolutely nothing

Chapter IX
Introduction to Our Friends

Winds swirl up snow in dazzling circles
Trees stand tall in white heavy mantles
Ice stars blanket windows and benches
Winter is here, through cities … in spirits

After a month of dating, it was time for Tudor to meet some of my friends. Laura, one of my closest, worked out of our London office. Our company had made the decision not to extend her U.S. work visa due to the recent recession and rising corporate costs. She had been transferred to London (though not without a fight!) a year earlier.

I had met her a few years back on our company's shuttle bus. She was teaching an American colleague how to say *yellow duck* in Romanian. Don't ask me why. The two were seated behind me. When I heard the Romanian words, a burst of joy followed by a cloud of melancholia wrapped in homesickness swept over me. She repeated the words a few times more. I burst into laughter, turned toward her, and said *hello* in Romanian. We became the best of friends right then and there.

Laura introduced me to my two other Romanian friends, Jake and Bogdan. She had a joyful, optimistic, witty and ambitious character. Her motivation was inspiring. She complimented my own personality perfectly. We clicked from the very start and never had a single negative thing to say about one another.

Olivia helped me plan a Saturday evening of dinner, drinks, and dancing in honor of Laura's visit. I was in charge of making restaurant reservations at one of her favorite places.

January 21, 2009
Adelle - Olivia' s sister, Laura, is coming to town next week. Olivia and I were planning a dinner and a night of clubbing on Saturday 31st. Laura is one of my closest friends. She's also the one who introduced me to most of my few Romanian friends. Would you accompany me?
Tudor - Sure. Count on it!

At the last minute, Luke announced his own plans for his birthday celebration on the very same evening. I had to scramble around in order to reorganize the events to accommodate everyone.

January 30, 2009
Adelle (Morning) - Hi baby! I changed the restaurant for tomorrow eve. It was too late to make reservations for such a large party. We're going to Adobo instead. See if Luke is interested and I can call them to reserve a larger table for all of us.
Tudor – Thanks. But Luke is set on his place. I'll let you know where and when. If you already have plans with your friends it's OK, I'll go by myself and not stay too long. We can meet later. His dinner is at eight.
Adelle – The timing is bad again. See if they want to meet us at the club Z on Randolph after ten. Olivia can place everyone on the list with no cover. I wanted to be there with you. Can you make it then around nine to our restaurant? Some of the guys don't want to go to the club and I really wanted to introduce you to them. We'll work something out.
Tudor – We'll see. No promises.

Tudor – (Later that afternoon) If you wanna be my date tomorrow night, you'll have to ditch your friends. Luke made reservations for a limited number of seats. If you think it's important to not be able to drop your friends at such late notice, then we'll have to meet another day. I'm not going to any clubs on Saturday, so it's your decision. Either way, I will not be mad at you, but please, let me know. Thanks!

Adelle – It's not about ditching!!! I haven't seen my friend since last March and she is here for only one week. I also want to be with you, so here's a plan: I will meet them at eight for an hour. I already rented a car for the weekend and I can drive to where you are to spend the rest of the eve. Laura will kill me, but at least I'll get to see her.

Tudor – No. Stay with your friends! It's ok. I'll go by myself. Thanks. Sorry for the short notice. Luke told me about it a month ago. He never decided on a date and place until two days ago. Have fun!

Adelle – Look, I want to be there with you! How about if we do this: come over to Adobo, we spend some time with my friends and then we both go to Luke's.

Tudor – NO! Have fun tomorrow! I will too. We'll meet another time.

Adelle – You mean a lot to me and if being at Luke's thing at eight is that important to you, then I will go with you. I'll call Laura and see if I can meet with her on Sunday.

Tudor – No. I already invited someone else. Forget it. The gal I invited is only a friend, a single mother, who is eager to go out. I don't need to sleep with her. Just company since everyone else has a wife or girlfriend. Have fun! I'll see you next week!

Adelle – Well, what can I say? I am easily replaceable. If you care to be with me, then please don't show up with some other woman at our friends' dinner parties. I told you I can be there and I will if you want me to.

Tudor – Too late. Go and have fun. These are Luke's friends and I couldn't care less what they think. I see them once every three years. They don't care about my reputation.

Adelle – Tudor, I CARE about US!

I was fuming, but I left it at that.

I left my office around four forty-five in the afternoon to pick up the car I rented for the weekend. I had a couple of other errands to run, in addition to driving to Tudor's house if he came to his senses. The car rental place was right across from my office.

Adelle – (Later that day) Just picked up the car. Do you want to get dinner some place?

Tudor – No, thanks. I'm having dinner with Luke.

Adelle – OK. Let me know if you want me to join you later. I rented a sweet SUV hybrid that begs for driving.

Tudor – Enjoy driving and be careful! Don't drive like me.

Adelle – It sounds weird but drives well. I miss you, my darling!

Tudor – Me too! I'm drunk already. Enjoy!

Adelle – (After parking the car) Do you have any idea how to unlock a steering wheel?

Tudor – Some cars have a button on the side of the steering wheel. Try to press it first.

Adelle – You just saved me! Thank you!

Tudor – As they say in Romania: "A pebble can turn over a carriage".

Adelle – I have so much to learn from you!

Hmm … it appears as if the beast does have a soul after all, I thought.

I fought my way home through the snow and Arctic winds and, after making the rounds with Luca around my island bar, I opened a box with the Crucifix sculpture that I had ordered from Tudor's website. It was only a reproduction of the original in his home. He had been quite disappointed with the limited edition, which had been made in China. The last time I'd gone to his home, he asked me to compare the reproduction to the original and note the profane discrepancies between the two. He had hung one of the copies next to the original on his hallway wall for comparison purposes. I had to admit that, with my untrained eye, I couldn't see any differences, aside from the obvious overall size difference between the two and perhaps a few other minor details.

I studied the copy after hanging it on my reading-corner wall. The definition of the veins, the expressive position of the fingers and toes, the sadness on Jesus' face, the posture of the crucified body and the manner in which the muscle mass was sculpted were astounding. Tudor was a sculpting god! I sat in front of the piece as tears formed in my eyes. The sculpture symbolized man's inhumanity to man and expressed Christianity in a unique, arresting and august manner. I imagined churches would go crazy for this piece.

Adelle – I opened the Crucifix … It is simply marvelous! Every church, every Christian should want one on one scale or another.
Tudor – Thanks!

With little hope of seeing Tudor that evening, I took a hot bath and crashed on the sofa with a good movie. I turned in, and when Saturday arrived, I was revitalized by the sun's strong wintery glare. But the January sun in Chicago can be deceitful. The temperature dipped well below freezing, and the Arctic blast that swept across the city from Lake Michigan could turn a man into stone in a heartbeat.

I dressed quickly, as warmly as I could, and set about getting an army of chores done as quickly as possible. I checked my watch and sent Tudor a quick message.

January 31, 2009

Adelle – Hi! I am running around like crazy. Just wanted to say hi.

Tudor – I don't wanna see you anymore.

Adelle – I understand. The fact that I want to see you is of no importance.

Tudor – No.

I was stunned. His cruelty sliced through me as if he'd used a knife. I wondered if he measured his words on occasion, whether or not he ever stopped to think about the irreparable damage they could do to me. After many minutes without a reply, I confronted him. I had to know what made him tick.

Tudor closed himself up in a glass cube of pride and coldness, the perfectly sealed cocoon, protecting himself from all interaction with others, protecting himself from me. But why? And why couldn't I simply let the matter drop? Even if it meant laying my head on madam guillotine before him, I was going to find out. I had to find out.

Adelle – I wanted to see you tonight. Good night! Your words really hurt.

Tudor – Maybe I just want to be alone, how about that? You may be cheerful; you've got a car. You didn't do it to come see me. You got it for your friends' enjoyment. I just want to be alone. I was your Plan B, anyway, your appendix for the night. No, thanks!

Adelle – Why do you always draw such conclusions? I wanted to take you on a road trip tomorrow to Wisconsin, the House on the Stone. I haven't driven in so long, and you need to relax. It sounded like a fun thing to do. I thought you'd be pleased.

I waited for several minutes, and when I didn't hear back, I sent him another message.

Adelle – You knew about Laura's visit. She is one of my dearest friends and I have told her about you, about us, and how happy I am now. Yet, if you want to spend the evening alone, I understand.

Tudor – Fine. Have fun with your friends. House on the Stone is a frightful monstrosity that gave me chills the first time I saw it ten years ago and I don't intend to repeat the experience. Really, you should focus on entertaining your friends as I have to do mine. Good night!

Adelle – And by the way … Olivia already has a car. I didn't need to rent one for Laura's visit. Olivia drove to your New Year's party and that's how we came to your house. We can go anywhere else you want tomorrow then. Let me know if you have any good ideas – hills … forest.

No answer. Perhaps there was no way for me to break through his armor, the walls he had built from his age, knowledge, experience, and pride. He wasn't willing yet to rid himself of it voluntarily. Why did I think I could help? He most likely considered me inferior to him in many ways. I was far younger, headstrong, ambitious and independent. Did he see in me only one more silly young woman, perhaps more independent than most, who was destined to succumb to his power and be crushed beneath his boot heel? Was I no more to him than another conquest to be used and discarded at will?

I couldn't allow myself to believe that.

I continued holding onto my phone for dear life, watching for the little red flashing light and waiting for a new message. I was ecstatic to spend time with my friends, but torn by a million painful questions I had no answer for regarding Tudor. I was running totally on instinct. He was on my mind, drilling through my emotions, making a hole in my heart, burning with the ashes of desire, a fire that could be extinguished only by a word from him, or a look.

I had so much to tell him. I had the world to confess and the universe to learn from him. I wanted to breathe the air he did, drink the water he did, think his every thought ... be his and only his.

February 1, 2009
Tudor – (3:00 a.m.) If by any chance you decide to show up tonight, the front door is open. Luke and Anna will be there. The address is 150 Destiny Lane, Wood Dale.

Tudor – If not, I will see you tomorrow.

Tudor – Actually don't bother. They changed their mind. Luke fell asleep in their car. Anna wanted to go home. I'm going to sleep and I locked the door. Talk to you tomorrow.

I had fallen asleep and I was devastated when I noticed the three missed messages from earlier in the morning.

Adelle – Just got your last messages. There's no way I could have driven after drinking wine at the club. Laura and Olivia dropped me off at home and I went straight to sleep. Of course Luca decided to wake me up at 7:00. I'm trying to get a couple more hours of sleep. I want to be at your place at nine, if that's OK with you, so we get an early start on our little road trip.

Tudor – No road trip for me. I'm just going to sleep soon. I've been watching tennis all night.

Adelle – If you would have allowed me to plan the darned evening properly I would have driven to the club, not had any wine, and then driven to your place before midnight.

Adelle – Can you wait another hour before you go to bed? I can get in the car in like fifteen minutes and then we can fall asleep together.

Tudor – No. Nothing early. I'll call you when I'm ready.

I lifted Luca onto my bed and she dug her way under the warm covers next to my belly. We fell asleep together for another couple of hours; when we woke up around nine, I got dressed to take the rental for a drive along the lake. Lunch would be a good time to see Tudor.

I hopped into the car and took Lake Shore Drive to Montrose driving through the park alleyways to my favorite spot. I went there every now and then since moving to the city, admiring the magnificent all-encompassing views of downtown, the skyscrapers and the glass and steel towering monuments.

The city, immersed in a gloomy dark winter fog, had an aura of peace and quiet on Sundays. Downtown Chicago imposed upon its panorama an air of a cozy American city, elegant yet unpretentious. Lonely and hungry seagulls floated above the icy crust glazing the lake, searching for a trace of food.

Why wasn't Tudor there with me, holding me in his arms? The usual strange feeling of belonging to this man was overbearing, though he was far, far away, farther away than anyone else has ever been to me, anyone who ever meant anything in my life.

That early afternoon he wanted to get lunch together. There was a "mom-and-pop" Greek diner close to his house that made irresistible feta cheese and spinach omelets. When I arrived at his home, food was no longer our primary source of nourishment. We were both starved, but for more than mere sustenance. I threw myself into his strong arms the moment he opened the door, and we kissed and stroked one another and began slowly undressing each other as we fumbled our way up the stairs to his bedroom.

Everything else vanished into nothingness. Everything else disappeared from life. Every fight, every hurt, every attack, every put down, everything dissolved in a fluid mass of bliss whenever we made love. All the grief he caused me, all the pain disappeared beneath our carnal desire for one another, a voracious physical belonging satisfied only when our bodies met. And joined.

His old bed covers were soft and luxurious. His pillows were a plush womb of heavenly feathers that molded into any shape or form. His body was strong and unyielding, or perhaps it was his mind that made his body appear so. We collapsed in one another's arms for an indeterminate time of exquisitely deep, satisfying sleep.

We might well have slept forever except for Luke's telephone call. He was hungry, and since neither Tudor nor I had eaten anything yet that day, we jumped at his suggestion to meet him for dinner in Old Town.

We drove my car into the city, and as we headed to the French restaurant that Luke and his wife Anna had opted to visit. Tudor behaved strangely, agitated, happy, hipper, impatient, not paying any attention to anything I said to him, or responding with some childish remark. I had never seen him that way before. No matter what subject I approached, I couldn't keep him focused on it for more than a couple of minutes before he switched to something completely unrelated while grabbing my right leg and caressing it obscenely. I was distracted and uncomfortable, even though I had made love to him the entire afternoon. It was as if he was not himself. Was he overly excited about our afternoon together or was it something else? He calmed down a bit by the time we stopped to shop on Michigan Avenue.

Was it me? I wondered. Perhaps I'd imagined the strange behavior. He seemed all right a couple of hours later as we were waiting for our food. Then Tudor made a comment that took me by surprise: "It says in your horo-scope that you are getting married this year." We all laughed. When I looked into his eyes, I saw what I had never seen in my ex-fiancée's eyes in all the time I'd known him, not even after he'd proposed to me in Paris. Passionate love.

Maybe *that's* why he had acted so strangely earlier. Maybe he realized just how perfectly we fit together, what a magnificent couple we made. Perhaps finally he had decided, against all odds, to trust me. And to trust in his own feelings, as well. His *true* feelings.

I wasn't able to find a reply to that. Not a coherent one anyway. I was mildly amused by his statement, as the grain of *what if* which he had planted on the couple of other occasions the subject came up, sprang out into a tiny fragile snowdrop. And just like that, I was the one spacing out for the remaining of our dinner conversation, missing half of the jokes Luke and Tudor threw across the table.

While driving him home, he asked: "How do you see your life's picture a few years from now?" My heart shivered for a moment. After a long silence, I finally uttered: "Frank-ly … I don't know. I have too many things on my agenda, and yet no decent level of certainty that any will come to fruition." I directed the discussion into art, avoiding any further elaborations on *my life's picture.* The thirty or so miles to his house were behind us before we knew it. I rushed out to get home before midnight. Another day in the office and an early morning alarm clock were a good excuse; what happened and was said that day needed serious mental regurgitation, ideal for saving me of half a good night's sleep.

Tudor held my face in his hands, kissing me good night while gently massaging my forehead; his penetrating stare, the cult-like intensity of his eyes, caught my own, captured them, ensuring that I was still his hostage, one he still dominated. His intense supremacy, his unrestrained willpower melted my very soul. I could not possibly resist.

I had always considered myself strong enough to face anything without fear. The man standing right before me, though, was something I did not understand and could not defend myself against. His charms, his power, his authority.

I sometimes missed the simple and uneventful life I had enjoyed before him, yet, he was an illuminating element within my existence. My life's portrait would have been painted of pale shades without him. Was this the substance that my teenager dreamy mind secretly entertained while starring at the high waves and the grey cloudy sky on long walks by the godforsaken Black Sea shore in winter?

Weakened by the long day's experiences, I gladly accepted the cup of coffee he offered me on my way out of the house. He poured it into a blue mug that I took along for the long drive home. I lost myself in thought all the way back along miles of nearly deserted highway.

Tudor – (As I drove home) Stay up!
Adelle – Did. Just got home. Thank you for another perfect day!
Tudor – Thanks for the same! XOXO!

Chapter X
Every Drop of Ink Hurts

What is the truth and what is a lie?
What keeps us going and why do we die?
Why spend a lifetime decoding our wants
When all lies before us, within our ardors?

Not knowing true love ... what else worse can be?

A second, a minute, a day or a year
How long has it passed since I have been here?

February days are short in Chicago: snowy, windy, dry and blisteringly cold.

Most Chicagoans hate winter. Me? I love it. I love the snowflakes dancing around my windows and melting on my coat. I yearn to jump into the tallest pile of white fluff I can find and bury myself. I love the soft, cold, pure texture of the snow. Live in a tropical climate? Are you kidding? Sorry, not for me. I love snow too much. How it makes me giggle when I see it out the window or dip my boots into the fresh flakes covering the streets.

Unfortunately, not even the snowiest winter in Chicago's history could save me from the hectic schedule I faced at work. It was year's fiscal end. And that meant it was *my* busiest time of year.

I needed a break. I found just enough free time at work to look up some classic Romanian poets and came across; a melodious verse I hoped would brighten Tudor's day.

February 2, 2009

Adelle – (Translated from Nichita Stanescu one of the greatest Romanian poets):

"When we saw each other the air between us
pushed away all of the sudden
the image of trees, indifferent and empty;
we allowed them to over-shadow us.

Oh … we ran in the other's arms
Screaming our names, so fast
that time crushed between our chests,
and the hour, broke into little pieces".

Adelle – *Bonjour mon amour*!
Tudor – You too, thanks!
Adelle – How is your day?
Tudor – OK.

He left it at that. No explanation. No details. I dared not ask any further questions. He was busy … but busy with what? My heart couldn't help but wonder. Regardless how busy I was, I always found time to reply to his messages with specific details, sometime more than needed. Work was one way to stop obsessing over the various scenarios running through my head, so I dove into my job and tried not to give it any more thought. Until I got home, at least.

Adelle – (Late evening) The evening is empty, the night will be a cold and dark place until my eyes close and I can dream of being next to you.

Adelle – (Half an hour later) Anyway, you don't seem to fancy nice words.

Adelle – (Three hours later way past midnight) Tudor???!!!!

Still no answer. I went to bed though I knew I was not going to get much sleep. Any sign from him, good or bad, would have made a world of difference. It was his silence that brought me to despair.

February 3, 2009
Adelle – (4:00 a.m.) Are you OK?
Tudor – (8:13 a.m.) I'm OK.
Adelle – Good. Have a wonderful day! On my way to work and it is bright, shiny and coooooold.
Tudor – Stay warm!
Adelle – Yes, my baby bear.
Tudor – Stop it! I'm not a two year old.
Adelle – Fine grumpy!
Adelle – (Later that day) I want you to kiss me.

His silence nearly killed me. We'd only just started dating. Was my kiss no longer desirable for him? Already? Every second I stared at my phone and saw no reply was a wrecking ball slamming into the wall of my self-confidence. And the wall began to crack just as an idea came to my mind: would texting him an elegant *good bye* in French salvage anything left of us before it was too late? According to an old Romanian custom, key expressions in French had the potential at least to warrant a response. I wondered.

Adelle – (Twenty minutes later, no response) – *Adieu monsieur*!
Tudor – *Adieu.*
Adelle – Your cruelty has no limits.
Tudor – Yes.
Adelle – I will love you until the day I die, regardless.
Tudor – You do that!

Adelle – Yes! I will do that!

Adelle – At least I don't run away from what I feel.

Adelle – Tudor!!! It all makes senses now ... the rumors about you .... women are disposable to you, not worth your ultimate pursuit.

Tudor – I'm tired. I don't have time for this crap.

Adelle – I have already given in to my feelings for you ... your words are incredibly painful sometimes.

Adelle – It is difficult for me to read your mind, to see what you are going through when we are not together, we only communicate through texts. Talking on the phone once in a while would help. I wish I could be closer to you, to be able to help. I understand if you need your space.

Tudor – My diagnosis for you is different: you are more in love with the idea of love and you need someone to be the subject of your fantasies. The reality is that this person could easily be anyone BUT me and the more I prefer to keep my distance from you, the more you are enticed to pursue the fantasy.

Adelle – You always conclude the exact opposite because you are biased in your experiences. I only acted with you as genuinely as I felt ... if it is too wrong ... I expected you to guide me through what I need to do. And if you have chosen to put distance between us, it is because you fear unleashing your own feelings as loose as I have mine. Just let it be if you love me, love me as you want to. I am yours with every particle that I exist and that is why it hurts when you put this synthetic distance between us.

Adelle – And you apparently have to make me cry at least on a weekly basis!

Tudor – Maybe you're right. Maybe I don't love you. It was an infatuation that expired too soon. Better luck next time!

Adelle – Do you really believe your own words? Your actions certainly can lie because you learned how to control your behavior with women in time. Your eyes can't. Your eyes have spoken to me from the moment I walked through your kitchen on New Year's eve and you were sitting in the corner, by the sink, with company. Your heart met mine then as mine met yours. I couldn't even say goodbye to you that night because I shuddered at what I instantly felt.

Adelle – Your hands when you touch my skin do not lie. When your lips touch mine and you are inside me, when we are one, as you know it as we both feel it. Why are you torturing us?

Adelle – Yes, there are a million things we need to learn about each other, but that is the fun of life, of a relationship, learning each other's imperfections and loving them as much as the qualities, aligning things important to both of us and pursuing our dreams together. Take all the time you need to answer this. I have patience.

Adelle – (A couple of hours later) I feel like throwing up. My belly hurts and I have an irregular heart beat. I am glued to my phone, and I am seriously starting to question why I even feel what I do for you. I hope one day it will make sense.

Adelle – As you wish my love … over and out.

Tudor – My phone was out of battery for the last few hours. I like you, but I am sorry, I can't feel love for anyone anymore. Nothing personal. I don't know what's wrong. I've been totally de-sensitized.

Adelle – You only need some time with me. It is a challenge of my own to love you as much as I do and also be able to open you up to your own feelings, whatever they are For now, you are covering yourself under a defense shield and attacking every single time I am getting near. Please … give us some time.

Tudor – No, I'm feeling-less.

Adelle – This world has some good left in it that is far beyond material mass. It is in our minds and feelings … if we purposely avoid feeling the most basic and natural emotion between a man and a woman, because we might get hurt again, then life has less sense. You are not empty yet! It is there, within you. It comes out of you in your amazing work and the things that you've chosen to surround yourself with.

Adelle – You are a work of art in yourself, and you have more feelings and passion in you than anyone I have ever seen or met before. You just choose to keep it locked away for now.

Tudor – It's safer under lock and key.

Adelle – Yeah … self-made prison … sure it is. Yet it is the very essence of existence, if released and met with the same, to make it sublime, complete, the very meaning of life!

Adelle – When out of the two minds and passions that met and became complete forms a third life, a baby, there is nothing that will surpass that feeling.

Tudor – Well, yes, a third is a blessing if both lovers want it.

Tudor – Go to bed! Good night!

I had to think hard about what I would type to get a reaction out of him. He made my mind work for him, for what would raise his interest in me. There was no time to get used to him, be lazy, comfortable with my feelings, as one might in a stable relationship. Every expression I typed had to be something to motivate him to reply. This did not wear on me. On the contrary: I felt startled, antagonized; and I wanted more of it as much as I hated admitting so. This man was something else, someone who forced me to rebuild myself, stretched my thoughts, worked my imagination and creativity, and nurtured my thinking, bringing to the surface things that were mummified in insecurities deep down within me. He forced me to exhume that tiny portion of my brain so used to vegetating when things went well. But when they didn't...

February 4, 2009

Adelle – Hi! Are you OK?

Tudor – Why wouldn't I be?

Adelle – I don't know!!! Just asking. I am feeling incredibly crummy – still like throwing up, belly hurts and so do my breasts ... something is definitely off. My doctor is not in the office today.

Tudor – I'm sorry to hear that. So you want to come over? Maybe you should stop taking those pills. They're obviously not the right type for you.

Adelle - I'm at work ... will try to make it through the afternoon. I have an audit closing meeting with senior management at 3:00 so I need to be here. What are you doing later?

Tudor – Just working till tonight. I have to give an invoice to the sports bar later and collect a check, after five anytime.

Adelle – Do you want to get dinner? Although I don't see how I can even touch anything but light chicken or miso soup if I still feel the same. It would be lovely to see you.

Tudor – We can meet when I go to Wrigleyville to get my check. I don't wanna eat either. Just coffee and maybe some club soda.

Adelle – That sounds great.

Tudor – OK. I'll see you after five sometime. I'll call you when I leave my house.

Tudor – (Soon after five in the evening) I'm sorry, but we'll have to push this meeting till tomorrow. I'm feeling sick too. I hope you feel better.

Adelle – No worries … get some hot tea and lots of sleep. The weather should be a little better tomorrow, I hope. I'll probably go to sleep early. I don't even have enough energy to make it to the gym. I hope we'll both be better by tomorrow. Call if you need anything. Sweet kiss!

Tudor – Sleep well and be well by tomorrow. And don't put stuff in your body that's toxic. Your body tells you what's good for it.

Adelle – I miss my dearest sooo much!

He canceled or rescheduled our dates again and again. I purposely refused to rationalize the grim reality. How could I, without going crazy! I looked for any excuse I could find, just to keep me in the game. His aloofness, his display of insensitivity and cruelty were remarkably blunt and even offensive. But why didn't he let go? Selfishness? Callousness? A desire to see me suffer so? And why didn't I tell myself, "Enough! I will suffer him no longer!"

Ahh … but my heart, my heart said no. Instead of being repelled by him, I was attracted to him like a magnet to another of opposite poles. I vaguely recalled a legend I heard during my childhood of a girl who embarked on a journey wearing iron shoes, a journey that changed her outlook on life and taught her what true love really is. The shoes are burdensome and dreadful to wear, and the adventure is a dangerous and agonizing one. Was I the girl? There was something exquisite about that excruciating pain.

February 5, 2009
Adelle – (I sent him a verse)
"We will have happy dreams
And a tune will be sang to us
by lonely springs
and the gentle breeze.

112

We will fall asleep in harmony
Of the forest covered in thoughts
Flowers will fall upon us
In many layers"
- Translation from M. Eminescu.

Tudor – You have too much time on your hands. I don't.

Adelle – It's not always like this – these are some of the benefits of the corporate world, a little something to help balance all the other negatives.

Tudor – See you later, bye!

Tudor – (A few hours later) You know what, I don't think it's a good idea to see you again. Something doesn't click with me emotionally. There's something missing.

Adelle – Tudor, my instincts never deceive me. I want to be with no one other than you for the rest of my life. You made me see sense in life again. It's the note on Facebook … isn't it? The note is referring to you.

Tudor – There is no note. It's how I honestly feel.

Adelle – It's how you want to feel not how you truly feel. I don't want anybody else in my life! I can make you happy, as happy as I am now just because I met you.

Tudor – As you say, but I have to go anyway.

Adelle – Just let it be! Let our love be!

Tudor – I envy you for feeling love. I don't. It's beyond my control.

Adelle – Then just let me love you! Otherwise I cannot honestly picture life without you. I'm only asking for time.

Tudor – Oh, don't make it sound so melodramatic! You'll be fine. Take care!

Adelle – Enjoy continuing to hunt for ghosts … the real love you chose to crush because its purity and honesty and immensity overwhelmed you. I am not as superficial as you want me to think you feel. I'll hold onto my love for you as long as I live and breathe.

Adelle – (An hour later) Tudor!!!!!

Adelle – I will not touch food or water until you see what we mean to one another. I believe in us more than I ever believed in anything in my entire life.

Tudor – Stop it, snap out of it. You will do no such thing. You are skin and bones as it is. Besides, if you continue, I'll have to give you an Oscar. I'm not the one for you. I'm sorry. It was nothing more than a straw fire and I apologize. I cannot fall in love with anyone anymore. I don't know why and I don't want to stick around and ruin your life in the hope that I'll find out.

Tudor – My battery will die any minute, I don't have a charger with me.

Adelle – You've already ruined it to the point that my life means nothing to me anymore. I wish I could explain how, at my age, a man can put me in this condition ... my will for existing is diminishing with every second. It is not my fault you don't believe me. If you'd see me this second you'd understand.

Tudor – You'll go out with your friends and find someone this weekend. I'm no good anyway.

Adelle – Don't you understand? Without you, I don't want to exist anymore! You should see me now.

Tudor – No, I shouldn't. That wouldn't solve anything. You've just developed an obsession and you know it. We don't have enough in common to make it work. I know ... I can tell after two dates. You need to find someone else.

Adelle – Obsession? That can only be over things, objects ... I never had an obsession. I am disintegrating particle by particle since you wrote your cruel words to me a few hours ago. You call it what you want, I can only define it as I feel it.

Tudor – Obviously pain is a good stimulant for creativity. Maybe you should start writing.

Adelle – Yes, I will, you bring this out of me. The pain does … losing you does … I want to write one day, about all the pain, to be followed by blissful and wonderful times … so whoever reads the story will have hope in life, and live for true love, to find it and live it as I want to … as I found it … in you.

Tudor – If you are happy, you lose your creativity, I am helping you here.

Adelle – I have never known profound and fulfilled love before. How can you say that? I want to leave behind something that will inspire and give hope, not depress and demoralize a reader even more than our monotone lives are now, without what I feel right now … what we both feel.

Adelle – I can't show up in the office tomorrow after so many hours of crying this way. I will call in.

Exasperated and sobbing, I tried to fall asleep. Nothing made sense. Why did he feel the need to break up with me every so often, when I knew clearly it was not only a physical attraction between us? But above all, why was I reacting so? I could not understand myself. Why didn't I just give up … draw a line in the sand, put an end to my own misery? Such humiliation on my account was hardly anything I ever thought I would allow myself to endure. There were other men around, but my heart and my mind were already soaked in my adoration for him. Why?

February 6, 2009
Adelle – I am home today, and having already reached a pretty low level of ridicule as far as you think of me already, I suppose that letting you know I meant every word yesterday evening is probably not going to make me look any worse than I already do. Passion has no limits to what it

endures and what it can achieve. Have a wonderful day my darling!

Tudor – You'll be a skeleton soon then. Go eat!

Adelle – I am serious about this, you brutal creature!!! You will at least have the courage to say the words to me directly not in a text and not over the phone. I should be in a hospital by Monday if I don't pick up your messages anymore. I love you to death and for that I at least deserve you to be honest and human to me.

Tudor – That's it. You are getting an Oscar. I prefer to write because I can barely hear you on the phone or in person, I do not want to say this to you in person. It'll make it worse.

Adelle – Worse than this? Worse than denying your feelings for me because you misinterpret what I post on my darned Facebook wall? Worse than me losing my will to live because the man to whom I am giving my all crushes and humiliates me constantly? Worse than all of this salt poured on an open wound?

Tudor – I'm your vehicle to creative writing. Pain is good.

Adelle – Is it too difficult to believe, to comprehend that someone is capable of loving and adoring you for who you are … with all your quirks and imperfections???

Tudor – Yes, it's beyond my comprehension that you can be so hooked after only three dates.

Adelle – Yes, I think I already have a bookful of all our text messages from the past month!!! I experienced more pain from you than all the cumulative pain for all my previous relationships combined! I want to write about love, as insane and irrational as ours is … and live it, and be happy at the same time, while making you happy.

Tudor - You do that!

Adelle – You say this??? You were as hooked as I was since the moment our eyes met on New Year's, you

Gabriela Sbarcea

know it! You were aware that I might get pregnant the second time we made love at your place. You even asked if I could give you a baby for your birthday only a week-and-a-half ago ... and then I asked you if you meant it and you told me that you did ... I know you did!!!

Adelle – OK ... you tell me what makes you happy then! I won't try to guess anymore. I thought I understood at least a little about what makes you tick, what you live for. What can I do to make you happy? And hopefully it's before I pass out and die malnourished because you won't open your mind and heart to your own feelings.

Tudor – Now it's becoming comic, your malnutrition! I can see you smirking. Just take a break, ok? Take a deep breath, go outside and take a walk. It's nice outside.

Adelle – I was planning on taking a walk ... Luca would be happy. That's not going to change my determination to make you believe I mean every single one of the words of love I have for you. I will not touch food nor water until you come see me. Until your skepticism will no longer keep you from loving me even half as much as I love you!

Tudor – Blackmail doesn't work on me. Besides, the only person hurting from hunger is you.

Adelle – Blackmail??? Only you could look at it that way. It saddens me even more. I say these things so that you see you must quit denying your own feelings. To call it blackmail is an insult. And yes, it hurts not to eat or even to have a glass of water in nearly twenty-four hours. What do you want of me so you stop questioning my feelings for you and stop trying to break us apart every other week? Don't you think I want a peaceful, quiet, magnificent relationship filled with joy and love? The kind where we cannot wait to embrace each other and spend as much time together as we possibly can? To make the best of this short life we have here on earth?

117

Adelle – (Several hours later) Just forget that I exist ... that's what you seem to want. I wouldn't want to make you hate me. I found you ... my darling love, but cannot go beyond what I already have. Don't worry about me ... I am a strong character and usually do better than most people I know. Best of luck with everything!

Tudor – To you too!

The idea I should begin writing a book grew like the new leaves on trees under the blazing sun, reflecting in the snow and caressed by the freezing winds of early March. Writing a book had been on my mind for some time. I had never found enough inspiration before I'd met Tudor, before our maniacal exchange of texts.

I opened up my laptop and started typing a title to the book about Tudor and I and our twisted love story. He made the perfect central character. The rest I was to figure out in time ... this was a beginning, illuminating my deeply pessimistic outlook for us, of what may come to be in the end. Maybe that was it, that was the answer ... the truth about a maddening love in one book, exposed to the world, to the harsh opinion of anyone and everyone.

Resolute and weakened by both lack of food and my marathon text message fight with Tudor, I decided to call Olivia. We made plans to meet for drinks later that day. My life had to be dragged back to normalcy, even if a man had trampled all over it, regardless of how difficult a task that was.

Adelle – (Later that day) I am meeting Olivia in a bit and I would like to see you. Do you have plans or want to join us around eight thirty?

Tudor – I have plans.

Adelle – Alright. Have fun! You know where I would rather be though. I just can't bury myself in my apartment in the meantime.

Tudor – Of course. Go have fun.

Adelle – That's difficult to do when I'm not with you, when my mind sees only you.

Tudor – Keep your mind in check and look forward, not behind.

Adelle – Yeah … you managed to change that for me … my mind will be where my heart is. Unfortunately it seems.

We met for dinner at Satire Bistro, one of the city's hot spots that constantly scored well with both locals and tourists: great service, amazing food, fancy but not pretentious, located in the heart of downtown Chicago. It was open until four in the morning a haven for everyone from celebrities to club-hoppers who have danced their shoes off and need that 3 a.m. fix of burgers and fries. No matter how much I dreaded the sight or smell of food, my friend Olivia thought I would find something enticing on the menu.

I spaced out repeatedly during my dinner. We carried on a lively yet pessimistic conversation: all men were doomed to hell. Between our recent past and our near future, we both saw deep darkness in our matters of the heart. An additional Martini and a strange look from a creepy man sitting at the bar made it all the more confusing and flat out depressing. "Are there any normal ones left out there?" Olivia asked as she glanced dreamily out the window. I grimed and replied softly, "I don't know, doll. I simply don't know. I wish I could say yes as much as I wish you'd also believe me".

I kept watching my phone. My next heartbeat depended on that message light blinking. I snapped back into lucidity for a moment now and then realizing how pathetic I was, how pitiful my situation. Both Olivia and I were in the same boat and sailing with no winds into stormy seas. Modern technology had transformed us into a different breed of people. Social interaction happened less in real life and more in cyber space. Electronic devices from blackberries to iPhones turned us into their faithful slaves.

I barely touched my food. My appetite shrunk to dangerously low levels. I needed to force feed myself just so people wouldn't think I was ill, or actually became ill. I weighed less than 100 lbs and was five feet four inches tall. I was seriously underweight.

One of Olivia's friends dropped by as we were finishing our second round of drinks. "Ha! Looks like I have some catching up to do," Michelle squealed as she threw her coat and purse on the empty chair next to Olivia. They planned the rest of the evening out in minutes. I kept to myself while sipping my drink, not paying much attention to the flurry of details. Michelle's enthusiasm would have normally been infectious. Instead, I found it all the more depressing. I excused myself politely and jumped into a cab to go home. I would rather have withdrawn from reality and slipped into solitude than suffering through a night of false faces and phony cheer. I required little more than my own thoughts to fall asleep, my tears staining my pillow. Why pretend I was content, wearing the old "I'm OK" mask while dancing in a club with a dozen different dime-a-dozen guys I really wasn't interested in?

He sent me a text to invite me to a party; it was Jake's sister's birthday. My head was whirring from lack of food. I felt weak, as if I had the flue. But it didn't matter. I had to see him.

A 25-minute, $20 cab ride later brought me to the mystery address Jake had forwarded me. I followed the distant sound of party noises in the rental building to the second floor, up a dark and dingy staircase. Two somewhat familiar looking men descended the stairs. I pasted my best courtesy smile on my face and said good evening; the two directed me toward a door from behind which the party sounds seemed to be coming.

I entered the room. My eyes searched for Tudor and Jake. Tudor was dancing with Neli, Jake's older sister. When his eyes met mine, he froze in place, stunned to see me there, although I had come at his invitation. My legs clutched the floor. I dared not take another step without him coming to greet me. Our eyes never left hold of one another's. He slid across the room to welcome me. Jake fell in behind him.

Jake took my coat and Tudor went to get me a drink. I looked for Neli to offer the usual birthday greetings and hand her my gift. She played the kind-and-cutesy smiley card well, appearing delighted to see me there. She evidently embodied yet one more victim of Tudor's charms.

I looked around for him.

He returned before long with a glass of red wine, and we stood together, drinking and making small talk, for some time. Finally we sat on the couch, he holding my hand and gently stroking it; I hardly finding the words to express my excitement in seeing him again.

When I finally rose to search out Jake, four other girls quickly took my place. One, in her late twenties wearing a body-hugging cotton shirt that looked like a pajama top. Poor thing must have had dementia, because she forgot to put on a bra! Every man in the room, including Tudor, focused on her small pointy breasts. How could they not?

I had to take him away from that … fast … before he'd be completely smothered in this girl's superficial charms! He must have read my mind, because he popped off the couch and extended his right hand to me to dance. I glowed with joy as he pulled me tightly to him.

After we danced, he sat on a chair and placed me on his knee, and I wrapped my arms around him and let my head lean on his shoulder. I was the princess and he was my knight in shining armor. We left the party and drove to his house.

Our love was fulfilled …

At sunrise … the morning's rampant desire for one another … we explored again and again before we rose, showered, and headed to the restaurant for another kind of nourishment.

While driving back to the city that afternoon, Tudor turned to me. "If I drive really fast into a wall, all my troubles will disappear."

"But you'd have to take me with you," I said. "I don't want to live if you're not around."

Tudor clenched down on my left hand. "We could do it now, and we'd be like Romeo and Juliet. Neither one of us would be left behind to suffer after the other. Let's do it!"

These words of a lunatic sounded surprisingly sane to me. "Why not?" I replied.

We looked at one another soulfully. We were the last remaining unknown quantities in the ample equation of life, and we were aware of it, of its meaning. Why question everything in life? Why not just go along with it? Why does our human nature always push us to crave security and fear the unknown? Yes, there may be more pain involved in walking on moving sands rather than on smooth asphalt … but those sands may inspire us to take a leap toward our future, toward our dreams, to avoid the turtle pace to the end of a mediocre existence.

Chapter XI
Valentine's Day

Too bad I love an empty soul, a wicked mind
A shallow creature of the swamps
Who'd sell me out to anyone without a second thought
For little less than dust

Too sad for all I have is his, not only that
But all he wants and would dare ask for
And all I get in turn is nothing more than hell

It is pathetic all I want is him
When all he wants is anyone but me

I wonder sometimes, why he even bothers lie
For what, I ask now, why?
The truth hurts less
I hope he'll learn one day

A dazzling sunny weekend day in February was a gift from heaven. The sun's rays shone brilliantly over the majestic open spaces of Lincoln Park, only beginning to fill with families off for a weekend day trip to the zoo. I wondered what Tudor was doing.

February 8, 2009
Tudor –Good morning!
Adelle – *Bonjour mon amour*!

Tudor – You must have this expression in your quick dial settings.

Adelle – Yeah! That's right! No, silly! I am finally getting into polishing my French and want to learn more ... reading Andre Gide's *Isabelle* as we speak, and looking up words in the dictionary. And besides, I've always hoped one day to find someone I'd be comfortable calling "mon amour."

Tudor – OK, *alors, on parle en Français, si vous voulez*!

Adelle – *Oui ... mais ... n'est pas possible.* I am a total disaster.

Tudor – *Pas problème.*

Adelle – *Qu'es que vous faites maintenant?*

Tudor – I'm not doing much, driving to my mother's house. *Conduire. Chez ma mère.*

Adelle – *Très bien – s'intéresser de une promenade dans Lincoln Park?* I know it is a little cold, but still pleasant enough for a walk in the park.

Tudor – *Plus tard c'est bon. Plus tard la semaine pro-chaine, pas aujourd'hui.* Later is actually not good - maybe later next week, not today.

Adelle – *Évidemment! A tantôt!*

Tudor – A bientôt, peut-être? Did you actually mean to say I'll see you soon ?

Adelle – *Oui.*

Adelle – Actually NO – *A tantôt*! Is what I meant – sometime.

Tudor – Never heard of it.

Adelle – It's in *Larrousse*. And I don't think there is an exact equivalent translation in English or Romanian. An interpretation would be ... I'll see you sometime ... indefinite.

Adelle – The expression correlates well with your lack of reliability.

Tudor – *Je suis très fatigue.* I'm too tired. *Tout c'est-que je t'ai promis autrefois n'est pas vrais maintenant.* Everything I promised you before will no longer happen.

Adelle – *Oui, je sais.* I see. You need not tire yourself with someone like me. Anyway ... I want to apologize for acting like a raging mad woman last month.

Tudor – I knew you'd recover. In that case, have a good life and be happy!

He liked to let me go on with my messages of bloody exasperation and borderline madness for hours and sometimes even days without addressing them. My words sailed aimlessly on dark waters for long periods of time before he picked them up, examined them, and chose to respond only to a few that really got to him.

I hadn't yet mastered that perfect combination of thoughts and ideas to goad him into answering more promptly. Either that or it all depended upon what kind of mood he was in, his surroundings, the company he held, and such. I figured he was more compelled to answer when he was alone and rather disinterested or unengaged from everything else. I was running out of fuel for him, for us. His uncaring blandness ripped my nerves to pieces and consumed what was left of my rational mind. I was becoming an emotional wreck.

It had taken some time to sink in, but I recalled using his guest bathroom on Friday night. As I brushed my teeth, I spied from the corner of my eyes a garbage can without a lid on it. An empty pink box of tampons was quite visible in it.

Perhaps that, I thought, accounted for his refusal to see me or share his emotions, his feelings with me of late.

Adelle – It hurt to see the tampon box in your trash in your bathroom yesterday. It just hurt like hell!!!

Tudor – I just woke up. The tampon box? I threw it there. I got some supplies from that closet and the damn thing was in the way. It was empty anyway.

Adelle – Does a bachelor normally keep tampons in his house for guests? Then you cancelled seeing me so many times, spending all those Friday and Saturday evenings apart, but for the last one. I mean, come on … I wish I was dumber than this, or cold enough not to care, to simply close my eyes and my mouth. But I'm not made of stone.

Tudor – I swear on my life I threw that box in the trash. Yes, I had that tampon box for at least a year. I don't know who used it last, but it certainly wasn't recent. As far as my last two weekends apart from you, it was my choice. I wanted to be alone and alone I was. I knew you'd suspect otherwise but I didn't even leave my house. Either out of laziness or depression, I'm not sure which.

Adelle – Thanks for the explanation. That makes me feel better.

Tudor - Me, too.

Adelle - I feel that, wherever my heart is, you're there with me. I could live in the middle of the desert or in a cave and be perfectly happy if you would be there, next to me. I would need nothing else. Just the thought of having you next to me warms my heart. But if you don't feel the same toward me, there is nothing more I can do. My feelings toward you are real, and yours need to be as well.

I was born stubborn. I realized that. But where Tudor was concerned, my stubbornness was more than I had expected, more than anyone could expect in a normal healthy relationship. I realized that. I just couldn't do anything about it.

It was an inexplicable instinctual feeling, making me accept every one of his lies, every malicious, thoughtless, callous word he aimed at me. My own resilience shocked me sometimes. I was like a mighty oak tree standing in the

126

middle of an empty field, pushed in every direction by strong winds. Branches would fall out, leaves would be burned by the blazing sun of summer and the stinging bitterness of winter, but at the end of the day, it stood up still, proud to have had the power to endure it all, and looking forward to another summer and winter to come, as long as its roots continued to feed off the potion created by this mind-numbing love.

Tudor – (A few hours later) I had a weird nightmare with you. I didn't want to sleep anymore for fear it was too real. I was coming out of my garage at night, snow on the ground, and at the end of my driveway a car with the lights on was blocking my exit. There was no one in it, so I got out of my car to go move it out of the way and in doing so, the lights fixed upon a little Yorkie shivering by my window. I assumed that you must be around, collapsed in the snow somewhere and that I may have backed the car over you. I woke up terrified.

Adelle - According to the dream dictionary, dogs mean enemies. The car is the good part of your dream – it denotes a journey, and a change in direction. To get out of a car means that you will succeed with some interesting plans.

Tudor – I hope so.

Adelle – God, I wish I would win the darned lottery!!! But would that solve any real problems? You have to look and see the beauty in this very second you live in ... once gone we never get it back; and all the riches in the world won't buy you back this second you are throwing away by worrying and stressing out about finances.

Tudor - You could be right.

Adelle - I know I am.

His thoughts of me were the oxygen that swelled my lungs, although sometimes it soured by the way he expressed them. There was one consideration I tried to factor in - he was about to lose his home to a short sale. He was worried that he might be facing foreclosure, bankruptcy, and who knew what else! He might avoid them if he could only reorganize, sell off some of his other investments, shift them to where they would do the most good.

I had a modest income, and had he allowed me to help him, I would have done so gladly. But he wouldn't hear of it, so I struggled to find a way to ease his emotional pain. I was concerned about his emotional state, his mounting depression, but I dared not let my worries show in my messages.

> February 9, 2009
> Adelle – *Bonjour*!
> Tudor – Not so.
> Adelle – Why?

Tudor – I don't know. My realtor called. She'll have a signed offer this afternoon. It's a relief and a concern at the same time.

Adelle – I thought that's what you wanted. Is it far less than you expected, or why then?

Tudor – Yes. *Far* less.

Adelle – Can you keep it then? I know this is really off, but I could sell my place (very easy to do in my building), rent a studio for a year, and help you with the mortgage payments on your house if you really want to keep it. Later on you can sell it for a lot more, enough to pay me back and realize a nice profit.

Adelle – I mean it.

Tudor – That's sweet. Thanks for offering, but I can't. It will go away. Time erases everything.

Adelle – I know it does, but from a business perspective, I know the real estate market will bounce back eventual-

128

ly. Then you wouldn't lose the money you've worked so hard for. We both work for every penny and to throw it all away is silly. It's your decision, I know. But I want you to realize that I could afford to help you out.

Tudor – Don't worry. I don't wanna be here anymore anyway. I'm just depressed because of the attachment and all the work I put into it.

Adelle – Perhaps that's a good reason to keep it. Your place could look amazing with a few decorative touches. I would never be able to drag my parents out of their house even if I built a castle for them. People do get attached to the places they put a lot of work and heart in. I think yours deserves to be saved. My place is still relatively new to me and frankly I am not that attached to it. Cheer up! You'll come up with a solution.

Tudor purchased the house nearly fifteen years earlier, hoping the woman he'd been dating at the time, a ballerina, was going to marry him. He thought it would be a nice place to raise a family.

But she turned him down and married her ballet instructor. Tudor's self-esteem was crushed. That's when he started playing the field. He'd meet young women, break their hearts, and abandon them on the side of life's road. One after another, extracting some sort of venomous vitality out of doing so. It kept him going. His family and friends told him to find one good woman and settle down, but that advice only irritated him. In time, he became aloof at that thought; he was no longer cared about what anyone said to him. Or *about* him.

I wanted to do something, *anything*, just to make him smile, to calm his fears, to soothe his troubled soul. I sent him a message in French on my way home, hoping it would make him forget some of his problems and smile.

Adelle – *Ca va?*

Tudor – I have no drive at all.

Adelle – At least you have an option to get out without losing everything you own. You're one of the lucky ones. A lot of people these days aren't so fortunate.

Tudor - I don't feel all that fortunate.

Adelle - What are you saying? What is wealth, anyway? Money is temporary and if you have health and motivation, not only will you make it all back, but also you'll look back at all of this one day and laugh.

Adelle – Of course, you could also ignore everything I just said because it's not worth much. I don't walk in your shoes, so I don't have the slightest idea of what you're going through.

Tudor – Gee, thanks for the motivational speech. I'm all teary eyed.

Adelle - Yes, I guess it did sound a bit rah-rah.

Tudor – Seriously, I appreciate your optimistic outlook. We'll see what happens next. I've had worse. Death does not scare me. The rest up to that point is only filling.

Adelle – I don't know. Do you want to hear my ideas on this, or not? I want to help but I don't want to overstep my boundaries here. What can I do that would make you feel better?

Adelle – (A few hours later) Are you alive?

Tudor – No.

Adelle – Baby … you're not planning to spend Valentine's day with me, are you?

Adelle – I am going on a road trip. You can co-pilot if you want.

No response for several hours. I had to bring up the subject of Valentine's Day again. I wanted to get an answer from him, either yay or nay. Perhaps, I thought, the direct route would work best.

Adelle – Enough!!! I have had enough of your silence and you have had enough of my noise. I need my sanity too, you know. If I don't get away for a vacation every so often, I'll go crazy!

Tudor – By all means, I think I'll take one of those cleansing trips myself. *Bon Voyage*!!!

Adelle – I am writing on empty walls that no one reads … you just don't hear me. You hardly ever say a kind word to me.

Tudor – I hear you. But how can I make you happy when I can't even bear myself right now?

Adelle – Sometimes you see a lot by looking, at least according to the world of Winnie the Pooh. What better philosopher in the world is there than he?

Tudor - Great. You're quoting cartoon bears now.

Adelle - Do you know what makes me happy? A smile from you, and nothing else.

Tudor – Maybe we can meet tomorrow to talk.

Adelle – I'd like that. I think that's a wonderful idea.

Tudor - Good. Then let's plan on it. But I'm tired now. I've got to get some rest.

That was all I needed to hear from him so I could get a good night's sleep. I woke up early the following morning with renewed hope.

My phone rang when I got home. Tudor invited himself, Luke and Anna for drinks at my place in a couple of hours since I didn't have a car to come meet them at a restaurant after they played tennis. I was amazed that he actually called me, and didn't text. He had to meet Rami shortly, a friend he comforted about men issues. He insisted on making it clear that he had no interest in her other than as a friend.

My first two guests arrived shortly after eight, with Tudor half an hour later. When he walked through the door, he was sweaty and still dressed in his tennis clothes. He apologized. I couldn't care less about his sweaty clothes.

The evening passed all too quickly, with the four of us gabbering away in our sweet native Romanian. I needed to refine my speech once again, since my years away from home had given it an edgy English accent. Luke and Anna left close to midnight, and Tudor and I hurried off to the bedroom where we cuddled among the pillows. That's when he dropped the bomb.

"Let's get married tomorrow!" he said. I looked at him as if someone had just socked me in the eye.

"What?"

"I'm serious. Let's get married."

"Why…how…are you kidding me?" I was petrified that he might have actually meant it. I mean, I loved him, granted. But this was a bit too sudden, too little time, and certainly not a good time to make such a radical decision with everything else he had going on in his life. He looked at me, and I saw his eyes glossed over by disappointment when I told him marriage was out of the question.

He smiled and turned his face to the pillow, burring in it for several long awkward seconds. I felt guilty for offering him the exact opposite answer to what I felt like saying.

He did not hold me in his arms that night.

February 11, 2009

Adelle – Tried sending some pictures but they are not going through – Going to a movie with my friend, Oly.

Tudor – Have fun!

Adelle – Allowed to laugh – we are watching "He's Just Not That Into You"

Tudor – I have to see it.

Adelle – Ha! Not a chance!

Tudor – Why?

Adelle – Chick flick.

Tudor – Enjoy!

Adelle – (Halfway through the movie) Aaaaaa … so stereotypical!

Adelle – Awful! Cheesy … waste of time.

Tudor – Thanks for the info. I'll skip it then.

Adelle – Going to sleep … the American dating game never ceases to amaze me with its hurtful, demeaning, senselessly useless nature.

Tudor – Isn't the dating game the same everywhere?

Adelle – I don't know … not too good at this … I guess I have never seen the rules so well contoured before. Maybe it is international, which begs the question of how cynical and superficial a society we live in.

Tudor – True. Advanced technology kills humanity.

Tudor – You made me curious about this movie. You seemed disturbed by it.

Adelle – Picks up on many things … mind games, some typical characters and weaknesses out there, nothing we haven't seen or heard our friends going through at one point or another … I think it's poorly done … simplistic Hollywood cinematic trash filled with clichés.

Tudor – OK, Roger Ebert. I'll take your word for it.

Unlike the actors in the movie, I didn't want to have to play a bunch of silly games to capture Tudor's love. I didn't want to lower myself to a level so many women did in order to get a man. To me, when a woman behaves like a cat with a mouse in its claws, she's not worth much more than the games she's playing. A woman who toys with one man's feelings will do so with another. And another.

I had shaped my character, my morals and integrity, years ago with the help of a stricter time, a more conservative ideology, where Jane Austen, Charlotte Bronte, Charles Dickens, and others held court. I wasn't about to trade my principles for a man. Not on my life.

Did Tudor really want to see that movie? He was better at the game than the writers of the script, even. I watched it both on the screen and unraveling in my life, day by day, since the day I'd met him. The game. The rules. The hypocrisy. After two long-term relationships of seven and four-and-a-half years respectively, I had run into the Master of all Games himself - the contemporary Romanian version of Casanova and Don Juan. Rolled into one.

And what could I do about it? About my feelings? About him?

February 12, 2009
Adelle – You have no IDEA how much I need you right this very second!

Tudor – I wish I was there to make you happy.

Adelle – Do you miss me?

Tudor – (A few hours later) Sorry, I'm too busy. Yes, I miss you.

Adelle – I won't bother you anymore. You and my kinkajou would have been best buddies schedule-wise. He slept days and played nights, too. I think I got a bad cough.

Tudor – I gave it to you, right?

Adelle – Noooo ... can't be – you didn't have it last time we met. This thing started this afternoon. Lots of germs everywhere, but I haven't had a cough this bad in a very long time. It will go away.

Tudor – In a month or so.

Adelle – You must be kidding! No, I am having some tea, can't happen.

Adelle – Regardless, it was still worth all the kissing.

134

Gabriela Sbarcea

A post-it note stuck on one of his wall decorations the last time I was at his house caught my attention. It was from Rita, thanking him for the unique moments they spent together. I avoided the subject then, not wanting to reproach him for anything, not wanting to set him off. It made no sense. He was going to do what he wanted with his time and life anyway; he was still a free man after all. As much as I tried to shelve the reality of it all for a while, the idea dug deep into me.

Rita posted some comments on Facebook as a reply to a friend, ranting about how happy she was that she had finally found "the one." I replied to her note, asking her to name the man who's been making our dear friend so happy, and she erased my words immediately. Her Facebook postings aggravated me the most, and they were the truest sign that *something* was happening between them: when I was crying and could not get hold of Tudor and, when I did, he was rude to me, her status was always extremely positive.

Another sleepless night and no messages from him.

February 13, 2009
Adelle - Enjoy having one less worry in your life.
Tudor – Bye.
Adelle – Say hi to Rita, and also tell her not to bother erasing my comments on her wall if she doesn't feel guilty. You two can go exclusive now that I am out of the picture.
Tudor – What?
Adelle – Come on … you are "the one" that's been making her happy for the last two weeks. Aren't you the one she moved here for all the way from Dubai? The post-it note hanging on your wall …
Tudor – You know better. I already told you about the tampon box. Anyway, I don't know about Rita, but I have OTHER preferences. Good bye!

Adelle — I would love to believe you. Yes, it was obvious for the past week or so you were not planning on spending Valentine's Day with me. How do you think I feel???

I couldn't focus on work. I emailed him.

Tudor, I was actually looking forward to this, but I cannot be a second choice for you. I felt like one for the past two weeks and it tortured me.

Maybe I spent too much time in the business world where reliability and dependence are prized commodities so necessary to achieve your goals. You are quite the opposite. I wanted to learn how to deal with it because you are YOU. In finance and accounting people are programmed to conduct their lives in a disciplined manner, according to a certain code of ethics. I've been able to submit to these rules and adapt to them easily because of how I grew up. A side of me has always been independent rebel and nonconformist. I see life differently than most people do, maintain an open point-of-view perspective. I want to know a little about a lot because I want to be able to see this life, this world, this society we live in from a macro standpoint, not from a narrow view.

My feelings for you remain to me a mystery ... how I felt so strongly so fast. I am sorry for not understanding you and for acting too emotionally.

You have to continue searching for what will make you happy eventually. Superficiality seems to work best in reaching into a man's heart. I am aware of the rules of this dating game, the rules of the dance, yet I refuse to become something I'd hate later.

Enjoy your new conquests, and continue living your life in a manner that makes you happy!

- A

P.S. When you are done with all the rest … you will find the meaning of life.

I found myself in the burning fires of hell. I became as sick as a dog with one of the worst flu of the season. I had excused myself from work early and gone home around noon nearly fainting on the bus on my way home. The world grew grim around me. I spaced out and saw nothing more. Things became fluid and melted into hot and dark matter, volcanic lava, creeping closer and closer to me until it covered me in my own grave, alive to feel and see it all before my eyes, to sense it, smell it, *feel* it. I ran a high fever and my sight grew blurry by the time I had reached my apartment. I don't remember much happening after that for about twenty four hours. Olivia desperately tried reaching me. THANK GOD I had friends!

February 14, 2009
Adelle – Happy Valentine's Day, baby!

Evidently, he did not bother answering my message on Valentine 's Day and I was still incredibly sick that evening. Olivia, however, was determined to drag me out of the house at any cost. She was *not* going to allow me to spend this special day alone. She had worked late at the bar that evening, until about two in the morning. Later, she planned on going out with some of her colleagues to a new sky lounge downtown.

Wretched as I was I still managed to get myself together, go to the hair salon, and put on my makeup that night. I couldn't show up in public less than perfect!

When I arrived at Olivia's hotel bar on Michigan Avenue, I was already tired and green with flue and disgusted with the human race. Nice start to a beautiful evening!

When a woman has that mindset, there must be some sort of negative energy around her, repelling men and keeping them instinctively at a distance. That was what I intended for that evening. I was alone, and I wanted it that way. No other men around me, forcing me to be witty. Olivia was the only person I wanted to see that night, to have a drink with her, confess to each other our troubles in the domain of love, and then go back home to my warm bed and cute little doggie, who was always so happy to see me.

We made it to Vertigo around two. Olivia's friend and her boyfriend sat at a low table on leather cubes. We joined them and ordered drinks; they were served promptly and were accompanied by a couple of roses. An ironic fact of life at that point, yet, still better to have a rose on V Day than none at all.

My plan for the next few days had originally been to spend a few days off work skiing with Tudor, Luke, and Anna in Michigan. But that never happened. I wasn't about to go on a ski trip with his married friends without him. Not in this life. I sat around instead, reminiscing about how much I loved driving through Michigan, blessed with all of that startling beautiful scenery. I got an idea. I would rent a car and drive up to Michigan all by myself. It wouldn't be my first crazy solitude trip. Nor, I was sure, my last.

The drive was easy, with little traffic. I ran the car at nearly a hundred miles an hour all the way there. Careless? Incautious? Stupid? Probably. But I kept fantasizing all the way there that I would get into a horrific automobile accident and die, and in that way finally I would no longer feel the blood burning through my veins and my mind easily slipping away from me.

The beauty of Michigan's landscapes absorbed some of my pains. I left them behind as I drove north, following a road around the lake. Plenty of snow covered the adorable small town of Charlevoix, which reminded me of Aspen and

Snowmass in Colorado, only on a smaller scale. There were little mom and pop stores, coquette bars, and elegant bed and breakfasts everywhere. It was a breath of fresh air.

I parked at the hotel, checked into the room, and took Luca for a long walk by the lake. The shore was frozen, an ethereal aura emanating from the lake's banks. I took some pictures with my blackberry camera and uploaded them on Facebook. I was sure Tudor would see them in the newsfeed when he checked his account.

Luca's little feet were getting tired and cold. I picked her up, put her in her fancy carrier camouflaged well in an expensive handbag, and carried her to the restaurant across the street from the hotel.

I sat Luca on the chair next to me and let her smell my hand through the carrier window on the side. A glass of red wine arrived shortly while I fiddled around on Facebook with my blackberry before dinner arrived. The red wine, cold weather, and magnificent view from the window anesthetized my agony. For a while.

And then the following message brought me to the Land of the Living:

February 15, 2009
Tudor – Can you send me your address? I want to return what's yours – a couple of Tupperware dishes and the little gold angel. Thank you.

Adelle – You don't need to. Throw away the plastic and give the little gold angel to one of your friends' kids. The PayPal payment for your Crucifix came back. I will send you a check through Anna. Michigan is cold and beautiful, just like the sculpture I lost my soul to.

Tudor – Keep your check. Don't bother writing it. I will not cash it. I don't need anything from you.

Adelle - *Adieu, mon amour!* I will print my memory of you in a work that will warm the marble monument you are, insane and magnificent, the one with which I first fell in love with and not the one I've grown to know over the past two-and-a-half weeks. *Bone chance!*

Waterfalls of tears ... I could hardly contain myself, despite looking pitiful while alone in the middle of a fancy restaurant. I gave him the tiny gold angel to protect him from evil. He accepted it and hanged it on the gold chain he wore around his neck with two other Pisces zodiac pendants from his mom and his brother. His brutish words were simply hot knives thrown in an open wound. The miles I had inserted between no longer helped.

Over the course of the following days, I explored the beatific surroundings in which I found myself, listening to loud music with Luca on my lap. I stopped now and then in rest areas and got out of the car to admire the magnanimous lake, rolling hills, and pungent forests for what they were: tributes to the One. A herd of white-tailed deer appeared on the right side of the road in a meadow between two vacation villages. The sight inspired some trace of hope in myself. Above all else, I had to make it. I had to make life happen for myself again, despite this monster who kept tarnishing my feelings for him and disregarding the fact that I was simply a young woman, madly in love with him. I also had a mind, which for some reason he seemed to despise.

My trip tired me enough to put me in a creative frame of mind. I spent the following days in my room, or in the hotel lobby, typing away, writing in longhand, inscribing anything I could remember that had happened between us from the moment we'd met, in chronological order. I drove back home two days later, feeling better and resolving never to send him another message.

Was I kidding?

140

Chapter XII
Tristan and Isolde

It is not your severe words that hurt
When thrown at me with recklessness and hive
Your silence craters deep down in my heart
And does not heal; it erodes its every part

The truth that blisters most my days
You know it clearly, and do it every time
To punish me for uttering fair truth
Enunciating what often works your mind

Distance doesn't break us now and then apart
But empty closeness when our passion's used
Your avid thirst of me is fully satisfied

The Chicago Lyric Opera is the one place in town one cannot miss during the winter season. In Communist Europe, the average child enjoyed less than an ideal upbringing. Not surprisingly, most families had to concentrate on providing the bare necessities: food, water, electricity, heat. When it came to educating their children about arts in particular, most parents left that job to the school system.

My childhood had been no different. When I grew up and moved to Chicago, I made it a point to scrape together enough money to buy a tick to my favorite opera that season.

The most memorable opera I saw during those four years was Mozart's *Die Zauberflöte*, or *The Magic Flute*.

Ahhh ... but not even opera could satisfy my need for creative expression. I had to make my own mark in the world of art, in the only way my love and personality inspired me to do it: through writing. And what better thing to write than a book about my relationship with Tudor. *If* he would allow me permission to use his text messages, of course.

February 18, 2009

Adelle – Just wanted your consent on using the texts between us in something that may or may not get published.

Tudor – No, you may not use them.

Adelle – Very well. I will use different words for your answers.

Tudor – Apparently, you overestimate the value of yours, since you think they deserve to be published.

Adelle – It's something I've wanted to do for a long time and this nonsense that's happened to me in the past two months just gave me a kick to start it. I did publish before in college and in limited editions. Not that it makes any difference.

Tudor – Honestly, our trivial correspondence would not interest anyone. But if you think you're such an outstanding writer, then by all means, get high on it! Who's to stop you?

Adelle – Thanks! I don't know what's going to come of this thing; I am NOT a writer yet. I would love to write something worthy of anyone's time one day, but as you know, if you don't practice, you get nowhere. I appreciate your understanding.

Well, it was a good start. I'd been expecting worse.

Suddenly I wondered what he'd say if I invited him to see Wagner's *Tristan and Isolde* opera. The dramatic love story fascinated me. Tudor was the only man I knew would love the experience. He was an artist, after all, and, as Nietzsche wrote in *The Birth of Tragedy*: "Art owes its continuous evolution to the Apollonian-Dionysiac duality, even as the propagation of the species depends on the duality of the sexes, their constant conflicts and periodic acts of reconciliation."

Adelle – Remember that I am still looking forward to admiring your sculptures in the Art Institute or even the *Louvre* one day.

Tudor – Thanks! Let me know if you ever get the urge to roll in the sack ...

Adelle - I love your sense of humor! Definitely NO urge of any rolling on straws or in sacks or anything of the sort, but I would still love to see *Tristan and Isolde*. Would you be interested? It's running for the next two weeks.

Tudor – Sure.

Adelle – Great. Check the Lyric Opera site, their calendar, when you get a chance, and let me know what evening works for you.

Tudor – Any. I'm FREE. Except from March first through the seventh.

Adelle – Alright then. As originally planned – this Friday since it *is* a weekend and I can dress up. During the week I've seen people wearing jeans and gym shoes. I am emailing you the details. Be at my place at five fifteen latest. We need to pick up the tickets at the box office.

Tudor – (About an hour later after I had purchased the tickets online) Oh shit, I forgot I made plans for this Friday. Damn!

Adelle – I bought the tickets already. Can you change your plans?

Tudor – Yes, I can. Rami'll be pissed off.

Adelle – Thanks! Send her my sincere apologies. Had I known, I wouldn't have booked them. She'll understand. I'm sure you'll find a way to make it up to her.

Tudor – It's done. She's OK with it.

Adelle – Wonderful. See you Friday then.

Victory! I wondered if he'd yet read the email I'd sent him before taking off for my Michigan trip in February:

Tudor,

I know for a fact that I will either hear a curse back or nothing at all, and this will make you hate my guts, however, as I love you more than anything, I would rather risk losing you forever than not letting you know about my untrained, obviously unprofessional, but deeply emotionally involved observation. I want you to be happy at any cost, please check out the link below.

Friday came all too quickly. He got my email on Thursday afternoon and refused to honor his commitment. "If you think I have ADD, why don't you find someone normal to accompany you to the opera?", he texted me as soon as he read my email. I went to the opera by myself, enduring the all-consuming misery that only intensified through the sadness of Tristan and Isolde's story. I hoped he would have shown up before the play was over. I even left his ticket at the window. He never did. Although Wagner's opera was exquisite, it only exacerbated my distress and anguish. My own immaturity and stupidity brought his anger upon me, and it hurt like nothing else before.

A week later, I called him on a whim, not quite expecting he'd pick up after his last words to me, but he actually answered my call.

A couple of hours later, Tudor showed up at my front door with a built-in smiley face and an adorable look that sent all our previous vexation and dismay scrambling. We blended into one as our lips locked with feverish intensity. The candles all over my apartment and the flickering softness of the light produced a sense of chic glamour. His hungry hands eternally unsatisfied of my body moved up and down my waist, hips and back, searching, sensing. We were poison to one another; we intoxicated each other's being with no antidote but succumbing to our own weakness.

We opened our eyes at sunrise. The primeval instinct to be one was far stronger than anything we could have contained. I was serene and truly happy next to this man. He held me in his eyes as if I was one of his masterpiece sculptures. There was an aura about Tudor that made him deistic. I couldn't explain it. He treated me as if I were disposable, yet, his love, desire and affection for me ran deeper through his heart and mind, deeper than he wanted to admit even to himself.

I took the following day off work. On our way to his house I floated through the land of dreams. It was a dark, foggy cold day, yet, somehow, the blazing sun of our love made it seem as if we were on a tropical island without a cloud in sight. Time was again irrelevant. We could have been locked up in that house for centuries. My phone was shut off and forgotten at the bottom of my purse. My worries ... have I ever had any?

We swayed to the rhythm of our love. Worn out, happy and sleepy, we dozed off. Time stopped in our reality as in our dreams, only for us ... we lived in a multi-dimensional universe of our own; we could have spent days, months and years in that same fraction of time.

His main lobby with vaulted skylight ceiling was his work area as well. The light was better there than in his studio on the opposite side of the house. He put his head-

145

phones on and began working at the sculpture he was commissioned to complete for the US Army. It was a hero's strong, imposing arm reaching out through the three-dimensional geographical map of the United States, like Michelangelo's *David*. Every vein and every muscle strained deftly, with an accent on the hand's long bohemian fingers, spread in his struggle to emerge from the underneath ground's surface as he breaks through the Rockys. The scene was symbolic of a soldier's victory, relentlessness, patriotism, vigor, even through the hardest of times.

I made some space on his table, cluttered with all kinds of things--a fruit bowl, books, some papers--and grabbed my laptop out of the bag. I began typing away at what I had started on my road trip - fragments of our time together from the very evening we met.

Tudor tip-toed his way behind me and read a few phrases of what I was typing.

"Oh!" I snapped. "You scared the hell out of me! What are you doing?" I nearly jumped out of my seat when I'd felt his breath on my ear.

"I'm sorry. I don't wear contacts and can't read well from a distance," he said.

"So ... do you like what you see?"

"I can't believe you remember all that. I can barely recall what I did yesterday. Except for a few grammar mistakes, I think you might be onto something. But why are you doing this when you're an accountant? You seem to be good at your profession. Why mess with something else?"

I put my head down. "I told you before ... I want to do what I truly love one day. On my own terms ... even if it takes me forever to do it right." Tudor did not reply. He lifted my hand and gently pulled me next to him, making me a prisoner to his affection. I hoped forever.

He ran his lips down my back and explored every contour of my body with his strong wide palms and curious

146

fingers. My already weak resistance dissolved beneath his embrace as he guided me up from the table and across the room. We settled into his leather couch and, in one free-flowing motion of kisses and caresses, surrendered all thoughts of sculpting and writing to the immediacy of our pure insatiable lust for one another.

After what seemed like hours, we settled back and smelled the aroma of our spent and exhausted bodies. Neither one of us wanted to make a move back to reality.

In time, we pulled away, instinctively dressing without uttering a word; was it our love's pure adrenaline that had given both of us such an incredibly powerful rush of inspiration? I wasn't sure ... but it felt to me like the flow of a furious river on the edge of a cascade.

I sat down at the table before my laptop again, and Tudor, before his sculpture. We poured ourselves into our work ... into our passions. All we had, all we were, all we had become together was something that we somehow had to express through our art, to mold it, form it, build it from the ground up. Would others, by reading those words or seeing that sculpture, experience the same rush of life that we did? Would their imaginations take flight through our creative energy? I wondered.

Chapter XIII
Many Words and All In Vain

We employ our days, have little free time
To finance life styles not ours to have
We want trifles there's really no need for
To build up an image and vain souls to cover

We flip through blank pages of pretty books covers
Reading long stories and fluffy old novels
If asked of the essence of all that we've read
We'd answer: "Your question, I don't understand"

Tudor asked me to accompany him to a baptism the following weekend. Luke and Anna were godparents to one of their relative's children. Baptisms for Romanians are smaller scale weddings, and, sometimes, even more elaborate and fancier. Godparents play a crucial role in the celebration and an invitation from them to such an event often carries more weight than an invitation from the baby's parents.

I was unable to reach Tudor that day until an hour before we were supposed to be on our way. He arrived right on time ... *physically* ... although mentally he was someplace else. His voice held an artificial tone. I retreated into a shell and detached myself from the conversation, my eyes following the unfolding lakefront architecture out the car window.

We were seated at the designated dinner table when my ex-fiancée Peter called and asked how I was holding up. It was the date we had planned on being married. Tudor was at the bar getting us a glass of wine and socializing with

Gabriela Sbarcea

some friends. Peter and I made some small talk, and as
Tudor returned to our table, I quickly hung up.

I must have had one too many glasses of wine that
evening. Everything seemed so confusing. That evening I
should have been Mrs. Peter. Instead, I was dancing with a
strange man who'd proven to me on more than one occasion
that I was not much more than a fling to him. An awkward
tension enveloped us. We avoided speaking of it. We danced
in an effort to smooth things over. The Romanian folk songs
helped to lighten the setting. But they didn't do much for
Tudor's mood. He threw me around the floor as if I were
made of straw. Little wonder. I weighed less than 100
pounds what with all the stress and turmoil he'd brought to
our relationship.

My heels slipped on the floor and I lost my balance
for a moment, stumbling to the ground. Tudor picked me up
and continued twirling me as if nothing had happened.

Luke asked me for a dance. He was a large and tall
man, with no patience and not much more grace. He picked
me up and circled the floor with me in his arms, putting me
in an even worse position than I'd been in before.

Tudor looked me squarely in the eyes as I sat down at
our table. "Have you talked to your ex recently?" The
question caught me off guard, and I thought for a moment
about lying. He must have looked at my phone call history.

"Yes, earlier this evening for a few brief moments." I
don't know if it was all the alcohol talking or the need to
hurt him as he had hurt me earlier. But I found myself
relishing the moment. "We were supposed to be married
today."

Tudor said nothing in response but merely motioned
for us to leave. On the ride home, we barely said anything at
all.

It was the very first evening we had spent in each
other's company without sleeping together. He went home

and so did I. My pride was tattered. I doubted there would be any left by morning.

I shook the ice off my shoulders and sent him a message the next day.

March 1, 2009

Adelle – Sorry, I behaved like a brat …

Tudor – As Luke so eloquently put it: "You guys are just so not synchronized together!" (How true. It applies to more than just dancing, I think). It's been nice knowing you. I have to move on.

Adelle – He thinks the opposite. You can move on. Patience and passion …

Tudor – Yeah, you had the passion and I had the patience …

Adelle – I have my passion still … for you, for us, for what you bring out of me, and when you will have the patience to handle me, you'll find the fire between us will NEVER die down like it does between other people.

Adelle – Face our love darling … rationalize and admit it … what makes it perfect is the insanity of it … all conflicting elements bound together. You keep hanging on any little irrelevant detail coming your way to justify it to yourself … give us time … just think how grand, splendid were the few moments we spent together so far. This is only the beginning.

Tudor – No. This is the official end. I don't feel the connection you say you do. I'm sorry.

Adelle – You make me smile with your last remark … you fear what life would be like if days like last Wednesday would happen again and again. I f that's a sign of how bad we are together, then by all means, go ahead and enjoy yourself by picturing it when you do it with other women, with whom you think you are more compatible. Be my guest.

150

I did not send him another message that day. I knew I was wrong and had made my own bed, but he always refused to admit to his own faults. The following day, I sent him an email. There was still much left unsaid. Texting does not contain enough acronyms to express my feelings.

Email chain between March 2, 2009 – March 5, 2009
Darling love,

I had to gather my wits and write you a note. I am not trying to explain my actions no more than excuse my bad French language skills. I've acted out of impulse and allowed my feelings to overtake my reason too many times since I met you. I cannot blame you for letting our affair get so far. It was what I needed perhaps, after four and a half years of stale life; I was beginning to despise the comfort of a stable relationship. That lifestyle was the opposite extreme of what I wanted. You taught me a life of complete abandon. You lifted me to a different level of consciousness, a phenomenon I never experienced before.

When we lock horns, you undermine everything I built myself to be until the moment I met you. I've grown accustomed to your salty language and find it amusing at times. Yet, I want to conduct my life in a manner that will make me content with myself: with respect, class, according to propensities and principles that will lead me to higher ends and help others around me where I can.

Our opposing character traits can build an extremely unique and beautiful connection. I embraced this because I understand its magnitude and importance to my life. You are not ready for us. .

I've always believed in quality, darling, not quantity ... it has been the guiding principle of my life. Your light blinds me; but you are still exhilarated by the novelty of the chase. The thrill of it hasn't tired you yet. I respect that ... I respect you for not pretending you are in a serious relation-

151

ship, marrying someone simply to obey the rules and expectations of our society.

I will let this go in peace. Luke was only a spectator though ... the surface barely exposed the force of gravity binding us together. You preferred to continue feeding on the adrenaline rush you find in new opportunities. I saw and felt it beyond that: us at our full potential together, eliminating impurities and temporary factors our passion for one another could overcome, if there is a will. No one can deny we are different and our life styles are by a significant length apart, but the things we do have in common overshadow those discrepancies by far.

I will continue writing this book ... who knows what will come of it ... it will need a lot of work and editing for a fact, but don't we all before the page in front of us reflects beautifully and blends gracefully with our own lives?

Tudor's response:
Oh, the euphoria of self-glorification!

I will not be quick to diagnose your delusions, but you are obviously in a drunken stupor from your own writing! I am nothing more than a hook on your wall of inspiration, on which you are hopelessly hanging some very thin clothing.

There's nothing more deceiving than your delusions of grandeur. Perhaps you take comfort in being your only critic, with nothing but positive reviews every time, but to make an analogy to dancing, if one doesn't listen to the music, which has a rhythm and a beat and a clear structure, or one doesn't let herself be lead by someone who understands those things, one is bound to end up off balance and flat on her ass in the middle of the dance floor...

I noticed you don't accept any outside criticism, or direction, at least not from people who mean well.

You are so content with yourself that any guidance seems to disturb you like an alarm clock going off in the middle of a wet dream. Yes, I may be vulgar sometimes, but I believe that the endless embellishments of your writing or speech are anachronistic. The 19th Century is gone! The Industrial Revolution already happened! Wake up!

Honestly, what I see happening here is you taking refuge into writing (mediocre, or not) as a means of escaping the tedious and stressful routine of your job. In that case, don't let me interrupt! By all means, carry on with your psychotherapy!

I am not, however, your Prince Charming, nor do I suppress my feelings for you, as you so eloquently suggested. I also do not suffer from any Attention Deficit Disorder. I simply feel nothing for you anymore and that is the truth, as painful as it may sound, and this is my last response to your emails, or text messages.

I wish you a speedy recovery, and if writing makes you happy, by all means write away!

All the best!

Tudor

Adelle's reply:

I can take criticism Mr. Popescu. In fact, I have always welcomed it. How else am I ever going to improve anything in my life if I don't? I take constructive criticism, if you know what that is, which differs greatly from insult, arrogant bluntness, jumping to conclusions, or misinterpretation.

Self-glorification ... *not* ... you'll find the contrary if you read between the lines of everything I ever wrote to you. You will find a scared, insecure, vulnerable character trying to fend for herself with NO protection around. I would hate to victimize myself here ... but try walking in the shoes of a nineteen-year-old woman who left home to follow her heart.

I didn't *have* to, unlike most other people immigrating to the states, but I *wanted* to for the sake of finding myself and my independence with one hundred dollars loaned from her dad. I accepted NO help here from anyone, other than ADVICE.

There is no such thing as emotional shelter in a man. I loved him and followed him to a brave new world, an entirely different continent. But pathological lying and cheating are things not even the greatest love can ever cure.

I traveled to random places on my own for a few months, questioning everything about myself, who I was, why I was here, and where I was going. I knew one thing. I couldn't stand the thought of ever showing up at my father's door with my bags in hand crying my eyes out after doing exactly what he had advised me not to do when I was nineteen. My father begged me to return home. But I knew his reproaches wouldn't be worth the temporary comfort my parents' home would provide.

I swore I would NEVER again be buried in my own love for a man. Another long term relationship where I found anything else BUT true love, the very substance of life seemed to be a good idea. Most people would have gone through with that wedding under pressure from friends and family to later destroy their lives. Weakness prevails. .

Someone once said, "Outside of a dog, a book is a man's best friend." I found it to be one of the fundamental truths of life. Hence the choice of words and the "endless embellishments" to my writing, as you call it.

I've never cheated in a relationship … not worth it for me … not worth the baggage that comes with it; it ruins the beauty of being with the person who actually matters. It's a simple principle I learned from my very youth. Unfaithfulness can hurt people more than ANYTHING.

Regarding the "wall where I hang thin clothes" as you love to insult me - sorry Tudor, but I have nothing to hide; nor am I afraid of being judged. People who know me

154

also know that my remarks on my Facebook wall are for my FRIENDS, as friends. As much adversity as Facebook brought between you and I, it has reconnected me to some of the people I spent countless hours with in an office, on weekends and evenings until our red and tired swollen eyes would fall out.

You, on the other hand, erase EVERYTHING on your wall ... a good junkie knows how to hide evidence. You've learned the tricks of Facebook in time. When we started seeing each other in January, your comments on your friends' pictures were fed into my news on a daily basis like a bitter pill because you had no idea I could see them. I took it ... and never said anything about it until now, because in the end it meant nothing compared to my feelings for you.

I landed flat on my ass because I had on five-inch heels for a dance partner who threw me around like a puppet on a slippery floor. Your moves were out of synch with the music. Dancing isn't one of my strengths, as you well know. But even *I* could tell that much.

You can go ahead and make whatever you want out of your feelings for me. I, on the other hand, refuse to hide and lie to myself when I feel like this.

Does writing help distract me from lamenting over the ongoing grief you give me? Even though our true feelings dictate otherwise? Yes it does. And who can tell? Maybe something good will come of it. Maybe an example of what NO ONE should do for the love of her life ... maybe disarming every single shield to be able to feel pure love again is not worth the pain and humiliation associated with it. It is particularly useless when the other person not only refuses to put his guard down, but also closes his eyes to make sure he doesn't even see what's in front of him, let alone FEEL it!

Our ... well ... I can't even find words for it ... brief *story* ...., was by far, the most meaningful event in my life and the trigger for me to start the climb toward my dream. My blind love for you will be the light to keep me going until I consider my book done.

No words or insults will ever change my feelings for you. Have a good night … or should I say good morning … already time for me to wake up and go to work.

Adelle

Tudor's response:
Poor, little victim,

Apparently, you haven't heard the expression, "Less is More."

Your uncontrolled word debit can easily be reduced to two paragraphs. The rest is just fluff, irrelevant information that would be best left out.

You obviously didn't understand my metaphor about the "thin clothes." It had nothing to do with Facebook. It had to do with exactly all this puffy language and elaborate love to use. Let me tell you, there's a level of tolerance in narration, beyond which the reader becomes impatient and annoyed. If you do not keep it in check, you risk having that reader fling the one thousand pages over his shoulder in boredom.

I know that these words will mean nothing to you. Your stubbornness will prevent you from absorbing them. Keep writing thousands of pages. *War and Peace* doesn't contain that many. As a matter of fact, don't forget to omit any details in your stories, even the time it took to purchase your flight ticket online, the travel website, the airline and seat number, the temperature of the plane's cabin, the meal you were served and if it was too salty, or not salty enough, the cleanliness of the bathrooms in it, the pilot's hairdo, the duration of the flight and the meaningless conversations you had with the person sitting next to you on the way to the States... The people in your auditing department will be proud of you and the fact that you didn't leave anything out! It'll make for great reading. Perhaps the book (should you finish it at this pace), might come with a blade attached to it, in case anyone wants to slash his wrists before finishing it.

As far as my feelings for you go, they are still the same...

I will have no more time to respond again.

Tudor

Adelle's reply:

Alright, there is no offense taken. I do need to learn how to dance. We talked about taking a class together. As for the fluff and detail ... well ... for one, a book is not a TEXT message, which you are so fond of, or an email and not even a letter. The substance in it is the whole story, with its every little detail defining it. A building structure is composed of many bricks and fillings, as I recall.

If you think you can get to know a person through monosyllabic exchanges of ideas based on a vocabulary of fifty words max, physical interaction on the dance floor and looks, good luck to you! If staring into a woman's eyes to get her in bed and derive some measure of temporary satisfaction is your life's meaning, well then my darling, the rest of your days may leave you a little disappointed.

That relationship will expire in less than a year after you signed the marriage contract, went through a wedding, and had a crying baby to turn your nights into days and vice-versa. Once you have a family, your life is not about you anymore. Children are existential substance, if conceived and raised in true love. Parents must interact and carry on conversations beyond mundane facts of life while still enjoying things they both love--history, geography, muse-ums, fine art, theatre, etc. These not only help to make their lives a beautiful experience, but also help their kids to grow to be strong and independent, well-formed personalities.

But, if a good looking, simply mindless good looking woman can make a man of your talent, intelligence, and knowledge spin his wheels through life ... well ... fasten your seatbelt.

Regards,

A

Tudor's response:

Honey, you need help, really!

Adelle's reply:

I should have been frightened to go out with you in the first place. Your insistent stare on New Year's Eve and your messages got me. No ... I cannot say I have ever been approached in this manner before. Yes, I am a frightened animal.

I was nothing more than someone else you wanted to satisfy your ongoing need for novelty. You put into this brief story as much dedication as you put into a new waitress to conquer.

Patience? How do you conclude that, darling? Really? Was it in between your other concomitant games while you knew I might posses the intellect to comprehend your moves? Patience is when you actually spend time with a person, *real* time, not a few hours a week after you infinitely torment them so that normal behavior between the two of you is out of the question. You rattled my cage every time you realized you could not be free of me emotionally. At least not until you momentarily cut me out of your life once more. Or maybe it wasn't momentary. Maybe in your head it was final every time, but my love for you and my stubbornness kept drawing you back again and again.

When we met, you said you were tired of cheats, idiots, and liars. I knew your character from the moment you pointed your stare at me the very first time. Your eyes are your favorite weapon of attack, as I learned soon enough, but I was up for the challenge, and one day you'll understand why. For now, you've done enough to put me down, hurt me, teach me things I may never have wanted to learn.

Adieu!!!!!!

Adelle

On my way to work that day I typed the following draft email which I never sent to him:

Most people have "skeletons" in their closets, two or three at least. You on the other hand, have them all over the Romanian community, Espresso, Elephant's, Bella, everywhere. They are walking all over you, tromping on your grave. Some you still foster in your life deliberately. I felt them lurking everywhere we went. You keep them close as if you don't want them out of your life or as if it gives you great pleasure to have them around. That in itself was what turned up my self-defenses, my shield, and I reacted accordingly. I undermined our relationship without even knowing it.

You will find relief and happiness when you finally decide to leave them behind. Then you can prepare for a new beginning. Until you do, they'll continue lurking around and defeat everything good that comes your way.

Let me be clear. I, too, am trying to build a wall between my past and my present. It's not easy, and I was hoping you would be in a position to help me, and not take my every mistake as an offense or a weakness. I want to leave in peace and not be haunted by remorse later on. You have to make peace with your past to truly be able to move into your future. I am getting there because I want to, and I have nothing to look back upon. You on the other hand prefer to live with your past and somehow combine the future with it ... It will never work.

Tudor' s email on March 5, 2009:

I don't get it, if you suspected that I was a game player from the start, why did you join in the dance? Curiosity?
Self-punishment? Or simply carefree abandon?

If it's any consolation to you, I didn't regard you as
just another trophy on my wall, and I had all intentions of
making it work in the long run. I thought you were intelligent, sensual, and elegant. I thought you would be a
complement to my image in public and a comfort in private.

The only problem is that you try too hard. You cannot relax around me whether in bed, on the dance floor, or
watching TV, and that makes me nervous and uncomfortable. I didn't think I was that intimidating. I can't understand if that's the way you are in general, or if it's just the
way you are around me. Either way, I cannot be myself
around you. I need to feel at ease around people. I cannot
cuddle with you when you are perpetually obsessed with
your own image. You are paranoid even about sitting in the
right position in my lap. You pose as if you are constantly in
a photographer's studio in front of a camera. I don't want to
be with a model! I used to date a ballerina who during sex
would admire herself and do splits, while totally oblivious to
my attempts to satisfy her. It's narcissism of the highest
order! It is very, very annoying! It's a neurotic condition.

This is the one and only reason I cannot be with you.
I don't suffer from ADHD - Attention Deficit Hyperactivity
Disorder nor did I want to play you. As a matter of fact, I
had every intention of taking this relationship slowly and
seriously.

Tudor

Adelle's reply:

I did not try ... that's me because we hadn't spent
enough time to get to know each other. I told you I need

Gabriela Sbarcea

time with a person to feel comfortable. I was hurt and was sick at the time and was anything but rational.

It sounds as if we both need time to move on with our lives, something you alluded to long ago.

Adelle – I replied to your last email. You don't seem to check it frequently – I have it on my blackberry. You are right on many things, aside from the self-image thing. Time is the only answer to that. I always felt as if I am with a Rodin of today when with you, all within the most amazing lover.

Chapter XIV
Sweet Curse

Like the air blast may the thought of me
Swirl through your mind every day
Like the sun blaze may the ardor of our last kiss
Burn your lips every time you sip water

Like the desert sun may the last time we made love
Turn your heart into ashes
When you'll hold someone else in your arms
And your thoughts would dare turn away from us

Come back my love, come back to me and stay forever!

Days without Tudor crawled. Every second was another obstacle dropped on my path to happiness. I worked
not in a clean office environment but in a salt mine. I dug
with my bare hands, sore blisters forming around my fingers.
That's how painful the minutes and days were without him.
Every now and again, when one of the blisters popped and
salt got into my blood stream, I wanted to scream out loud.
Instead, I sat dutifully silent, a prisoner of my own mind,
rejecting reality, refusing to admit to what was happening to
me or to bow to it: he did not want to be in a "normal"
relationship. Not like other people did. That was too
mundane for him. He was an artist, and he needed the

excitement of life experienced to the fullest to bring out who he really was, for his genius to manifest itself in his creations.

I knew all that in my head; I felt it in my soul. Yet I couldn't stop interiorizing an absurd amount of pain because of my feelings him. Still, I couldn't move on to someone or something else for dear life. He worked his way into my psyche like a larva in a ripe apple.

He was probably right to call me a masochist for returning to him again and again, every time he beckoned. And sometimes when he didn't. The best way I can describe it is to say I was in withdrawal. Tudor withdrawal. He was a narcotic, a drug, one that I never thought I would allow into my life. I found myself addicted without even knowing it.

I looked at the calendar to see if my period was due. I was late. I had stopped taking the pill a month before, and I told Tudor. He was turned on by the concept while denying it, rejecting the very idea when I brought it up.

I was a few days late.

March 7, 2009
Tudor – The heart is dead.
Adelle – I can't tell you now … on Wednesday you may find out why it is more alive than you think.
Tudor – You're not pregnant, I hope!

The phone rang a couple of minutes later. His tone was emphatic, rude and condescending. I asked him if he knew what I wanted to discuss with him. He got it without me ever uttering the actual words. He said that he thought I'd been on the pill. He told me to try to get rid of it. That moment I felt he had thrown me into the fire pit. Perhaps, I thought for a moment or two, I had misunderstood his words. "Whaaaaaaaat?" I sat staring in disbelief.

163

Tudor ended his rampant discourse with, "Alright, let me know soon then."

"Fine," I replied. I hung up as he was preparing to say something else.

Adelle – It was a mistake telling you. You take no responsibilities for your actions. It was wonderful to find out your reaction to it. I have a life too and it doesn't have to include this. Enjoy yours now that you won't have me around anymore.

Tudor – I DON'T NEED THIS KIND OF FUCKING STRESS NOW! GOD DAMN IT! I don't even like you anymore. What is the point of all this? You know what, I don't need to know any results. I don't want any more messages from you, EVER! You are crazy and I don't need a crazy woman in my life.

Adelle – You knew when I was off the pill – way before last time we were together, and why. I am peaceful and happy about it. You can curse, insult me as much as you want. You made this neurotic instant texter out of me because of the way you behaved between the times we were together. Do as you please. I can't hate you, but I am extremely upset with you right now. This is not a trap! You aren't even welcomed to stay if this is not where you want to be. I'd prefer to carry the burden and enjoy a baby's smile and happiness on my own rather than with someone who would dread each and every day together with us.

Tudor – You are not as smart as I thought. You're also evil and irrational on top of it. I hope you come to your senses soon. Go explain your wonderful deed to your dad. I'm sure he'll be proud. And good luck with rebuilding your life afterwards.

Adelle – Thanks! Insulting me, making me out to be stupid and crazy might make you feel better about yourself. I made a capital mistake to trust a man who fed me nothing but lies all the while I was falling for him. I already explained to my dad how much I love you. I will handle my "deed" to the best of my abilities. I have not destroyed my life ... and I had enough of the specie of man for a lifetime. I am sorry for the timing ... and you having such a low opinion of me, but these are the only things I will ever be sorry for. The little life that might be growing inside of me will be the greatest gift I ever had from the love of my life who never once offered me a modicum of support. You criticized me instead, put me down and judged me harshly every time I made a mistake.

It's all right. I can live with it.

Tudor – You're a fanatic and mentally imbalanced woman. The biggest mistake of my life was touching you. You are out for revenge, nothing else. What do you know about love? You're nothing but an egotistical showoff. This will never be who I love, on the contrary.

Adelle – Darling ... I would never stand in the way of your happiness. Go on. Continue looking for it as you have been doing since right after the third time we were together. On the other hand, as inexperienced as I may be in many other regards, I recognize and come to terms with my own feelings and do not expect to be told that I don't know what I feel. Not by you or by anyone. You may deceive me with what you want me to believe in any other sense, but NOT by belittling my feelings. Love what you want, whom you want, and carry on with your life as if I never existed ... I will be as far away as I was before we met. You have my word on it.

Tudor – From this point on you're on your own. I should give you my cousin's number, so she can tell you how easy it is to find a mate when you already have all that baggage with you. I don't want to hear from you again. Do as you please. Just don't bother me anymore.

Adelle – I don't need any mates! In case you missed my earlier statement ... three relationships have been three too many. Men seem to be of only two kinds – liars and cheaters, or just plain old boring. So I'm fine, don't worry about me.

Adelle – How could you ever have suggested my disposing of the one thing you told me so many times you wanted??? And how could I have fallen for it? And relied upon the one method of contraception that I knew was least reliable? How and why did I ever fall in love again when I swore to myself that I wouldn't? Not for anything in this world!

Well, I guess that's more than one question. Just some rhetorical ramblings ….

March 8, 2009
Adelle - Look - I wanted to say this yesterday, but the meanness in your words prevented me. I AM SORRY! I didn't want this for myself at this point in my life any more than I wanted it for you. I understand your position and anger. If you think I did this to get to you or out of revenge, you should think again. It's not in my character. I would never deliberately hurt myself to get back at someone and then hurt a third innocent life in the process. I KNOW this is not how you make someone love you, quite the contrary. I was not born yesterday. It happened ... What's done is done. I feel like throwing up right now. But I never have and never will consider doing what you suggested for all the reasons I already told you. Be at peace with this, please. Relax. It's going to be OK, regardless of your decision.

Tudor - I've never been more depressed in my life. You're about to ruin what's left of it, just to satisfy a selfish whim. I don't love you. I love someone else who doesn't want me. If you are pregnant and decide to keep it, you will do everyone a disfavor. There will be no end to my hatred of you. You are old enough to know that things said during sex mean nothing. It's only hormonal. I don't want to have kids with you! I hate irrational and stubborn people! If you decide to punish me for not loving you, you are nothing but a sadistic fanatic. I will deny you and your offspring for the rest of my life with no remorse. I don't want you knocking on my door, or even letting me know of your stupid decisions. If you make decisions on your own, you have to live with them yourself until the end of time.

Adelle - Tudor ... I am sorry ... I wish things were different. I am sorry to hear you are in love with someone that doesn't want you, I am sorry about your financial situation, I am sorry to hear you are in such a state. That's the reason why I don't want you to worry about me. I will NEVER make ANYONE have me in their life if they don't want me or if I don't make them happy. No one will know who the father is, aside from my family and Olivia. I will deal with the rest of the social stone throwers at work and such. You try and relax ... You will be better off with a clear mind. Go on a vacation. I needed nothing from you before and will need nothing going forward.. Good luck with getting to fulfill the love you want! Forget that I exist. Pardon me for intruding in your life for as long as I did.

Tudor - You're such an evil bitch. I want you to get an abortion, do you understand?

Tudor – (A few hours later after no response from me) How the fuck do you think I can have a clear mind and go on a vacation? Are you retarded? I don't want to even have you on my conscience anymore. How can I erase you from my memory?

I chose not to respond to his last messages. Despite my strong impulse to reply. Besides, there wasn't much I could say anymore.

I sensed his internal struggles as if he lived through me.

Our minds were one, though he refused to accept that concept.

Later that afternoon, I sent him this message:

March 10, 2009
Adelle – You far exceed the limits of monstrosity generally observed in people, Mr. Popescu. How do you live with yourself? I am not pregnant and quite relived to find that. The thought of you turns my senses upside down at this point.

My period finally arrived. I checked my Facebook account that evening and there were some comments from Tudor on one of our mutual friend's pictures leading me to think he might say awful things about me, about us, to our friends. I resolved to send him a message after a couple more days.

March 12, 2009
Adelle – Yes, it's over. No need to drag it through the mud. I won't. Let it be what it was. Despite your demeaning words, I still have some respect left for you. Continue your life in peace and I will mine. It was honest. Don't tear it apart.

Tudor – "It's over"? It was over the day you started blackmailing me. That is not love. I never ruined anyone's future who didn't love me in return. Why would I punish them for something only God has control over? I was never bitter. If anything, I always absorbed the dealing of a cruel fate into self-blame and self-pity. The opposite is just bad karma.

I just could not wrap my mind around Tudor's logic. It was blown to pieces. I responded to the rest of his message, to the accusations filled with injustice and hostility.

168

Adelle – Yeah … bad karma. Blackmailing? You never took the time to learn who I am. All I ever believe in is that the one bad thing one does to ANYONE will come back a thousand times worse on himself. I spoke the truth … what I believed in at the time … the existing evidence. Maybe I should begin lying for a change, maybe I learned a bad habit.

Tudor – We can alter things that fate throws our way. God gave us a brain to do that. Unfortunately, we cannot change feelings.

Adelle – I agree.

Tudor – Why would you be so sadistic not to give me a way out, anyway? You obviously don't know me either. Messing with my conscience is worse than messing with my body. I cannot concentrate on anything. I am an inch away from either killing myself, or the one who is torturing me. You have no idea what criminal thoughts go through my head at a time like this. As desperate as I am right now and cornered on all sides by disaster, I may just snap. I have nothing to lose. *Nothing*.

Adelle – I exposed my presumptions to you thinking, based on your words, that this would bring a ray of light to your life. I was late.

Tudor – You don't understand. There's nothing that scares me more in life than being tied down. If you ever plan on keeping another man's baby, someone who feels trapped by the concept, don't ever let him know you're pregnant. Weighing his conscience down with the possibility of it happening is the worst form of torture. I've been unproductive for a week. I've lost a ton of hair and all my joints hurt like crazy. I'm a mess.

Tudor – When did you get your period?

Tudor – (About an hour later with no response from me) Ironically, in the middle of all that stress and loathing for you, I was still having sexual fantasies about you. I don't know how science can explain that.

Adelle – I got it about half an hour before you got my message. We are the same in that regard, remember? Wild mustangs? I was going nuts as well … but trying to keep my senses about me. If I'd been pregnant, it would have been because of love, not chance.

Adelle – Because you want me … and I want you. Everything else is nonsense.

Tudor – Right. I almost killed you.

Tudor was derailed that night; I sensed he might actually consider doing away with me and I instinctively bolted my door. I looked around me on my way to the bus station in the morning. Even with my paranoia exploding, I knew he could never find the malice within him to commit such a barbaric act. Or maybe he could have. He was on the edge of sanity … my love for him only made things worse.

What to do? Where to go next?

It dawned on me. His birthday was coming up. I sent him a gift.

Adelle – I sent your birthday gift earlier today through Amazon. When you get it, you may understand that none of what happened last week was ill intended. And if you decided to kill me, which somehow I expected … well … that's life. No pun intended. Maybe I would have deserved it.

Tudor – I don't know if I'll be fully recovered by my birthday. I have nothing to celebrate. I am *not* celebrating actually.

Adelle – I know … I don't celebrate mine either, it's just a gift. It might come in two separate shipments though. This life is too short … enjoy every moment no matter where you are, what you do, how you feel, and with whom you share it.

Adelle – I am falling asleep and have to go to work tomorrow, but before I turn in, I want to say one last thing … all I ever wanted to do was to be able to be there to hold you in my arms through the most difficult times in your life. And be there through all the glorious times, as well, to push you even further. I am far from perfect.

Tudor – Good night!

I gently placed my guard on the ground … again. I had already considered our relationship a lost cause and was beginning to console myself with a life spent without him. Somehow, the wheels of our deranged relationship were once again in motion.

And just as quickly and unceremoniously as that, I arrived at his home, and he opened the door and a few moments of silence froze between us as we stared into each other's eyes. All was said then: fragments of thought transferred from my mind to his and from his to mine. I threw my arms around his neck and our lips parted to receive more and more of one another.

We caressed each other through the living room where he pushed me hard up against the wall. My legs wrapped around him. I was in bliss when I smiled. He paused before speaking.

"Why are you laughing? Did you think that was funny?"

My mind wanted to answer, but my body was already disconnected; it had surrendered to his will. I was his.

Chapter XV
Happy Birthday, Darling!

If I shall never send a message on your way again
Will you forget last night you had me in your arms?
Will you block off my legs around your waist
When you said: "My love, you are only mine"?

If I abandon scratching walls in narrow caves
To break volcanic rock and reach your soul
Will you capitulate to my imploring eyes
Pleading for me to stay and always be with you?

Tudor was born on March seventeenth under the sign of Pisces. He was fascinated by the Zodiac and knew the signs of most of his friends and family. As for his own sign, Pisces fit him like a glove.

Pisces. If you were born between March eleventh and twentieth, the Scorpio will dominate your nature through intense passion. A highly demanding character, an input of one hundred percent is hardly good enough for you; be less possessive and jealous in your relationships.

I often wondered which came first: the Pisces or the man.

The last time I saw him before his birthday, I asked him if I could take him to dinner as a gift to which he responded cautiously, "I'll just go to dinner with my mom and brother and don't want to see anyone else that day." My hands were tied.

On the day of his birth, I awoke early and texted a message to him.

March 17, 2009

Adelle – Happy birthday darling! I am wishing you all you want from life, health, happiness, and, above all, to be famous for what you love to do. Wishing you to be surrounded by people who truly admire you for who you are, soon in your own gallery of magnificent sculptures, as soon as this year or next. Then we will have a cup of champagne together. Smile darling, you are worlds apart from everyone else. Have a wonderful day!

Tudor – Thanks. I am overrated.

Adelle – The one sculpture you have – the man undressing his skin - is absolutely brilliant. It makes the mind think far beyond what the eyes actually see! You are far better than you think.

Adelle – The Munch Exhibition is great – check it out. I would even go see it a second time. And I was not too fond of his work before I went.

Tudor – Thanks for the invite. I wanted to go see it this week.

Adelle – I can only go after five or on the weekend. Thursday is the only day it's open until eight, and the site says there's free admission between five and eight.

Tudor – OK. Thursday then.

I had gone with my friend, Harra, to the Art Institute to see the Munch exhibit the previous week. The artist was renowned for painting the souls of people, exposing their sins, and illuminating the darkest corners of their minds, places where most people rarely let outsiders in. I just knew that Tudor would love it.

March 18, 2009
Adelle – *Bonjour!* How is your day?
Tudor – (Several hours later) OK so far.
Tudor – I have to pursue my ideal, or die alone.
Adelle – I completely agree with you. "The Vanity of this life, each longing for what he or she could not get." - W. Thackeray
Adelle – (An hour later) If you don't see it until it hurts, so be it. I wanted to make it easy for you. Suppose I was wrong. My endurance has a limit. Pursue your dreams. Just make sure you have nothing to look back to before you do so. Who am I to say all this? You already know it.

How many times had he already said those same words to me? How many more were to come? It was beyond me. Nothing got through to him. It was over. Except that I felt deep down within me that it wasn't. I'm not even sure why.

March 19, 2009
Adelle – Great! You might get a laugh out of this – now my sister is trying to set me up with some University of CA professor, in his 40s, who left from Constanta many years ago. Hmmmm … what draws out that pity in your family when you pass the age of thirty and are still single?
Tudor – Well, there's a Romanian saying – "Until you turn thirty, you get married on your own, between thirty and forty, your relatives will try to get you married, and after forty, not even the devil will get you married."
Adelle - I remember that one – haven't heard it in a while. So funny!

Adelle – Do you still want to see the Munch exhibition this evening, as friends? I completely understand your point of view on pursuing your ideals – I hold similar beliefs.

Tudor – I can see the exhibit on my own.

Adelle – Very well. You might get it one day, but until then, happy hunting!

Adelle – This life is so bizarre … you are EVERYTHING I want from it, and for a brief two weeks at least, I was in heaven because I knew you were with me and felt the same. Let it be what it may. I don't play games with whom I truly love. I can play them well, but only with those I want to crush and care not about. *Adieu!*

Tudor – I will never be happy. I don't want to bring you into my misery.

Adelle – I would be more miserable in a house of gold without you. That is not it though … I just don't do it for you. You got bored.

Adelle – I never expected fidelity from you. Misery feeds inspiration, you probably need it. You asked once why I joined the dance … it was for that very reason, unconsciously though, and because your mind overpowered mine the minute I was walking out of your house on New Year's Eve. A text message cannot contain what I got out of it.

Tudor – I didn't get bored. I'm just in a constant search for God knows what, cause I don't know anymore. Even girls who I thought would be ideal (you), are not good enough.

Adelle – Thank you! There is nothing more rewarding than the truth. I am glad you finally said it … I knew it a long time ago. Unhappiness and constant searching indicate progress. Perhaps one day you'll find that better version of me and she will finally be the one thing you need. Don't feel bad about it though … the chase is better than the catch.

Tudor – You see. That's why I let you do the chase. It's the only way I could keep your interest peaked.

Adelle – Clever … perhaps genius I should say. If you want me alive at the end of it all, you should probably wind it down. Remember how skeptical I am about you.

Tudor – And you remember who's the doll maker and the puppeteer here …

Adelle – True … my strings are now quite tangled up. You run the show well.

Tudor – They're tangled up because you always fight the rhythm …

Adelle – Yes … I do need direction, and I respond to good reason and a skilled hand.

Tudor – I'll let you know when I feel like dancing again.

He was a master puppeteer in all power of the expression: he made gorgeous dolls for a living. They helped found his wealth and provided him a comfortable lifestyle. Why did I feed on his nonsense like a love-famished woman? It was profane … but I ate up every one of the crumbs without looking up to him with anything less than complete gratitude.

He had me by my strings, hanging from up high, and would only allow me to touch the ground to clear my head for a few seconds at a time before the next show began.

I walked out of my office building at lunch and saw his car parked by the front entrance. A man dressed up in police uniform leaned casually against it. The man was his younger brother, Virgil. Tudor sprang out through one of the massive doors of our office building like a deer in rut. He grabbed me and hugged me, introducing me to his brother.

We ran across the street to Café Hazelnut and had a cup of coffee and some water. I didn't need any food. Tudor's venerable smile was enough to keep me nourished throughout the day.

Gabriela Sbarcea

We kissed and hugged like teenagers in a movie theater. I should have felt embarrassed, carrying on like that in front of family. But my passion for him was impossible to harness. He was as hungry for me as I was for him.

Tudor invited me to a last minute party for a bunch of his friends who all celebrated their birthdays in March. He was hosting it at home the next day, Saturday.

On Friday night, I planned to go out to help Harra celebrate the Persian New Year. It was a unique event, the first one I would experience.

Adelle – We'll be at Aperitif 21 close by my place on Lincoln and not planning to stay long past midnight. Can you pick me up on your way here?

Tudor – No, it's OK, have fun! I'll pick you up tomorrow afternoon around three.

Adelle – There's only one place that I'd rather be and you know it.

Tudor – Well, I'll probably be in bed by then.

Adelle – Come by and meet her and have a drink with us, or I can leave my keys with the doorman and you can snoop around my place until I get home.

Tudor – OK, sorry, I was installing some cable at my house. I wish you had a car, or I wish I lived closer. The way things are going, I'll be out of the house soon. This life sucks ass! And the banks always win. I'm not feeling in the frisky mood I was this morning.

Adelle – (I sent him a picture of me all dressed up and looking *hot*)

Tudor – (A few seconds later) I guess you can come to my house after midnight!

Adelle – OK. I'll take a cab.

Tudor – No. Got a better idea. I'll come to you and we'll leave your place in the morning. Call me when I should take off for your place.

Adelle – No later than eleven forty-five. Send me a text when you are close to the city.

Tudor – OK

Tudor – (An hour later) Actually, I just ate some lamb and I am stuffed. I'll pick you up tomorrow. I won't be good for anything tonight besides deep sleep and snoring. I'll spare you that and I'll see you with a clear mind and stomach tomorrow.

I went out that evening with my friend. He kept texting me. Should I have felt flattered that he cared for me not bringing anyone home? What spins the wheels of a player? Was it the male marking his territory syndrome or actual jealousy? The feathers in my pillows were not as soft that night. My restless mind jetted from one question to another, leaving me with no comfortable answers. Who was I to Tudor, a man who had women at his fingertips, granting him favors left and right?

March 21, 2009

Adelle – (Passed 3:00 in the afternoon) The battle of the wits ... I'm liking it. How are you darling?

Tudor – What are you talking about? I'm leaving my house. I'm sick of cleaning the whole morning.

Adelle – I wish I could have been of some help. I'll help tomorrow with cleaning after the party. See you soon.

Tudor – I'm sick and tired of these parties. I'm already tired literally. I'm not in the mood for any fucking party. It's Dorina's idea. I'm waiting to see if Vlad can pick you up on the way here. He lives by the lake.

Adelle – I can take a cab.

Tudor – I'm done. It was supposed to be a small, ten-person get together, nothing fancy. Now there are thirty. This Goodman bullshit! *I* may not show up.

Adelle – Grumpy! It will be fun. I already bought some gifts.

Tudor – No. No gifts.

Adelle – They're not a big deal – just some gift cards from Victoria's Secret for the girls.

Tudor surprised me with a quick telephone call. He said he'd pick me up at home in about an hour after he got something to eat at Espresso's.

Tudor – (About an hour later) – I can't do this. I can't meet you anymore. Why am I doing it? I don't want a relationship with you. What's the point? Don't come.

Adelle – I am all dressed up! You'll understand when you see me why you want me.

Tudor – I don't care. No! I left. I don't want you, dressed or not. Better to hurt you now than in the long run.

Adelle – It's not about the dress … when we are together is what I mean. You want me as much as I want you, and US TOGETHER is perfection. Think about yesterday – the few moments we were together.

Adelle – I can only be happy with you.

Tudor – Too bad. I'm sorry for stopping by yesterday, but I'm sure you're not the one for me. Not even physically.

Adelle – Right … that's why we cannot take our hands off each other. That's why you light up and smile when we are together. That's why we carry on conversations to no end and everything else around us vanishes when our eyes meet … because I am NOT the one for you.

Adelle – Talking about bad timing – the man who pestered me last night to give him my number just called me. He seemed well put together.

Tudor – Go for it! Don't waste a good chance!

Adelle – Yeah ... I am yours even if you put me through hell!

Adelle – I was about to walk out the door and do the most insane thing I would ever have done. Wanted to take a cab and come to your house, have the cab driver deliver the gifts for you and Dorina, and send you a text on my way home to go to the door and pick them up. Why would I do that? Instead, I am taking ten sleeping pills and hope I don't wake up till Monday morning when I can go to work and take my mind off of you.

Tudor – You're insane. Fine, come over if you want. I could care less. I don't wanna be here myself.

Adelle – I know. You draw this out of me.

Tudor – Fine. My God, you are resilient!

Adelle – I guess I am ... you made me so.

Tudor drove out of his garage right as my cab pulled into his driveway. He stopped his car next to the taxi and lowered his window. "I'm out of here." I started laughing. Out of all the scenarios going through my head, the one where I went to his house for a party and he had just left never entered my mind!

"Where?"

"To get some ice and a couple other things."

I got out of the cab and walked over to Tudor's car. "Let me go with you."

"Kiss me when Rita is around. And go ahead and go inside. The door is open."

I didn't get it. If he had invited her to his party, why would he want me there to help make her jealous? Hardly anything that came out of the man shocked me. But this one made me stand up straight, take a step back from him, and stare blankly. I had no reply. He smiled emphatically, pressed the gas pedal and drove away. I stood out there in the cold March afternoon and contemplated the naked forest across from his house. *There is still time to run* I thought. But my ungodly attraction to Tudor weighed a thousand tons on me. I turned toward the house and walked through the door to find two of his friends in frantic preparation for the party. I set my purse and coat aside and helped them set up the table. My mind was far, far away. I responded to their pleasantries mechanically.

Before long, Rita, Alex and the rest of Tudor's Gang arrived. I was washing the cherry tomatoes when Rita walked in. Alex whispered just loud enough into her ear for me to hear:

"You're going to be sooooo jealous tonight..."

I heard his remark and couldn't help but chuckle. Tudor told me how she had pushed herself into his life once she'd learned we'd been seeing each other. There was no love lost between the two of us.

Tudor was remarkably well behaved that evening, the perfect gentleman, treating me like royalty around his friends. We made the perfect couple, and all eyes were on us, some with envy; others with jealousy. We cared not about any of them. We were just so happy to be together again, despite our earlier spats.

Spats, I thought to myself. *That's what we have. Little spats. They're not fights, not knock-down, drag-out royal battles. Just little disagreements.* I suddenly felt better about our relationship, our future, everything. Suddenly everything seemed workable, manageable, doable.

I took hold of Tudor's arm and laid my head against his shoulder as I squeezed it gently. In the background, the jazz quartet he had hired for the evening was playing, softly, sweetly. It was a relaxing, elegant, quiet party. It was the same ambiance that embellished his living room at New Year's Eve, but with fewer people, and in a much more intimate atmosphere.

181

As midnight came and passed, Rita and another girl were putting on a belly-dancing show for several people who had gathered around them. I thought that vulgar and tasteless, but I also found her efforts to impress Tudor quite comical. Obviously she hadn't known that I was going to attend the party, and I thoroughly enjoyed watching her carry on so foolishly. Until I looked more closely at her.

Sadness masked her face.

Tudor's brother stood right behind us during the show. When it was finally over, I turned to them and began making small talk. Virgil picked up on the subject and told us about some recent gang bust operation he'd been part of.

Tudor excused himself and went in the kitchen. Five minutes into our talk, Virgil announced, "You should probably keep an eye on him. I think you're getting to know him better."

He was right. I found Tudor carrying on a discussion with another one of his more attractive exes whom he'd invited to the party. I worked my way across the room and snuggled in next to him. He took my left hand into his as he talked to the woman about art.

Most guests were gone by three in the morning. I surrounded Tudor with my arms as we stood in the doorway, saying goodbye to the last of the guests. We must have looked like an old married couple, melded to one another by time and love. I submitted involuntarily to that sentiment several times that evening. And I sensed Tudor did as well.

An unmistakable sensation that I was home <u>washed over me, drowning me in a sea of delight.</u>

It was the sweet, warm, cozy feeling of a woman in love.

Perhaps for the very first time.

I closed my eyes and lay next to the man I loved, but all I could think about was the episode we'd just gone through, Rita's dance, and Virgil's advice. My earlier

Gabriela Sbarcea

feelings were beginning to butt heads with all these things. We were walking on thin ice … how long before we'd sink or maybe reach solid ground?

Chapter XVI
Vacation Apart

You took some time away from me
Away from us, on foreign seas
To find what I've taken from you
Your heart ... though that I did not do

I volunteered mine instead
With it you also took my head
To crush them both under your foot
Disgrace me where I proudly stood

You came back after many days
To say "I'm not home, never again"
It wasn't long till I was cast
Together with your putrid past

Reading on my way to and from work helped me to unwind, to remove me from the oppressive military routine of the office. On one particular morning, well into my third bus stop, I settled into a seat and noticed a nerdy looking man in his mid-twenties who sat next to me and opened up his *Financial Times* somewhere in the middle. The young man's ears began to twitch, rotating like the ears of a rhinoceros, the muscles in his forehead rising and falling in unison. I hadn't noticed him doing it at first - only after he opened the paper and began to read. He seemed as normal and content as most people otherwise. But I couldn't stop staring at him. I could barely contain my amusement. *Only Tudor would understand my view.*

The markets kept swirling down into a black hole peppered by one day of rallies followed by another of even larger downturns. The lavish lifestyle most Americans took for granted was not sustainable long term. The writing was getting clear.

I knew Tudor was taking off within a day or two for a vacation with his brother. I wanted to see if there was a way for us to see each other one more time before he left. What better excuse to spend some time together than watching one of the two DVDs I gave him for his birthday?

Yeah ... why not another "no"? *After all, I can just watch the darned thing AGAIN by myself,* I thought. The idea occurred to me for a split second that he might actually plan on going on vacation with some other woman – a possibility not to be entirely excluded from consideration. I shook my head in denial ... *it can't be.*

Ah ... yes ... his brother. I was relieved. He went on trips with Virgil once in a while; he posted some of the pictures in his Facebook albums. It was actually somewhat comforting to see him close to his family. I wish I had that kind of closeness with my older sisters. The age difference had often made me feel like I belonged on a different planet while I was growing up. Living on another continent for a third of my life, in an environment so unlike the Romanian one in so many ways, only weakened the connection I might have had with my family.

Adelle – Little by little, good things will start happening.
Tudor – Right.
Tudor – Can you come over tonight?
Adelle – Yes. Around 7.

Tudor – OK. Can you take me to the airport around 3:00 a.m.?

Adelle – Yes I can. I'll rent a car overnight – it's far cheaper than a cab. So that will be perfect.

Tudor – Thanks! I'll pay for it.

Adelle – You don't have to! See you later.

I arrived at Tudor's house on time. He seemed surprised. I'd only had enough time to let Luca out of the pet carrier bag and put my purse down before we were all over one another. We left a trail of clothing on our way to his living room couch. We couldn't hold off long enough to reach the bedroom.

After we were done fooling around, we put in an old movie. I laid my head on his lap. By the time the movie ended, I found myself somewhere in between reality and dreamland. He stood up and gathered me into his arms like a precious possession. He carried me upstairs, depositing me gently on the bed. I whispered, "The lion is carrying his victim to his den," and he smiled.

He woke up grumpy and irritable around at two-thirty in the morning, packed up the rest of his luggage, and watched as I tried to tip-toe my way around the house so as not to upset him even more.

"Definitely separate bedrooms when we get married," he said.

March 27, 2009
Adelle – (A verse from Eminescu)
"And if the branches knock on windows,
And the trees tremble
It is to have you in my mind
And slowly bring you closer."

Poetry was close to his heart, nearly as close as it was to mine. Every cell of my body and brain missed him, ached for his return. I woke up early the next day, a Saturday, and attempted to write. I ended up watching *Quills*, another one of our favorite period movies. The sound of a new message coming in jolted me.

March 28, 2009
Tudor – (Sends a picture of the beach shaded by a cloud looking as if it was going to rain) Not too much sun today, but yesterday there was plenty.
Adelle – I am watching *Quills*. It's a typical quiet and cold weekend here.
Tudor – Enjoy. I am.
Adelle – Love to hear that! Thanks, I am as well, though I miss your eyes and smile.
Tudor – (Sends a picture of a man that seemed to be his brother on the small phone screen, on a beach chair under a straws umbrella with his pants on).
Adelle – Hmmm … defining vacation. Though who-ever that is on that chair, tell him to take his pants off and jump in the water at once!!!
Tudor – We both burned to a crisp yesterday.
Adelle – Oh love … sun block!!! SPF 40 or 50! There's got to be a convenience store in the hotel. Now, put lots of lotion on, stay in the shade for a day, and wear light shirts and shorts, no jeans.

March 29, 2009
I sent him a picture of Lincoln Park covered in snow.

March 30, 2009
Adelle -
"Could so much desire
In night disappear

187

When the spring waves
Haven't ceased crying?"
By M. Eminescu

I heard nothing from him in nearly four days. He said he'd be gone for a week, so I figured he'd be back by April 1.

April 1, 2009
Adelle – Welcome back home!
Tudor – I am not home. I'll never be home again.
Adelle – I thought you were on your flight back already and you'd get this when you landed. I know it's April's Fools Day, but you will be home. Where are you?
Adelle – (A couple of hours later) I am an empty shell.
Tudor – Even empty shells are pretty. I'm in my own world, that's where I am. Have a nice day!

April 3, 2009
Tudor – Do you have time to see me tonight?
Adelle –What do you have in mind?
Tudor – Straight sex, all night long. Maybe some Thai food and some water during breaks.
Adelle – Excellent! Your place or mine?
Tudor – What do you prefer?
Adelle – How about the city for a change? Six thirty-ish at my place?
Tudor – Do you have a place that delivers Thai?
Adelle – Only good one I know is sushi. Do you like sushi?
Tudor – Sure.
Adelle – Super! I'll see you later!
Tudor – (Several hours later) It'll have to be later. I DON'T WANNA BE STUCK IN RUSH HOUR TRAFIC!

Adelle – No problem. Drive safe. It should clear after six or so.

Tudor – I hope so …

Tudor – Cancel plans! I can't do it with you anymore. I want more than carnal attraction. I'll never bother you again. You left your necklace here last time. If you give me your address, I'll send it to you.

Adelle – Do you remember the last time we were together? How about if we actually have no time pressure? Just us – 24 hours or the whole weekend?

Tudor – No. I want it to be over. Truly. If it didn't happen this far, it never will. You are a narcissist with no remedy. You cling to me out of stubbornness more than affection. You aim to please, but you can't really live and let yourself loose in the moment.

Adelle – Every sense in me is in absolute state of ecstasy whenever we make love. I have NEVER experienced anything of the sort before. It's just that I am not used to you yet.

Adelle – I told you there will always be something new when we are together – otherwise you'd be bored. Good things get better with time, remember?

Tudor – I am leaving my house.

Adelle – Or I might just go out with Olivia and maybe have sex with a stranger!!!

Tudor – Better. Have fun!

Adelle – YOU SUCK!!!! I WANT YOU, you fool! Will you ever get that?

Adelle – (A couple of hours later after no response) I love you more than I love my own life, the air that I breathe, the light that I see, but you have it all and want none of it. I have taken too much of your time. *Adieu!*

Adelle – (Passed midnight) EVERYTHING hurts! And I don't even know what it is. I hope you do, because I never felt it before.

Tudor – Pain sucks, I'm sorry. I'm drunk as a skunk.

Adelle – I was trying to fall asleep, but it's not working.

Tudor – I'm not drunk enough for that.

He abnegated our love by denouncing our pleasure. He sullied me and vitiated the most sublime moments we had spent in one another's arms in complete abandon to our passion.

Through it all, I continued to take it in, to absorb it. Perhaps it was out of stubbornness that I did so. At least partly. But mainly I think it was because of my colossal adoration and love for the man.

Give up? For what? Accept defeat in front of the only stream of vibrant emotions I had ever known? Why?

As much as his anger with me hurt, it wasn't enough to convince me to step back from our bizarre connection and abandon our transcendental attraction for one another. And neither, I knew, was it enough for him.

Chapter XVII
My Perfect Birthday

When glacial death will come my way
I want your arms to be my only cover
My last vision of life to be your eye
White mantle through eternal winter

When my left hand will clench your palm
I want your ardent fingers nestling mine
My frail body will rest upon your arm
As my last breath will conjure up to heaven

He told me so many times he wished I had a car. I re-solved to get one in the end even if I wasn't convinced I really need it. Tudor's reproaches bothered me. Why should I buy a car simply because he thought I should? But, in the end, I decided it was easier to give in than it was to keep butting heads with him.

April 4, 2009
Adelle – I found a car. Would you test-drive it with me?

Tudor – No.

Tudor – Don't buy a car just because of what I said last night. It won't make any difference between us anyway.

Adelle – It seemed to be an issue you've had with me ever since we met. You said several times you wish I had one. Relationships are NOT easy. Sometimes you have to try to work out a few things that stand in the way of the rest.

Tudor – Relax, I don't wanna work on this relationship. I have someone else in mind.

Adelle – You found the crummiest excuses to run as fast as you could from me. I won't stand in the way of your happiness. But don't think I'm going to sit around in agony waiting for you to open your eyes and see me. Not forever!

April 9, 2009

Adelle - I do need to grow up. This is my last message to you. Most people never feel what I feel. I'm lucky that I have at least experienced it once. I have gone beyond all limits for you, gone to the END of the world, lived in hell, and allowed myself to be dragged through mud. Enough! *C'est la vie! A tantot, mon amour!*

Tudor – It's better this way. Trust me. I'm only doing you a favor by rejecting you. I'm no good.

It was a gorgeous April day and I was out on the Lake Shore path rollerblading when I thought back to his last message. It resonated so loudly in my heart that I simply had no strength left to reply to it. His saying "goodbye" seemed to have no end. It had lost its meaning. It was just another one of his acts of desperation, but one I had no willingness to confront. *Fine, have it YOUR way,* I said to myself and rolled my way to the Gold Coast. When I finally returned home, I threw myself onto the couch and cried.

And then it hit me. Tudor had said the last time we were together that he planned yet another trip, supposedly for business purposes, to Romania with his mother. That meant I'd be spending Easter and my birthday without him. I could picture him in Romania, with so many carefree beauties running after his money. Some things never changed.

192

April 10, 2009

Tudor – Well, I'm home, I'm beat, but if you want a drink, we can meet half way to Elephant's. I want some avocado salad too. Are you up for it?

Adelle – Sure. I can be there in about an hour.

Two hours, many stolen kisses, rapacious looks, and two glasses of red wine later, we left Elephant's for my place.

April 11, 2009

Tudor – I am glad I left when I did. I had a message from my brother. My mom was in the emergency room because of a kidney stone. She has to have it removed. The trip will be postponed.

Adelle – Is there anything I can do?

Adelle – If she's still there, what hospital is she in? I can stop by anytime if you think it would make sense.

Tudor – No. She's home now. I'm with her. It's OK now. They gave her medicine, but she has to get rid of it this week. Thanks anyway. I'm going to sleep now. Good night!

Worried and exhausted, I was ready to get dressed and go to the hospital if he needed me to. I did not know his mother yet. He always spoke extremely kindly and affectionately about her, and I imagined she must be a very nice lady.

I fell back asleep and woke up early that morning to phone my older sister and see what practical advice she might have for Tudor's mom.

My sister was as much as a doctor in my family. We always turned to her whenever anyone needed help. I texted Tudor as soon as I was off the phone.

Adelle – How's your mom? My sister gave me some tips on the kidney stones. They dissolved my dad's with medication over time. Far better than surgery.

Tudor – My mom's is too big, seven millimeters.

Adelle – I can make some good chicken soup for her, if you'd like.

Tudor – Yeah, bullshit.

Adelle – Why? I can cook you know, and I would love to do it, especially now. You can pick it up when it's ready.

Tudor – I already bought a lot of stuff. Thanks for the offer.

I felt so helpless. What else could I do? I called one of my work friends who wanted to go to a small shop in Old Town where we'd design and make our own jewelry. Jewelry-making is a tedious process that requires a little bit of creativity and a whole lot of patience … a perfect therapy in a sense. Why not make a necklace for his mom? Tudor would probably only throw it in the trash, just as he'd done with all my other overtures to get closer to him. But maybe not.

The following day was my birthday. In my naïvity, the thought that he might not show never entered my mind, particularly not when I was planning on cooking his favorite food. I went grocery shopping after work and picked up several bags of food and a bottle of good wine. I looked forward to spending a delightful evening with two of the most important people in my life: one of my best friends, Olivia, and Tudor, my lovely wild beast.

Halfway through my cooking extravaganza, I received a message from him.

April 14, 2009

194

Tudor – Sorry about tonight. I'm too lazy to leave my house, and tomorrow my mother has surgery.

Adelle – I made so much food. I also made a necklace for your mom. Can you stop by for at least half an hour and have something to eat?

Tudor – When?

Adelle – Now?

Tudor – I'm watching *House.* Haven't even taken a shower today. I don't wanna do anything. I'm not even hungry. How about tomorrow night? I'll eat then. Just reheat it.

Adelle – I don't care if you haven't taken a shower.

Tudor – I could meet you at Espresso later, if you want. I'll be on the way to my mom's house later.

Tudor – Come with your friend too.

Adelle – That's a great idea. She drives. Around ten? What's the address?

Tudor – Does she drive?

Adelle – Yes, she does. That's how I got to your house on New Year's Eve!

Tudor – Yes. Ten is ok. On Harlem, south of Irving Park a couple of blocks.

Olivia's opinion on the matter was made quite clear to me: I was going overboard in accommodating Tudor, especially on my birthday. "You just didn't understand him! He is much more complicated than any other man I'd ever met. Come on … please please please! It's my birthday", I played my best card. She did not resist.

We drove to the Eastern European Espresso café. Tudor was by the window and watched us walk in. He hugged and kissed me as if nothing had happened earlier and ordered some coffee and water. He hadn't made any reference to my birthday - I wondered why. *Did he forget my birthday??????*, I screamed inside my thoughts. His gaping smile and surprisingly bubbly aura dispelled any clouds of doubt. Tudor's smile was enough to raise me from death, the best birthday present I could have gotten.

After an hour or so, he told Olivia that he would see me safely home. He suggested that we were closer to his place than to mine, so we went there. Once inside, we threw ourselves at one another. Up against the kitchen table, one of the chairs, the living room wall … His arms cushioned me against the cool hardwood floor. His eyes bore through me as he forced me down against the bathroom's icy granite. He was a god and his house was our temple.

I parted with my physical body and glanced over us from the edge of the moon. The rest of the universe gravitated around our exhibition of love. It was absolute, sublime, esoteric. I closed my eyes at one point and said out loud, "This is the most perfect birthday I ever had." He turned all red and looked down in disbelief. He *had* forgotten. I smiled and told him not to worry … I already had all I wished for. Still, he said we'd make up for it on Friday. I nodded and thought to myself, *Yeah, sure, if we don't break up again by then.* I fell asleep with my head on his chest and my heart beating softly.

The following morning, Tudor drove me home to change and take a shower while he waited for me downstairs to drive me to the office. I packed some of the things I had cooked the night before so he could have them for lunch at the hospital.

April 15, 2009
Adelle – How did the surgery go? How is your mom doing?
Tudor – In it now. Waiting.
Adelle – (Later that day) You must be exhausted.

Tudor – She's home sleeping. I'm eating with my brother at Espresso. Thanks for the food by the way. It came in handy at the hospital.

Adelle – Good. Glad to hear that. Say hi to Virgil.

Tudor – I did. Hi back.

Once I arrived home, I opened up my laptop and began pounding out my soul. My mind waltzed through delicate thoughts as they grew first into words and then phrases and finally complete paragraphs. I didn't know what came over me. I was fulfilled when Tudor was at peace. I had it all then. Not much else in the material world mattered but my love and my writing.

Somehow, within that short span of inspiration, a claw of fear grabbed hold of me. Was my happiness now directly dependent on his? Had I lost the spiritual freedom I had yearned for so long and worked for so hard all those many many years after coming to the States? Had my love for Tudor made me prisoner to his will? Had my own consciousness become a direct factor of his state of mind?

I shivered. Darkness, containing the key to whom I was going to become, swept over me. I lost sight of any hope for escape.

What am I doing to myself? And when will it end?

Chapter XVIII
Easter Like Home

A holiday away from home
In exile on a foreign land
You made it into bread and wine
As all I loved and left behind

April 16, 2009

Adelle – Have you ever heard of a Romanian car dealership on Halsted? On Yahoo Autos they have the Romanian flag as a logo. I found a really good deal on an Audi, but I'm not sure if I can trust them.

Tudor – I wouldn't trust any Romanian car dealers.

Adelle – True.

Adelle – (Later that evening) How is your mom progressing, love?

Tudor – Fine. Thanks for asking.

April 17, 2009

Adelle – On my way home.

Tudor – Good for you. And what does that have to do with me?

Adelle – Well … not a whole lot unless you actually meant what you said two days ago.

Tudor – I didn't mean anything. I'm sorry. I want to be alone.

Adelle – I was looking forward to a quiet evening, lazing in front of the TV together. I am too tired to go out, but I wanted you to hold me in your arms and nothing else would equal that.

Tudor – I'll be honest, I had no time to get you a present, so I don't wanna face you before I do.

Adelle – A present? Spending time with you is the greatest present life has brought me so far. Material things mean nothing to me. If that's it, we can just watch a movie home.

Tudor – I am so sick of my house, but I have no money or drive to go anywhere else.

Tudor – Maybe we can meet at J. M. café later and go see a movie at Music Box.

Adelle – Sounds perfect.

Tudor – Around nine. Do you promise to eat something this time?

Adelle – Thanks! I EAT! I want to look the way I wish until it's time to plan for a family.

Tudor – And then you can bloat. But wait. If you kill yourself, how will you reproduce?

Adelle – I am not killing myself. I want a life, with you in it, a family, peace and quiet, no more of this fear of saying or typing the wrong thing that might annoy you.

Tudor – I wish there was something I could do to help you, but I only lust for you on occasion. Not a good basis for a marriage.

Adelle – That's more than enough for a marriage.

Tudor – Aren't you supposed to meet Olivia?

Adelle – She has decided to stay home. She had a long day.

Tudor – She's smart. What am I doing driving aimlessly?

Tudor – I am heading to J. M.

Adelle – I am jumping in a cab now.

Tudor – Tonight I will torture you.

Adelle – Funny.

Tudor – Oh, I don't think so.

Adelle – You got me. I don't even know how to answer this one.

Tudor – With: *Yes, master!*

Adelle – The cabby thinks I'm nuts. I'm giggling here by myself.

Adelle – Just got here.

Tudor – He's on the money. He should drive you straight to the asylum.

Tudor – I'm here already.

Adelle – I don't see you.

Adelle – I'll be there in five minutes – I went to the other location.

Tudor – You're crazy. I'm on Addison and Lincoln.

Adelle – I just found out there are two locations.

Adelle – I am almost there.

Tudor – DUH!

Tudor – Right! I'm almost done eating and ready to go home.

Adelle – I'm almost there!

Tudor – Stop saying that! It sounds like you're about to cum.

Tudor sat at a table by the window with a cup of coffee, water, and some coffee cake in front of him. He always chose the nearby window seats, just as I did. I liked to have a view of what was happening outside of my surroundings.

We spent the night at my place watching and reliving the French movie I had given him for his birthday, *Perfect Love*.

Easter was that next Sunday, and we still hadn't agreed on a plan for celebrating it by Holy Saturday. He said he had to consult his family to plan for the Easter dinner.

Tudor called me shortly after he took off in the morning and said it would be great to have me over; his house was more spacey than my condo. Olivia and I wanted to spend Easter together regardless of where or how.

April 18, 2009

Tudor – You can bring Olivia tomorrow, if you'd like.

Adelle – Super. I'll make some goodies also.

Tudor – See you tomorrow then.

Adelle – Let me know around what time we need to be there.

Tudor – Like Christmas …

Adelle – Hmm … is this a riddle? Two or three?

Tudor – Two or three months from now.

Adelle – Fine. We'll have to sing some carols tomorrow afternoon then.

Tudor – Make sure they're good ones. Otherwise you don't get fed.

Adelle – Yes, master!

Tudor – (Later that day) What are you doing?

Adelle – At a south-side dealer with Olivia.

Tudor – Stop dragging the poor girl around for nothing. Or is she more than happy to see you buy a car?

Adelle – She's laughing at your message.

Tudor – Poor girl. It's the Passion week and she is the martyr.

Adelle – The Audi I came here for, listed today, got sold half an hour ago. Now I am test-driving a Mercedes C280 from 2007 with 50K miles.

Tudor – If you want a Mercedes, I can give you a name at Leed Motors. If you want to buy it from there, good luck! Olivia is probably saying buy, buy, buy!

Adelle – 18K and need to get extended warranty for 2K.

Adelle – Perfect shape, drives fabulous.

Tudor – Buy it!

Tudor – The dealer bought it for 12K someplace. Are you good at bargaining?

Adelle – Olivia is.

Tudor – A lot of miles for only two years of driving. It's 15K per year on a generous driving schedule.

Adelle – True, but the comparables with fewer miles are 4K more.

Tudor – Good. Let her talk. Walk away if they don't budge. They'll chase you out the door. I'd ask for 15K. You'll do fine. You're a money person. Don't look too excited. That's a no-no.

Adelle – I'm getting it. I'm doing the paperwork now.

Tudor – What's the verdict?

Adelle – I have a good credit score and I'm driving out of here with it tonight. I'll send you a text. Want to check it out?

Tudor – Come by then.

Tudor – (About an hour later) I hope you didn't leave already. I have to meet Vlad now.

Adelle – I did.

Tudor – OK. Come by first and we leave later.

The adrenaline rush of driving a Mercedes was far better than I expected. I got over my hesitation of owning a car and just enjoyed it for the fun of it, for what it truly was. It drove like a butterfly, yet it was one of those material luxuries I viewed as an unnecessary waste of money.

I pulled into Tudor's driveway. He waited outside with his arms crossed looking at me with a smirk of disbelief and bewilderment. I pulled to a stop, rolled down the window, and said, "Well … you knew I was crazy before. Here's more proof of it." He laughed out loud.

By the time we went back to his house following dinner, I was tired to the point where I almost crashed on a
chair and put my head on his kitchen table. He asked that I
get some sleep first and then go home to be in good shape for
the big Easter dinner he was planning the second day.

I fell asleep for a couple of hours before he tiptoed his
way in and sat by me on the side of the bed. He kissed me on
my forehead. I pushed the comforter away and threw my
arms around his neck. He giggled. The warmth of his hug
ran through my entire body like a flash of indescribable
happiness. Was he holding his beloved? It was difficult to
pull myself away from that blissful serenity, yet I had a lot to
do before Easter dinner. A few traditional rituals such as
cooking traditional dishes (sarmale or stuffed cabbage for
one) and making it to midnight mass were high on my list of
priorities, just as they'd been back in Romania during my
childhood.

A last kiss, and I was on my way, my heart filled with
joy. I skipped from one little cloud to another all the way
home. Olivia and I drove our cars to Tudor's house on
Easter. Virgil helped us get the food out of the car and into
the kitchen. I walked in and looked to see if I could recognize his mom from the pictures I saw on the walls. She was a
short, modest lady who received me with the kindest smile
and open arms. I melted in moments without knowing
anything more about her. I sensed all her sweetness,
affection, thoughtfulness, amiability combined with a shrewd
mind and stone-hard ethics, just like my mother. We bonded
instantly… she was just like my very own mother. I hoped
our relationship would continue, no matter what happened
between her son and I!

Tudor's uncle, aunt and cousin were all there. The
place sparkled, and the table nearly burst with food. Tudor
even dyed Easter eggs red and blue! He cooked an extrava-

gant meal, all by himself. I suddenly viewed him even more highly than I had before.

The magical combination of people, conversation and surroundings transformed the day into one of the most special I had ever lived. It took me back to my childhood, where everything was simple, modest, delicious ... my safe haven. We all spoke Romanian, cracked jokes, and I listened to our beautiful language with its mountain dialect, the Ardeal region, a slow and elegant manner of speech. His mom's accent was particularly harmonious and delightful, and the entire presentation touched my heart.

Tudor's mom remarked before departing, "Make sure you do not kill each other." I smiled amiably, connecting the dots: did he tell his mom that he wanted to kill me when he thought I was pregnant?

We arranged a couple of chairs around the fireplace and sat there for a while, fixing our eyes on the burning wood and chatting about nonsense. I sat in his lap, my favorite place on earth, and it all started from there on ... the flames of our passion matched those in the pit. Several hours later, while we watched TV, I rested my head on his chest ... another day in dreamland.

All the humiliation, tears, and agony I endured at the hands of Tudor were gone. Faded by the unique moments of love and joy we lived together. I finally felt at home. He brought it all together for me, in one place, where everything became perfect, comprising all the quintessential elements of life, everything that made a strange land finally feel like home, after twelve years of roaming the world, estranged from my family. It brought to mind one of my favorite quotes, one that Homer wrote in his Iliad:

"Where shall a man find sweetness to surpass his home or his parents?

In far lands he shall not, though he'd find a house of gold."

It was not gold that made it happen though, it was he, his genius, talent, insanity, affection, temper, the way he handled me, the magnetism drawing us together from the moment we fell into each other's universe on New Year's Eve, out of nowhere, like alien objects simply belonging together.

His magical home and my instincts about it had evolved into a reality far beyond what I had ever imagined possible, even before I met Tudor. All I knew for a fact was that I met the man capable of molding my dreams into reality, just as easily as he sculpted his own realities ... in a quarry of glistening white marble.

Chapter XIX
Flowers

Red rose petals fall on tables
Torn by battle from their buds
Elbows lie resigned on armrests
I am failing all your tests

Tudor confessed he wanted to learn the basics of accounting, something he'd found totally foreign in the past. I told him I'd be glad to teach him in my spare time to balance his business and personal accounts.

April 22, 2009
Adelle – I will be on my way soon. Have your QuickBooks® ready. I'm bringing a rather heavy accounting book!
Tudor – OK.
Tudor – (Half an hour later) Can we do it tomorrow, instead?
Adelle – Took off early from work and told my boss I'll work late tomorrow to make up for it. Wanted to beat the rush hour traffic.
Tudor – I just want to go to sleep now.
Adelle – It'll take me an hour to get there. Go to sleep.

The door was slightly open and he was asleep when I tiptoed into the upstairs bedroom, where the heavy velvet curtains were pulled, making it nearly impossible to see. He stirred, opened his eyes, and motioned me closer. He'd suddenly lost all desire for slumber, as my body heat drew near. I felt his own body covering mine with the immense unearthly blanket of sweet unconsciousness.

He fixed his eyes upon mine and then slowly moved his index finger to my lips, seductively tracing them before run a line down my chin, my neck, all the way down to my heart.

"What's in that pretty red head of yours? Your heart is running a marathon," he said.

"Do you really need an answer?" I smiled up at him.

"No. It's in your eyes and under my palm".

I kept my eyes open. I wanted that moment to linger in my mind forever, imprinted on my heart for eternity.

The following day I was in the office as usual when he sprang his predictable chain of messages on me:

April 23, 2009
Tudor – Do you invest in the stock market?
Adelle – A little. Why?
Tudor – I was just wondering if you're a good gambler. I used to. I used to do better than my stock broker. She lost me tens of thousands in options. I was wondering if it's a good time to buy stocks. I don't need a good credit history for that.
Adelle – I have my own picks on a watch list I sent you a while ago. One tripled since I sent you that email. I need to do some research on a few industries you might like, then we can develop a strategy based on your tolerance levels and then diversify (divide and concur). That's for any portfolio over 2K.
Tudor – Thanks. We'll talk more in person.
Tudor – What's your address at work? I know it's on Madison, but what's the full address?

207

Adelle – It's the main building. I'm in the directory and they can find me even though I work out of the Madison building.

I sent him my work address. I wondered why he'd asked for it.

April 24, 2009

Tudor – I'm sorry, I had to cancel the order. Those people are retarded. I've never had a problem with them before. I placed the order yesterday at nine in the morning and they couldn't find time to deliver it until after the bank is closed? And now they told me again before five, when I asked them to do it before noon? I told them to go fuck themselves. I don't trust them anymore. Sorry, I'm livid with these morons. I'll deliver it in person.

Adelle – Only if you have time for it.

Tudor – I'll wait till I see you. I won't bother you at work.

Adelle – You wouldn't bother me.

Tudor – I'm sorry, you're a wonderful girl, but it seems that even fate doesn't cooperate with this relationship. It's all messed up. I want to be alone and grind over this.

Adelle – I respect your wish.

Tudor – I have to return a few things. Can I please have your home address?

Adelle – No. Throw everything out, please. It is more appropriate. It is the easiest way to discard memories that might hurt in any way for either one of us.

Tudor – Your accounting book, Tupperware, pots ..?

Adelle – Yes! It all means nothing to me. Despite how exhausted I was yesterday, I had the most productive day at work because I woke up next to you. I was happy. Now, I am sitting at my desk, typing a text message, and wondering why the building doesn't crash down on me. Do you think I care about an accounting book and some damned pots??? It doesn't make any sense! But then again, being in love never does.

I sent him a dozen of red roses, hoping he'd smile and forget all that. Tudor's flowers were delivered to my desk within moments after I submitted the order for his.

Adelle – I cannot believe it! I am in shock.

Tudor – I don't even know why they delivered them. I cancelled the order this morning.

Adelle – OK grumpy. But then how about fate??? This is nuts!

Tudor – Read it as you wish. I don't want to see anyone this weekend.

Tudor – (About an hour later when he received my flowers) I give up. What's the point of all this? You see, that's why I refuse to give you any more gifts, because you'll most likely return something of equal or higher value. It just goes to prove you can't accept pleasures of any kind, because you're too paranoid having your balance sheet come out even.

Adelle – I sent them on a whim after your gloomy message. We don't equal by any means. What is happening to us is beyond logic.

Tudor – You must find someone who can absorb your paranoia and insecurity. I'm not it. We don't complete each other.

Adelle – Thanks for the flowers anyway! They came at an impeccable moment, when I expected nothing but another mean message from you, at best. Too bad you seem to like your women hot and cheap, as inscribed on your coffee mug. I like men like you, less them feeling offended if they receive flowers once in their life time. Flowers to one another the same day. That's class.

April 25, 2009

Adelle – (4:00 a.m.) You are right. I am an idiot, of phenomenal proportions. I don't need to send flowers to cheer you up, nor buy a car I have no other use for, just to drive to see you, especially in *this* economy! I also think clearer in the morning. Have a good laugh on my account. I deserve it. I allowed my feelings and not my reason to guide me.

Harra talked me into going to one of Tudor's friends' party where I was invited. My social life needed to go on, even as my personal life was disintegrating before me.

Tudor showed up an hour after we arrived, and he graciously kept Harra and I company for the remainder of the evening. We danced for hours, while his eyes wandered in a dozen different directions. He was wearing me down. I took Harra off to one side and asked if she'd be okay leaving in a few minutes.

"Yes ... I can see why," she said.

I turned to Tudor. "I think Harra and I are going to head home. Feel free to stay if you want."

"I've had enough for tonight," he said. "I think I'll head out too. I'll walk you to your car. This isn't exactly one of the city's safest neighborhoods."

A quick peck on the lips, and Harra and I were on our way. As was Tudor, to his home, I supposed. Or possibly not.

I knew no more humiliation ... I lived past it.

The night pressed on my shoulders like a mountain of granite. The city lights flickering through my sheer curtains were fading away in the darkness of my loneliness. I heard the red rose petals falling heavily, burned, onto my coffee table. I wanted him. Only him.

Would he keep tomorrow's promise?

Chapter XX
Je t'aime!

I want not to want to belong to you
This place, this month, this year
I have to free myself of us
This self made solace prison

I want to be oblivious to life
To everything grow alien and cold
To chose the hearts I want to break
And tie them all together in a knot

Stop me from dancing to our music
Responding to the rhythm of my heart
I want for once, again to reason
And not flow on emotions for a change

I need to feel the snow cold on my skin
Not let it melt without a sense
To feel the rain drops crawling on my back
Not thinking they are our passion's sweat

One day this and one day that ... we were only a matter of time. I was drenched in sadness like a terminally ill
patient sweating blood. I found comfort nowhere – friends,
parents, work, literature, philosophy ... it was all blended in
one unbearable mass ... too heavy, dark, suffocating, with no
end.

April 27, 2009

Adelle – If you weren't you, as complicated as anyone can ever be, this would have ended long ago. I know you don't give a cat's ass about me.

Tudor – You're so right

Adelle – You made me feel both extremes of life – horrendous pain and bliss.

Tudor – I'm at my mom's house. She's not feeling well, but she went to sleep. I can't talk. Come to think of it, I don't want to talk either.

Adelle –I want to be there. But I can't so long as you despise me.

Tudor – You are lost in space. I don't know how to console you. You need to hold hands in public to assert your territorial ownership; you need to kiss me in public for the same reason, although I tell you repeatedly not to. On the other hand, you insist on pleasing me, without accepting pleasure yourself. You constantly scrutinize every move I make. You are neurotic beyond hope; you are stubborn and inflexible and instill the same discomfort in the people around you.

Adelle – Don't get started on what's wrong with me, or yourself, for that matter! We both have our own insecurities and issues. NO ONE IS PERFECT, well, aside from you, in my love-clouded opinion, despite all advice from friends and family. I want you to tell me when I act dumb, when I suffocate you, when I stop thinking.

Tudor – You're a smart girl, but not when it comes to men. And I cannot be your guidance counselor. I'M TOO OLD FOR THAT SHIT. I need someone who's already potty trained.

April 28, 2009
Adelle – Is your mom getting better?

Tudor – Can you shut up for a minute?

Tudor – I'll drop your pots, Tuppaware, and book at the front desk, at your condo. It'll be in a cardboard box.

Adelle – Just don't make a special trip. Not worth it – only if you're in the area for something else.

Adelle – I cannot guarantee that I'll still be here when you're ready for US. You have had so many women who have been "potty trained" by those men who came before you. I bet you've heard that before, haven't you? Most women who loved you just gave up after a while.

Tudor – From what I remember, you've been potty trained by other men, bad trainers, but nevertheless. You were not a pristine package. What makes you think you're such an indispensable commodity? Your package is in the laundry room at your building.

Adelle – Why couldn't you just leave it with the doorman? You take back and deny EVERYTHING you say. How am I supposed to act?

Tudor – I'm not taking back anything I said. You misunderstand me, that's all. Sorry I didn't provide a dictionary for all the allusions I make.

Adelle – You said you hate women that reproach, so I won't go into it. If you care, you'll find at least half a dozen of them in the mess of a draft of the chapters I sent you, in your own words mostly. There's no point to it though. I obviously contributed to our problems with my own catastrophic blunders, at least to this point.

Tudor – OK, nothing makes me happy!

Adelle – I also told you once that I will do and say all the wrong things until I find the right thing to say that will make you want me again, just as you did before I gave into you.

Tudor – Yeah, well, I'm not your guinea pig. Practice your charms on someone else. I'm out of the picture.

Adelle – I don't care for someone else!

Tudor – Just have your friends take you to another New Year's Eve party. You'll find someone new to obsess about. Guaranteed.

Adelle – They tried taking me out, trust me, but I can't bear the thought of any other man in my life since meeting you.

Tudor – Well, do it! I'm not the one for you!

Adelle – Do you think I have endured all this for four months just because I'm a masochist? I love you, point blank. That's all there is to it.

Adelle – (Later that day) Exhausted, hurt, happy, humiliated, reduced to less than dust, certain of what I want, lucky, insane, agitated, aware, vulnerable, impulsive, open, lost to any other men but one, with no will of my own, dead to my family though still alive. Why live, why breathe, why love, to be crushed by it all?

I reached my limits of endurance. I was ready to capitulate. I had nothing left to fight for. I was alone.

April 29, 2009

Adelle – *C'est fini, mon amour, comme vous voulez. Mais je veux que vous pas disiez n'importe quoi de mal nous.* It was heaven. I will always be yours.

Tudor –What a pity! *Quel dommage ! Mais, je t'aime !*

Adelle – *Je ne sais pas, mon amour. Si vous m'aimez, vous savez que dire et faire, sinon, ensuite vous arretez, s'il vous plait !*

Tudor – *Tres bien.* As you wish.

Adelle – Where are you?

Tudor – *Dans ma maison* Come over. I'll jump in the shower now. I'll leave the door cracked open, just pull it hard behind you.

Another night on the plush feathers of love ... we forgot why and even that we had fought mere hours earlier.

We were passion's faithful slaves. The arguments only served to intensify our ardor.

I woke up at five the following morning and drew up a balance sheet and an income statement for him. He wanted to understand the basics of accounting for his businesses. When I explained it to him an hour later over coffee and breakfast, he was happy as a child with a new toy: he finally understood what he'd been missing all those years.

Tudor offered to take Luca to the groomer that day and I left her at his house. He spoiled her rotten, fed her salami, cheese, pizza, just about anything he ate ... she gallantly returned his sentiments. And why not? Who wouldn't?

Adelle – It's amusing to see a man like you with a little Yorkie.

Tudor – Right. Everyone thinks I'm gay.

Adelle – Or have a trendy girlfriend.

The intensity of our emotions was an enormous source of vitality. Yet our sporadic highs followed by the extreme lows sucked the very life out of me. He was a magnificent famished vampire feeding off his powerless victim, keeping her drained – but not drained enough to kill her. He'd leave just enough blood for her to go on, to recover in agonizing pain, and then he would return, again and again. The time in between his feedings fired up the creative circuits in my brain where love and pain were braided together.

But would the pulsing voltage charging through me cause irreparable damage to the circuits one day?

I didn't know. Nobody did.

Chapter XXI
The Last Kiss Before the Storm

It is all a white fog I walk in
I do not care
It is the most secure ground I ever set foot on
The most dreadful and divine ...
Two extremes have intersected

Tudor and I had vastly different political views. Once in a while we'd agree on something. More often than not, his radicalism overpowered my conservatism, and I was often left speechless in his wake. Most of the time I either agreed with him or refused to answer him in order to avoid conflict. Why anger him over small matters of subjective interpretations when at the end of the day his happiness was my main goal in life?

May 1, 2009
Tudor – We're heading for a depression. That's my prognosis. What's yours?

Tudor – When is the government going to pay back the Fed, from where they keep borrowing, and which ironically has nothing to do with the U.S. Government, despite the name, Federal.

Adelle – So frustrated. Sorry, I had no time to read the news this morning. I had to reschedule an important meeting and put a project on hold because of someone's carelessness.

Adelle – Well, anything is possible. But I also see the bulls sharpening their horns to push back. Some banks are ready to pay back their government loans, some are sounder than the panic made them look, and some are worse. The government will borrow from the Fed as much as it needs to keep things flowing. I want to think some good will come of it, only because if the U.S. goes into a depression, the rest of the world is doomed. Even the Arab world and the Chinese have an interest in maintaining America's stable to save their own investments in our treasury.

Tudor – That's what happens when Democrats run the show. And you thought the movie, *Planet of the Apes*, was a fantasy?

Adelle – There's something to do with coal. All my coal stocks went through the roof in the past few days, which could mean we're going back to using our own natural resources.

Tudor – No. It has to do with corruption and promises made to the coal companies, even though they pollute more than any other source of energy. And what? Are you going to power cars with coal?

Adelle – Things will change, that's certain. Good or bad, compromising long term values for short term solutions, perhaps.

Sometimes I wondered if he knew the definition of the word "compromise" … if he'd ever used it in a relationship, discussion, or anywhere. I asked him in a message, and he didn't answer.

My friends called on me to go for a drink someplace in Lincoln Park. I had no other plans for that evening so I went along. They were all modest, intelligent, educated people; always pleasant company. Jake didn't approve of my relationship with Tudor, based on his reputation as something of a ladies' man. But he was very discrete in expressing his views. He always made us laugh, a characteristic that put him high up on my list of friends.

Adelle – I know you might not care – I will be at Kelly's on Clark with Olivia, Jake, John and Bogdan around eleven. Stop by if you want.

Tudor – Seems like you already have enough male company. No, thanks. I don't want to be around people anymore.

Adelle – These are friends I've known for years and all of them know I am with you. If I'd had the option of spending the evening with you, I would have been there, wherever you are.

Tudor – Have fun! I prefer to be alone.

Adelle – (I sent him a picture of Luca) Luca still smells like an angel. Thank you!

Tudor – You're welcome, and so is she.

Why hadn't I simply ignored him, put him behind me, pushed him in the abyss of all forgotten things forever, just as he deserved? The idea that I might have cared because he rejected me, as some of my friends so kindly suggested, disturbed me. No. That *couldn't* have been the basis for my resilience. That wouldn't have been enough to justify all the degrading emotional abuse I so stoically accepted, like the volcanic rock of an ancient crater, cast in time until the very end.

Chapter XXII
The Proposal

Forgive my questioning the wondering eyes
To any easy prey who walks you by
Your apathy of safe commitments
Your constant search for new indulgence

May 4, 2009

Adelle – This is nuts, my little coal stock is up another 20%.

Tudor – Good for you. As they say: lucky at gambling, unlucky at love.

Adelle – *Au contraire, mon cheri.* I am lucky in everything I truly and honestly want from life. We shall see.

Adelle – As everybody that cares about me has said … you'd destroy my life. Unless some sort of miracle happened and you awakened to what we could do together and mean to one another, which at this point is as remote as me moving to Mars in a couple of months, I'm lucky to have overcome my own stubbornness and accept an end to us here.

Tudor – Hallelujah!

Adelle – Fly away, my little butterfly, but don't forget your love of one wild flower might bring you back to her one day. Make sure you leave behind wind-driven words, when you do, and your heart is true. Hope that she will always be yours, no matter what other bees may come along to rest on her petals. I can't sit here, starring at my phone, thinking of you, wondering what other nonsense will cross your mind to justify our breaking up today. I spend my weekends in agony, wondering what woman you might be doing now – your ex, some waitress, or a new addition to your Facebook floozies while you could be sculpting and using your talent to your own advantage! *Je ne sais pas, mon amour, je suis perdu.* I don't know anymore. *Je veux etre le votre.* I want to be yours and I feel your love. Why are you torturing me?

I dreaded the life I had, the people around me, my work … everything. I hated having to talk to my own mother when I was on bad terms with Tudor. My friends were nothing more than cold shades of dark on a mournfully gray canvas. My physical presence in the world became insignificant not only to him, but also to myself.

My food lost all of its taste, my wine lost its body, my vision lost its depth, and I lost all of my soul. Why did I hang around for so long?

May 5, 2009
Adelle – On my way, my love. Are you up?
Tudor – I've been up for two hours.

I wore a white cotton dress with white leather shoes, accessorizing the outfit with a small white purse with a bracelet ring handle. We enjoyed the marvelous spring day at his place, in love, in paradise … live and see what happens next. It didn't matter anymore.

May 7, 2009
Adelle – Had such a long and crummy day. I was hoping to hear a friendly voice at the end of the line.
Tudor – Keep hoping.

Adelle – You sound like such a Romanian vagabond sometimes.

Adelle – One day, though, I might tell you to bugger off, just because I might have had a bad day too, and at the end of it, I would like to be hugged by the man I love.

Tudor – Jesus. Stop already! I'm busy booking flights in Europe.

It was a thin, invisible string that tied us together, easy to ignore and impossible to grab when I needed it most. Its strength, though, was irrefutable; and he pulled me back by it exactly when I was on the verge of renouncing us for good.

May 8, 2009

Adelle – This will be the last weekend we can spend together for a while, if you'd like. Either the city or your place. I can cook. I'll stop by the library to get a couple of French movies.

Tudor – You are willing to make it work, but I can't.

May 12, 2009

Adelle – God does have a sick sense of humor, Mr. Popescu, as you wrote to me five months ago.

Tudor – (Two in the morning) So he does …

Adelle – I have no idea what else I could do, not do, say, or not say to you.

Tudor – Just quit.

Adelle – Yes …. I am in love with a man without a heart.

May 14, 2009

Adelle – I'm going out this weekend with someone new.

Tudor – Good for you. Finally! I hope you two get married and are insanely happy.

Adelle – You are a player and a commitment freak. Live with it! Enjoy it!

The following day, Tudor was to take off for Romania for a month. Regardless of how upset I was with him, I couldn't find the heart not to make peace with him before he left. I couldn't imagine being able to rest my head on a pillow for all those weeks knowing that we were on bad terms, regardless of what he decided to do there.

May 15, 2009

Adelle – They say the road to hell is paved with good intentions. Have a safe and fun trip and a great summer!

Tudor - You too. Make sure you are married by the time I get back.

Adelle – I don't need papers and having kids could wait another couple of years.

I believed that assuring him of those things would help keep his mind off all those twenty-something Romanian girls. I knew he would be a hot commodity himself as an American tourist of Romanian origin. In truth, he couldn't discard my message quickly enough to suit him.

Chapter XXIII
Distance is Fire

A continent apart you thought we'd be
With miles of land and water in between
Instead, our hearts formed one that grew
In fire forged and cooled by morning's dew

Bureaucracy is the silent wall slowing formerly communist Eastern European countries from the natural pace of economic evolution that the West is fortunate to have. Communism left a heavy legacy behind to pollute the mentality of old and new generations. It will take a few more generations born in capitalism and democracy to clean out the dead wood of decay. The infrastructure system created by censorship had transported nations back to the Middle Ages and transformed their people into unethical, ignorant human beings, selfish, unmotivated, and short-sighted. It stripped away the vision of free will and free thinking. Running for nearly half a century on bribery and the worst human traits imaginable, remnants of the system are still there, nearly 20 years after its fall in 1990.

Tudor returned with his mother to this obstinately corrupt world to take care of family business in Romania. He said he'd be gone for three weeks.

May 20, 2009
Adelle – How is our dear homeland these days?
Tudor – I have no money to read or respond to your messages in Europe.

Adelle – Fine, though I could care less if you have any money. If you were homeless, I would still love you and make love to you just the same.

I stopped messaging him. His words crushed me. He was not a man caught up in counting pennies. I pushed the envelope far enough. I hurt myself far more than I had antagonized him, then took refuge from the grim reality in reading. Ever since I was a little girl, when I wanted to escape my parents' speeches and my friends' silly teasing, I'd pick up a book and isolate myself from the world. I lived through the characters in the story; I imagined my future and tried to picture what I would become when I grew up. Now, was one of those times … time to lose myself in other people's writings, other people's worlds, to find answers to questions those around me were no longer able to provide.

May 25, 2009
Facebook message
How easy was it for you to forget all this and move on? I've read Freud's book, *Sexuality and the Psychology of Love*. It was all common sense, including one striking thing I saw in your eyes the moment I met you: artists cannot ever commit. If they do, they lose any trait of creativity they might have. They need novelty in order to create new works of art, for their mind to remain vigil. I grew in time not to expect fidelity of you; although you mentioned last time when we were together that you appreciate loyalty. I hope you realize it is a heavy thing to ask for when you are not offering it in return.

I expected nothing less from you and wanted nothing more than I received. Nothing came as a surprise and it all felt as if I was simply fulfilling something that was predestined in me. Everything and everybody else in my life played only a marginal role to bring me to you.

A

When I heard nothing back from him for several days, I sent him another phone message.

May 30, 2009
Adelle – (Sent a picture of Lincoln Park and the lake off my balcony)
Tudor – Send me a picture of your ass, why don't you?
Adelle – You'll get to see the real thing when you get home
Tudor – It's OK. I'll be sick of all the ass in Romania by the time I get home. I'll be absolutely spent.
Adelle – Evidently.
Adelle – Why don't you call my parents and tell them how much you enjoyed my ass up until a month ago?
Tudor – Nah. It's old news.
Adelle – Insufferable!

June 7, 2009
Adelle – Is it true? Do you bring girls from home and have your way with them, then leave them? Went to a BBQ party. That's what I heard. It just made me cry.
Tudor – It's all true. Believe it. They know it all.
Tudor – Romanians, both there and here, are nothing but cave men. I can't wait to leave this hell. Never again.
Adelle – Chicago is not the same without you. Your friends and your life are waiting for you here.
Tudor – Friends, what friends? Oh, those who gossip and bad-mouth me? Yeah, I really miss them. Maybe I should throw another party to feed them and entertain them.

Why did it always have to be about him? The sarcastic tone of his messages garnished by his abnormally high opinion of himself took me aback. Could I possibly be so in love with a man so much in love with himself? More so than anyone else on earth?

225

Chapter XXIV
Who Am I Fooling?

You come and go, and then return to me
In time, that has become our mad routine
My friends think me a hopeless lunatic
And yours ... would try to bend our verdict

I burned with impatience and desire for his return. The month he was gone had been blue and gray and I wanted to forget it as I had already forgotten and forgiven all our past cruel exchange of messages. They were mere words ... simple thoughtless words, without substance, sprung from his temporary mournful moods, perhaps a result of his creative genius. No one understood me ... except for Olivia to whom I talked daily. She was the shoulder I could lean on. I withheld many things from my family. They lived entirely too far remote from my life style, culture and society in the US. I could not expect they would empathize with me and understand my little ups and downs with Tudor. My parents pinned me down with their routing discourse every time I called home – when are you getting married and have a couple of kids? This would be their only gratification.

June 15, 2009
Tudor – I am so tired. I just landed.
Adelle – Welcome home! I can imagine you are exhausted. Do you want to get some rest this evening?

Tudor – Of course. At least a shower. I'm going for sushi with my brother and mom.

Adelle – Tell them I said hi. And you don't need a shower, by the way. You always smell good.

Tudor – Not now. I've been in the same clothes for two days.

Adelle – I love your smell, regardless.

Tudor – Ok, I'll leave it then.

Tudor – (A couple hours later) I'll sleep over at my mom's tonight. My brother doesn't feel like driving me home. We'll talk tomorrow.

Adelle – You'll be up around two – jet lag. Sweet dreams!

Tudor – Ok.

It had escaped my memory that he hadn't ever responded to my Facebook message, until I received this:

June 16, 2009
Facebook Message
Tudor
You are incorrigible! There's nothing I can do to placate you...

Text Messages
Adelle – I see you finally got my Facebook message. It's about three weeks old.

Adelle – You can't change me, my love, as I can't change you. I can only admire and respect who you are, as you are.

Adelle – (A few hours later) Just make love to me ... no more words, no more meaningless excuses, no more antagonizing one another.

Tudor – When?

Adelle – Tonight.

The smell of his skin, the sweat particularly, intoxicated me. I didn't know if it was the distance, or our maniac attraction for one another, but one thing was certain: everything about Tudor, no matter how common or how singular, how deceitful or innately insincere, how repulsive to others, it was all an integral part of everything I loved about him.

Luke and Tudor got into occasional arguments and refused to speak to one another for months. Anna and I had become relatively close friends, and I went out for dinner with the two of them now and then. Strong advocates of the idea that Tudor and I simply did not belong together, they offered to introduce me to one of their fabulously successful single friends. I mentioned it to Tudor as I was walking out of his house to meet the couple that evening. He was amused by the fact and suggested I go along with it, remarking: "Why not, maybe he's better than I am!"

It turned out to be a pleasant party. Jason owned his own hair salon in the heart of the Gold Coast, on Oak and Rush, and was dressed up as if cut straight from the cover of a French fashion magazine. The summer evening was refreshing, yet I could not get my mind off Tudor.

Was he really going to sleep alone that night?

Chapter XXV
She Moved In

My day in love with you's a jungle
Behind that bush there is a tiger
Climbing a tree, a diamond snake
On top circles a starving vulture

I'm flanked by all the weird creatures
With shiny eyes and slugger features
Famished and meager looking things
I'm in their way, or so it seems

We had a few mutual friends when we met; two of them were a decent, modest couple, Roxana and Tiberiu. I had known Roxana for many years. Although we didn't talk often, we shared a certain level of respect for one another. Tiberiu and Tudor, on the other hand, were about the same age, had been really close friends for a long time, and roamed the same social circles and parties.

Roxana and I met for lunch, and I asked her if she knew Tudor. Right on the money! They'd all been friends for some time.

June 18, 2009
Adelle – We just got an invitation for Tiberiu's birthday party this Saturday. It would be nice if we went together.
Tudor – I didn't get an invite.
Adelle – Roxana asked that I mention it to you.

Tudor – I doubt it. I feel insulted for not hearing it from Tiberu personally. I'm not going. Have fun.

Adelle – Well, blame it on me then. I told you Roxana and I had rekindled our friendship in the past month or so, and since they may consider us some sort of a couple, and her being responsible for the invitations, she asked that I pass along the message.

Tudor – She should have done it herself. We're not an item.

Adelle – But whenever I try explaining to my friends that you and I are only friends with benefits who pretend to be something more whenever we talk to our parents, they don't get it. They just don't quite grasp the concept as well as we do.

Tudor – Well, I'm not going anyway. A friend of mine died yesterday of cancer, at 39.

Adelle – My condolences.

June 20, 2009

Adele – (Sent him a picture of the pool)

Tudor – Nice

Adelle – I know the drive and parking are a drag, but are you interested?

Tudor – I have to go to the wake soon.

Adelle – (A few hours later) I feel like a first-class idiot going to this on my own – YOUR friend's birthday party. The gossip will be spectacular.

Tudor – What gossip? They can all go where they came from.

Adelle – I know.

Tudor – OK, then shut the hell up and go see your friend, Roxana.

Adelle – We were both invited.

Tudor – There's no WE. Never was. Nobody in that circle knows we ever dated.

Adelle – I am aware of that, not so much the people that know us. Facebook might have given it away. If anyone asks about you, I shall kindly explain we only use each other for sex.

Tudor – You do that. I've used half of the girls at that party for the same thing anyway.

Adelle – That's easy to imagine. Only they tend to look rather, uhh, haggard …I assumed you'd require a little more sophistication.

He was there, in my hand, in my blackberry. The blinking new-message light gave it away. Everyone there knew Tudor. His reputation was well shaped by his own disregard for society and good old common sense. His eccentricity for the way he handled women, preceded him. I felt more like one of them than at any other time since becoming another one of his "dolls."

"Is it that important that you cannot put your phone down for a minute"? Tiberiu was visibly annoyed.

June 21, 2009

Adelle – (Sent a picture of Lincoln Park Fest happening across from my balcony) – Baby raccoons are far cuter, Lincoln Park is noisy, but not too bad.

Tudor – Good, enjoy! Find a husband!

Adelle – If a man has all the devices around the house to replace a wife, what makes you think the same principle doesn't function for the opposite sex?

Tudor – Good for you! Then you are already complete.

Adelle – As complete as you are, darling. See … I learned something new from you.

Tudor – Good. I am glad I am good for something.

Adelle – You told me several times that you would make a sculpture of my ugly body from your memory.

Tudor – You know your body is not ugly. Stop being modest. Your body is one of the only redeeming things about you. Your mind is where the problem is. I'll make a sculpture of your body when you come and pose for it.

Adelle – Thanks. That depends on the sculptor and not the model, if I am not mistaken. You know a diamond is the hardest rock. It can only be crafted by a skilled hand.

Tudor – I guess you would be the diamond? Funny. At least the head part. It's hard enough ... I prefer clay. It's a lot easier to mold.

Adelle – Yes, you are right. Clay is easy to mold, break, and reshape. Anyone can work with clay, which lasts as long as the first storm it weathers.

June 23, 2009

Adelle – I am not looking to find a husband. I'm looking to find someone to love. I may be little more than nuisance to you, but I cannot go against my insane instincts about you, about us.

Tudor – Christina moved in with me yesterday. I guess she'll be here with me for a while. A long while.

Adelle – If she is what you really want from life. I'm sorry for not being insulted.

Adelle - (Sent him a picture of North Beach that evening) – You keep playing with your old toy, darling. City life is still worth a couple more years till you get bored with it. Old foxes are never threatened by materialistic half-wits.

I agonized about Tudor all the rest of the day, into the evening. I picked up the phone and called Olivia, my only friend who was willing to listen to my deranged mind spill its tales. Between hiccups and tears, I explained the dreadful situation. After I hang up, she called me back a few times, just to make sure I was okay. I wasn't.

June 24, 2009

Adelle – You may screw whoever you want, while your mortgage payments are up in the air. At least consider getting some opinions from your mom and brother about this ... whatever it is you are trying to do.

Tudor – Hey ... Christina moved in with me and she's read your messages and now she's pissed off. She did move in with me, and she'll probably stay here until I lose my house. None of your business if that happens or not.

Adelle – If you're doing this consciously, then you deserve the half-wit.

Tudor – Since your head is so hard to penetrate, how much wit do you think *it* contains?

Adelle – You choose someone beneath you to bolster your own ego, and you hurl insults at me? She obviously has no respect for your privacy if she reads your messages, and no clue what's on your plate, least of all thinking of ways she could help you. Enjoy your clay possessions and your cartoon themed conversations around the dinner table.

I simply couldn't bear another word from him. The air that filled my lungs became acid.

Olivia asked me to go with her to a new bar that evening. I was hardly in the mood, but I jumped into the shower and reluctantly began preparing for the evening. Just as I was about to ring her to say I was on my way, Tudor called.

"Congratulations! You managed to drive the idiot away. I don't know if I should be mad at you or thank you. But I think it's the latter. She read your messages about my house and left."

"I'm sorry to hear that. Wow ..."

That had taken a lot less time than I'd expected.

Chapter XXVI
Wedding

I sent you off with who you want to be
Not sit around and trap yourself by me
You sat there for a minute, and then left
I ran behind you, sank in pain and wept

I cried for what I've said and what you've done
Abandoned me, our dreams, left me alone
Your last words were: "You underestimate me"
I never did, and never will, my love, forgive me!

In rain I called for your return
Expected you're a gentle soul in turn
Despair engulfed me like the cape of death
I lost you then, for dared I say the truth

That evening one of Tudor's friends had a bachelor's party on a boat on Lake Michigan. Tudor asked me to come to the pier and bring Olivia. I knew I should have been furious with him for how he'd treated me; but I simply wasn't able to hold grudge against him. For *any* reason.

Tudor – Bring your swimming suit, I want a lap dance.
Adelle – Funny.
Tudor – Seriously! Be ready to be picked up by a bunch of hungry wolves. I'm on the boat waiting for you.

Adelle – I'm on my way to get Olivia.

Tudor – I'm coming to get you. Belmont Harbor, G gate.

Adelle – Alright.

When our eyes locked, he shook his head as though he couldn't believe I actually came. I wasn't smiling. He took hold of my right hand as soon as I was close enough, pulled me toward him and we ignored the fact that there were any people around us for the next few hours. Everyone was staring at us ... a couple of his friends knew me, but the other twenty or so didn't. Olivia took quite a few pictures of us ... she gave up on lecturing me about Tudor. She realized that anyone's intention to pull me away from him, even for my own sake, was as a lost cause. Besides, she had rather quickly become preoccupied with something else--one of the Romanian boys she met on the boat.

June 25, 2009

Adelle – Do you know anything about Olivia's new friend?

Tudor – Yes, he was just released from prison a week ago on good behavior.

Adelle – She likes him and they're going to the wedding together on Saturday.

Tudor – Good. She owes me a commission.

Adelle – You owe each other. In fact, you might be even with her now.

Tudor – True.

Tudor – But what she owes me is an apology.

Adelle – For the pest?

Tudor – You got it.

Tudor – I can't make it to the pool. I have things to do and am so damned sleepy.

June 26, 2009

Tudor – I want you to wear your hair down and curly, with curls hanging over your forehead for the wedding. It looks a thousand times better than straight. I will not take no for an answer.

Adelle –Wasn't planning on making it straight anyway, not with this humidity. I'm going shopping for a dress with Olivia today.

Tudor – Good girls! What time should I pick you up tomorrow?

Adelle – Look at the invitation.

Tudor – Six.

Tudor – I have to finish two portraits by next Friday. I can't be bothered with anything else for even a minute after the wedding.

Tudor – (A few hours later) Is Olivia with you?

Adelle – She's home now. We came back from shopping a little while ago.

Adelle – By the way, she says Thank You! She and Paul hit it off really well.

Tudor – Do you guys wanna come by my bar on Clark?

Adelle – I'll call her see if she's up for it.

Adelle – How about around eight?

Tudor – Sooner if possible. I'm here now.

Adelle – We'll try.

Tudor – I had to change the blinds upstairs and that's why I'm here.

Tudor – Don't dress up or anything, I'm in swimming trunks.

Tudor owned a building that housed a popular bar near Wrigley Field. The bar was always busy and the business was doing well, making it one of his most profitable business investments. He was proud of it and brought his closest friends there from time to time.

Olivia and Tudor were from the same region of Romania, Ardeal – the Carpatian Mountains area. Their melodic accents added a special charm to their conversations in Romanian; I sat there mesmerized.

"How was last night?" Tudor asked Olivia laughing.

"Ah … Paul, you mean? Very funny! We're not there yet. But I hear you're not wasting any time when Adelle's not around." Olivia smiled triumphantly.

Tudor shook his head. "You got me. What can I say? Just remember: You're the one who brought her to my New Year's Eve party." Tudor threw a wink in my direction. I smiled behind my glass of Cabernet.

"So does the new boy have any potential?" he asked. "You two look awfully cozy together."

It was true. Olivia was 5 foot 11 inches tall and had a hard time finding a man to match her height. Paul was well over 6 feet, well built and relatively handsome. They did make a great looking pair.

"Well … I hardly know him," she said. "Let's not rush into anything yet. Now, Adelle here, learns lessons the hard way. I like to do my homework first, do some surveillance." Olivia threw her arms out and gave me a big hug. "Remember, Mr. Macho Man. Adelle has friends who would go a long way to protect her!"

"Yes, yes, I know … it's easy enough to imagine. No worries, though, on your part. I'm completely harmless."

"Just keep thinking that way," she said, reminding me one more time why I loved her so. She was literally one in a million.

Adelle – (A few hours later) *Bonne nuit mon amour!*
Tudor – *Bonne nuit!*

At the wedding reception, Tudor couldn't stop staring at a belly dancer. From her return glances, they apparently knew one another well. He went straight up to her, and they started chattering. I sat at a table, alone. When he finally returned, I told him he could be with whomever he chose. He stood up, his eyes glaring, and said, "You underestimate me!" and left. He simply walked right out of the restaurant.

I ran after him, tried to stop him, but he nearly ran me over with his car. After a few minutes standing in the pouring rain without an umbrella, I tried to hail a cab, without any luck. I went back inside and told his friend, Alex, what had happened and asked him if he would be kind enough to drive me home.

Tudor (Later that day) – Don't ever bother me again. *Ever!*

Adelle – Alex drove me home after I'd been standing in the rain for 20 minutes.

Tudor – I don't give a shit. He can even fuck you for all I care.

Adelle – He just felt sorry for me, that's all. Nothing more. He's your friend!

Tudor – Go screw yourself!

Adelle – Stop it! You know better, and you're obviously drunk. You've heard what I've had to say too many times in the past. I hate repeating myself, yet I do, for you only. I am nothing, I am dust in the wind and rain in the gutter without you.

Tudor – Listen, you two-dollar poet, you suck! Fuck you! You superficial airhead! You suck more than you know.

Adelle – If I were so superficial ... Tudor, would I still be here? Would I take every tear, hope, dream I ever had of us and build my only happiness from them. And when

238

that's no longer possible, would I write down every memory of us together in a book?

Tudor – Your pathetic book! You'll be the only one reading it!

Adelle – Perhaps you're wiser than I. Perhaps you're right. Perhaps we'll never end up together. Maybe you see things more clearly than I do. And you needn't worry. I won't bother you with any more messages. So go and enjoy life with your empty-headed trash. At least they'll bow to your every whim and fancy!

Tudor – Go die!

Adelle – You'll put me through hell again, won't you?

For the following couple of weeks I did all my head could possibly allow for me to get over him. I went out with my friends, I smiled when I hated my own image in the mirror, I cried, I ran, I wrote, I filled my mind with all sorts of other thoughts, even one of finding a job in Paris and moving away from Chicago for good. Away from him.

I know it seemed drastic. I know I should have been able to cope. It wasn't the first time he had thrown me to the pavement. I know I should have been able to forget about him and move on with my life.

But his presence only a few miles away was too close for me to bear.

And always would be.

Chapter XXVII
Training

"Are you my lover or my love?"
She queried him with teary eyes
He looked at her with cool and peace
"Why ask? Who feels it, knows"

July 14, 2009

Adelle – *Bonsoir! Ca va?* I'm going to be out of town for training the whole next week and don't have anywhere to leave Luca. Olivia's building doesn't accept dogs and Harra is out of town. I don't want to board the poor thing because she's not very social and she's tiny. Would you be able to take care of her? This is stupid work-related travel and I have no way out of it.

Tudor – No. I hate small dogs. I don't want the responsibility! Take it where you usually do on such occasions.

Adelle – I haven't travelled for work in over a year. If I were going on vacation, she'd go with me. She's low maintenance. I'm getting a girl roommate in a Marriott at Notre Dame in Indiana and we have to study a lot – there's a test at the end of the week. Some crummy investments certification. I don't take her where I used to a year ago, as you can imagine.

Adelle – No worries. I completely understand. She'll just have to learn to be sociable the hard way.

Tudor – Take her to your old fiancée. He bought it for you. He must like her.

Adelle – I can't. It's wrong for too many reasons. Don't worry.

July 15, 2009

Adelle – Hi baby!

Tudor – I am not your baby.

Adelle – I know. I just love spoiling you. Your responses are delightful.

Tudor – I am tired of this. Is that how you get your lovers, by tiring them into submission? Beating them into the ground?

Adelle – I just want you to undress me and take control until I scream … and disintegrate beneath you.

Tudor – I would treat you like a prostitute. Forget it. I would hate myself for doing that to you.

Adelle – I don't care. I will be anything you want me to be.

Tudor – You are insane. I have no scruples, I am egotistical and cruel. I will destroy you emotionally. Run, while you still have a chance.

Adelle – You are the only one I want.

Tudor – Fine. Then come over this evening.

Adelle – OK. I'll be there around 7.

Another magnificent evening … when we parted, he agreed to take care of Luca while I was out of town. He sent me updates on how they were spending time together, eating short ribs and cheese, sleeping all day and chasing the stray cats he had in his back yard. She was the daughter he'd never had! She did manage to find his comforter and any rugs lying around to be suitable places to urinate, and that just drove him nuts. When returned to town and stopped by to pick her up, we made love and had breakfast, and then we broke up yet again. We kissed good bye and he had tears in his eyes.

The last weekend in August I went to Las Vegas for one of my friends' bachelorette parties. Tudor called me on my way there and asked me if I could help him with some business project – setting up a trust. I told him I would when I returned. Before my flight home took off, he texted to ask if I needed a ride home from the airport. I said I didn't, since my friend's fiancée was going to provide transportation for us.

Two days later he asked that I meet him, with his uncle, also his real estate broker, at Café Armitage across from my place to discuss business. During dinner he declared to both his uncle and me that, aside from his mother and brother, I was the only other person he ever trusted in his life.

We got back together "officially" and went away for the Labor Day weekend to Lake Geneva with his aunt, uncle, and family friends. He taught me how to fish, commenting at one point how he likes to release the fish he catches back into the water … just as he does with his women. All in all, it was a marvelous weekend. We made love by the bonfire under the starry sky. And, of course, the inevitable breakup happened again at the end of that month.

Chapter XXVIII
The Book

A month later, I had to break our silence. I sent him a message on Facebook to test the waters, not exactly knowing what to expect in response. The billion negative thoughts of him carpeting my mind failed to weed out all traces of our love for one another.

Facebook Message
November 4, 2009
I know you'll say "I told you so," but the feedback from an expert on my sample chapters was similar to yours. I am not giving up. I wish you would help me edit it, but that would be too much to ask for.

Text Messages
November 5, 2009
Tudor – 'I TOLD YOU SO!'

I chose to ignore the arrogance in his tone.

November 6, 2009
Tudor – My Internet isn't working, or I'd respond more elaborately.
Adelle – *Bonsoir!* I am so sorry to hear that. Thank you.
Tudor – It bothers me when people consider my opinion second rate ....

Adelle – *Au contraire.* Your opinion is what got me into writing this book.

Tudor – Good then.

Adelle – It's not easy, but I'm determined not to falter, unlike so many other things I fancy temporarily and then lose interest in.

Tudor – How is your male-teasing going?

Adelle – Well, thank you. I just turned down someone today. That was fun.

Tudor – You are crazy. Your imagination is working overtime.

Adelle – I felt good doing it, even though he had the perfect Arian blonde hair and blue eyes. I doubt he's giving up, but at least he learned some things about Constanta to try get to me.

Tudor – Good. Play him though. All guys like that. But make sure you don't keep him dangling for too long. He might get tired and move on.

Adelle – It's fun to see men at their games when you don't care about them.

Tudor – Don't be cruel. It's bad karma.

Adelle – Trust me, I don't sleep with them. *That* would be bad karma. It's simply a matter of misfortune on their side and disinterest on mine.

Tudor – If you aren't, then turn them down gently and swiftly. Don't string them along.

Adelle – I do, as many of them and as reasonably as I possibly can. The problem is that I sort of like one or two, but it kills me to see them going nuts after me. I remain interested in them for no longer than it takes to have a dinner or a lunch. It's perfect.

Tudor – Oh, you player, you! If I didn't know you better, I'd actually believe your story.

Adelle – I am using manners I learned from the French and English period movies, and all the classical books

I've read, blended with my personal touch, and it works like a charm. It radiates out of me sometimes, subconsciously.

Tudor – You're incurable.

Adelle – There is only one man who has my saddle – the love of my life. The rest is pure fun!

Tudor – Funny. Speaking of saddle, I think I am due for a ride.

Adelle – I am watching a commercial for *The March of The Penguins* movie and one of the characters says: "Alright. I'm done. I'll see you in four months!"

Tudor – That's what I usually say.

Adelle – Sometimes you don't even need to say it. What am I going to do with you?

Tudor – Nothing.

Adelle – Then go on having fun. The only way I would have you back is with an engagement ring.

Tudor – I'm not marrying anyone. This world is too screwed as it is.

Tudor – I just gorged on two slices of pizza. Now I can slash my wrists.

Adelle – Eat the pizza, just don't touch those wrists. Those hands need to mold into clay and grasp the hammer to cut into stone. I will not have them otherwise.

Tudor – The tragic thing is that they don't even feel like doing that anymore.

Adelle – It's there. You need the adrenaline.

Tudor – I could use some adrenaline now.

Adelle – Watch *Crank*. It's adrenaline on DVD.

Adelle – Skiing and making love to you were the only other two ways I got it.

Tudor – No comment.

Tudor – I've seen it. Not impressed. I'm watching *Legends of the Fall*. For the second time today. Depressing. I have no will power.

Adelle – I love that movie! I have it. Montana or Calgary in Canada, where the movie was filmed, is where I want to retire – my dream.

Tudor – I just went there.

Adelle – It is paradise itself, isn't it?

Tudor – A mix of paradise and hell. Like everything else in life.

Adelle – I suppose that makes it ideal, doesn't it? I can't watch that movie without wishing I lived there.

Tudor – It is not easy there. Especially in the winter.

Adelle – It is the life I thrive on … simple work and nothing but books around.

Tudor – Such is the life in Wood Dale.

Adelle – Is it? Then it's perfect.

Tudor – No, there's one thing missing …

Adelle – What?

Tudor – Never mind.

Adelle – Ask what you wish for.

Tudor – I can't. Reason wins over instinct.

Adelle – Keep the reason. Just sculpt.

Tudor – I don't wanna sculpt on command. Will you stop?

Adelle – I don't give a damn when and how you sculpt. I just want to see you in your own gallery, whatever it takes.

Tudor – Calm down. Can't force nature. Just let it be.

November 7, 2009

Tudor – (Late in the afternoon) Luke wants to go to dinner.

Adelle – Sure.

Tudor – Talk to Anna and make the arrangements.

246

Gabriela Sbarcea

Luke and Anna were punctual, as usual. Tudor, on the other hand, arrived fifteen minutes late, wearing a white shirt, hanging outside his pants, with his eyes roaming around the restaurant as if I wasn't even there, until he saw me. We both froze for a minute, not knowing what to say, but allowing our eyes to conduct all the communication we needed for the moment. Our friends said nothing for a little while, knowing us both well enough by then.

Luke and Tudor broke the ice, and their impossibly vulgar Romanian jokes rolled out of their mouths like apples down a steep hillside. Anna and I compared pet stories, one of our favorite topics. She told me about their recently adopted cat who loved sleeping on their bed and waking them in the middle of the night to the inexplicable sounds of *mauuuuu – mauuuuuu.* Of course, I told her about my tiny Yorkie who fell off the couch a month before and nearly passed out, although she recovered well enough.

November 9, 2009
Adelle – The ball is in your court, my darling.
Tudor – The ball is out. I let it go.
Adelle – An experienced player who loses a game on purpose is to be admired.
Tudor – You're too good at this game. I'm an amateur. I quit.
Adelle – Reverse psychology just doesn't work on me.
Tudor – NO psychology works on you. I'm not out to play games. I'm really depressed, although it may not be obvious. The fact that I feel no motivation to sculpt is the biggest indication. I just want to sleep forever.
Adelle – Ok, don't call it a relationship, because, frankly, I wouldn't call it that either. Not the way it's been. I just want to be your light as you are mine. That's why I write, and I will persevere only because of you.

247

Tudor – Ok. Write then. At least one of us should be productive.

Adelle – Peace, quiet, a refuge from this world, work, unconditional love.

Tudor – I cannot work. I have no reason to work.

Adelle – You have yourself. Life is a privilege, not a given.

Tudor – I didn't ask for this life. Whoever gave it to me can just take it back. I don't even crave a reincarnation, or an afterlife. It's ok if there's absolutely nothing after death.

Adelle – No one knows what's after death, but we'll all find out one day. For now, we have this … look out your window, not to the high-rise you hate, but the yellow and red leaves, the little baby raccoons, then they follow their mom … what do you see?

Tudor – I see disaster. I see them starving to death in the upcoming winter. And through the barren trees, I see a monstrous high-rise that will never go away regardless of the seasons, unless God sends an 8.5-magni earthquake with its epicenter at Elizabeth and Wood Dale roads.

Adelle – We can fix both – plant the tallest trees that can take the soil and climate here; and buy the house from the bank somehow; and feed the baby raccoons so they grow up big and strong.

Tudor – You are optimistic. I tried that approach for too many years. You can't fight nature and corruption.

Adelle – The solution is somewhere in the middle. But if you decide to go with the current, then I may follow as well. It's too difficult to fight it on my own.

Tudor – Just find your own causes. I'm not a good partner.

Adelle – I may not be a good one either – but you are the only one I find worth allying with against the world.

I looked for the meaning of life. The more time I spent with Tudor, the more I found it unfolding before my eyes. It blossomed through my tears, and it gained volume and substance through the seconds he held me close to his chest, with his strong arms wrapped around me, protecting me from the volatility of the outside world, from its superficiality, from its lack of taste even with twenty packages of artificial sweetener and flavored creamer added to it.

Adelle – (A few hours later)
Let the world fall on my head
First I kneel and then I tell
I was loved once, now I dread
All but one, who gives me hell

Tudor – Who's the author?
Adelle – I am ... on the bus from work. Sad, sad sad ...

Tudor – Not bad for a beginner!
Adelle – Thanks. It's nothing compared to molding clay and chopping rock.
Tudor – Not true. It's the same, if not even more challenging, juggling mental images.
Adelle – Mental juggling ... that would be you, you, and you ... enough.
Tudor – Ok. Enough!
Adelle – Never!
Adelle – Cold! Should get my ass to the gym. Instead I'm watching the History Channel.
Tudor – What's on the History Channel? I am at Elephant's.
Adelle – Fort Knox. America's gold depository.
Tudor – I see.
Adelle – In this economy ... back to basics – gold. So sad ... we are regressing.

249

Tudor – I can't wait to move to the city.

Tudor – Come on over if you're not too lazy.

Adelle – You'll have fun. Ok … in an hour or so.

He waited for me with a glass of red wine and the new building plans he had worked on so assiduously. He introduced me to the waitress, a Polish girl who looked to be a couple years underage. She stumbled down the stairs carrying a large tray filled with empty glassware after cleaning the table behind ours. Tudor mentioned cavalierly that he was trying to make me jealous and had planned on taking a photo with her to send it to me, but his camera phone wasn't working.

It no longer affected me.

Chapter XXIX
Thanksgiving

I planned a holiday party in December. My Ritz-Carlton deposit was expiring at the end of the year, and I enjoyed spoiling my friends with special parties. More so because they took the place of a second family in my life, since my own family would never move to Chicago. It was a perfect opportunity to gather all my close friends and also, perhaps, if the winds were in my favor, introduce Tudor to everyone.

November 11, 2009

Tudor – What are you doing?

Adelle - I just finished the invitations. It took me a few hours to hand write.

Tudor – What invitations?

Adelle – To my December holiday party. You?

Tudor – Drawing plans at Espresso. The bar wants to expand and move the kitchen into my garage just as I was planning to reclaim it. Now I have to redesign it to accommodate at least a one-car garage, the kitchen, a new exit, and space for the garbage dumpsters. I have to work a miracle.

Adelle – I have no doubt you'll make it work. I'm going to run over to the gym later for a quick workout. The first time since Saturday – about time.

Tudor – Good for you. I am so lazy.

Adelle – Your mind works off calories, too, more than you might imagine.

Tudor – Yeah, I should be anorexic based on that assumption.

Adelle – You entertain a rather different kind of workout as well.

Adelle – If you'd like to watch a movie, stop by.

Tudor – I'm getting ready to take a nap.

Adelle – I'm reading – I love this book – Eliade's short stories. They dive into the same idea of time relativity as Hancock.

Tudor – Eliade lived at the same time as Einstein, so he's bound to be influenced by his ideas.

Adelle – Hmm … I'm sure. Never thought of it before. His stories then are even more profound. He combines folklore with science.

Tudor – That he does. OK. My sleep is gone. I'll turn in early.

Adelle – Oh … sorry. Sleep! Didn't mean to wake you up. I took a nap earlier.

Tudor – Egotistical!

Adelle – Yep – you're right.

Tudor – I don't wanna see you anymore!

Adelle – You never do, darling.

Tudor – That's right. It's OK, you have to fight all the contenders to your skirt with a stick. You have plenty of options.

Adelle – Yes, I do. You know what I want though.

Tudor – You want the crap that doesn't work. You're not out to find harmony, quite the contrary. You like to be on the losing end.

Adelle – I like to earn what I get.

November 12, 2009

Adelle – We are a gift for one another.

Tudor – You are exaggerating again.

Adelle – You told me once I would hate you in time. Well, it's the opposite. The more I look around me and see, the more I appreciate you. I can't explain it in a text.

Tudor – I am trying to make myself as undesirable as possible. You are just a pain mongrel. I like you. I admire you, outside of your political views. But, I can't go on loving a compromise.

Adelle – You are and always will be a free man, regardless of your social "status." Depending on who you have next to you.

Tudor – (Many hours later - around noon) – You're right. I need someone next to me who's not a burden. You may as well qualify. I don't want a commitment and contracts, no matter who's next to me.

Adelle – I will never dare ask or demand something that you will not offer yourself.

Tudor – No one will put up with my weird work schedule and moods. I'm a pain in the ass to be around.

Two of my friends invited me to go out with them for a drink. It was the first time we'd met since Elisa's glamorous Halloween masked ball-themed wedding. I'd found it all so exciting! The only thing that would have made it even more perfect was being able to share it with Tudor. He had rebuked my invitation on the pretense of yet another one of our breakups.

November 14, 2009
Tudor – I just woke up from a long nap. Not long enough though. I was planning on sleeping till morning.

Adelle — Harra and I are about to blow our brains out at a house party. Both Olivia and our new friend are into boxing. Flippin' magnificent!

Tudor – At least you are among people. Beats watching a movie at home.

Adelle – Not! I want to be there, with my head on your lap.

Tudor – I have a fear of being with anyone. I don't feel like having company. I feel for you. You deserve happiness, if there is such a thing. I can't give you something I don't have.

Adelle – You don't frighten me anymore. You are air, light, and life for me. This is the truth. I don't want to trick you into loving me back. I would never do something so based and unbecoming.

November 15, 2009
Tudor – Wanna do lunch?
Adelle – Yes – sure – where?
Tudor – I don't know. Somewhere close to my house. I have to be here at three. Some agent is showing my house.
Adelle – I am jumping in the shower.
Tudor – Don't jump in the shower. You might slip and fall.
Adelle – Threw on some clothes, and I'm on my way.
Tudor – I left the front door open. Just push it in closed behind you. I'm in the shower now.

I pushed open the heavy front door slowly. My hands were busy with Luca's pet carrier, my purse, and a brown paper bag with a bottle of red wine and just enough food to put together a light meal. The majestic white marble floors, arched high ceilings with towering skylights, and the Baroque staircase to the South wing of the house in the late afternoon sun cast their dancing shadows across the room. *Why would he let this house go?*

I set Luca's carrier on the chair and placed the paper bag on the cluttered table. The countertops and the granite island were cold; books, magazines, National Geographic maps, a sketch book, two empty glasses, a dirty plate and pan. The kitchen was the messiest I had ever seen it.

Suddenly the sound of heavy footsteps from the North wing stairway echoed across the room. Tudor stopped. His complexion was pale. Mine was flushed. My heart shrank for a moment. I opened my arms, my palms outstretched. We uttered no words. By the time that night was over, we had left our mark on every surface in the house where we could conceivably have made love. And a few others, as well. Soft, hard, covered, bare, it hadn't mattered to us. The only thing that mattered was our union, our oneness with the universe.

"Take me," I whispered as he lifted me up onto the table.

"Again and again," he said, "forever and ever."

November 16, 2009
Adelle – Was I hit by a train?
Tudor – Why?
Adelle – I am as stiff as a board! Feels like I worked out for 10 hours. Hope you feel better.
Tudor – Why? From last night?
Adelle – Yes ! It was formidable.

Later that day, I learned that Tudor had planned yet another trip without me; this time he was going to Miami. I didn't bother trying to wrangle an invitation to go along. It wasn't worth risking another argument. Our relationship was hanging by a thread as it was, and adding more weight to it was no solution.

November 17, 2009
Adelle – Are you taking off for Miami tomorrow?
Tudor – I leave on Thursday, not tomorrow.
Tudor – What day is your party again?
Adelle – Saturday, December 12.

November 18, 2009
Adelle – Don't forget your Speedos for the beach!

Tudor - LOL! With my gut, I'll get arrested for indecency.

Adelle – No, silly! You'll only break a few more hearts with that cute bottom of yours.

Tudor – Big ass of mine you mean. I'm at Espresso now. Just got a coffee. I was in Wrigleyville earlier. I can't wait to move there.

Adelle – My clothes are in the dryer.

Tudor – See me when I get back. You can heal my sun burns.

Adelle – I'll pick you up from the airport. Send me your flight info.

November 19, 2009
Adelle – Is it all you wanted and more?

November 20, 2009
Tudor – No. It's kind of chilly and cloudy. (Sends a picture of the cloudy beach.)

Adelle – At least the color of the water is beautiful. I hope you have a good book with you. Chicago is worse.

Tudor – I do. *Masonic Myth.*

Adelle – You'll have to tell me all about it. The one-sentence paragraph starting off *The Lost Symbol* drives me nuts, but the content is good. It's getting progressively better.

Tudor – (Sends a picture of a drink, the beach, and a bridge.)

Adelle – Fabulous! I love that!

Tudor – The only thing missing is you.

Adelle – I wish I was in your arms, doing what we did on Sunday night!

Tudor – Well … Sunday then, for our one-week anniversary.

Tudor – I wonder how you'd look as a blonde.

Adelle – Probably not very good with my complexion. I can try on a wig just for kicks.

Later that evening, I watched a documentary on Julius Caesar on the History Channel. I was alone, yet again, on a Friday night. It had become all too familiar. I numbed my pain with a glass of red wine and drew parallels in my mind between powerful men and the need to gamble.

Adelle – (Still later that evening.) Did Caesar really have the mind of a gambler?
Tudor – What?

November 21, 2009
Tudor – I still don't get your Caesar message.
Adelle – I was watching the History Channel. Something about Caesar and gambling. Thought of you – Roman emperors, gambling ... what's in the mind of a king – what drives a strong character. Also had a glass of wine.
Tudor – That last part explains it.
Adelle – Yeah. My thoughts over-extrapolate ideas after a glass of wine.

November 22, 2009
Adelle – How was your flight back?
Tudor – Not bad. I just can't stand Midway. The landing has to be so abrupt because of those short runways. Are you hungry?
Adelle – Who needs food when you're reading *The Lost Symbol?* Although my head is starting to hurt a little.
Tudor – Only intelligence hurts.
Adelle – The pain is all physiological, I assure you. Lack of food drains the mind.
Tudor – Then let's eat. Actually I ate already. But I'll do dinner.

Adelle – OK, where?
Tudor – Maybe sushi at Elephant's.
Adelle – On my way to Elephant's.
Tudor – Me too.

Pure and simple physical attraction - his dexterous and experienced hands possessed my body in the same way they did any sculpting medium he chose for his work. He was the perfect lover. Anything beyond or above was mere illusion. When we craved each other ... nothing stood in our way. Our love was fulfilled. It was ethereal, magical, frighteningly delicious. I wanted more.

November 23, 2009
Tudor – I'm sorry, I feel a fever coming on. I don't think I'll make it tonight. Can we try tomorrow instead. All my bones hurt.
Tudor – You know what. I'll come anyway. These guys who want to rent the garage need to meet after seven.
Adelle – A message as a bonus then.
Tudor – I need you to fill up the tub, so I can sweat it out pronto. I'll be there around seven thirty I think. I only had breakfast today.
Adelle – Hurry! Baked potatoes are getting cold. But drive safely, please.
Adelle – Advil Liquigel.
Tudor – Forget it. I have my own. I want to eat in the tub.
Adelle – A glass of wine, healthy food, and a good movie. How does that sound?
Tudor – Good.
We watched *Mrs. Parker and the Vicious Circle*, cooked dinner, and discovered again and again how easily we formed a physical and intellectual harmony together through all the

things we loved, everyday things that united us in one ethereal emotional being.

November 24, 2009

Tudor – I miss you.

Adelle – Miss you too! If you get hungry, I have so much food that I need help with. Need to finish making the eggplant salad when I get home.

Tudor – I wish, but I have work to do.

Adelle – OK. I'll freeze what doesn't fit in my belly then.

We were invited by my friends to spend Thanksgiving dinner at their house. Tudor accepted the invitation and was going to pick me up from home early that afternoon. Our hosts were two respected and well-established Romanians who had immigrated to the U.S. 20 years ago or more. They both had successful careers and had been married for many years. Although Tudor's age, they had two teenage children who were well educated and behaved. The family seemed to be idyllic: everything about them was perfect. I first met them while skiing in Lake Tahoe, on top of a mountain, as we all were immersed in the breathtaking views of the lake and the beautiful slopes surrounded by nature at her finest.

The night before Thanksgiving, I had watched *Titus*, the movie, and I was so repulsed by the manner in which it had been directed that I nearly shut it off ten minutes into it. It was nowhere near how Shakespeare had originally intended his play to be. I couldn't finish watching it. It was grotesque. I texted Tudor my opinion of the film as subtly as possible: he had recommended the thing to me. He did not honor my message with an answer.

November 26, 2009

Adelle – This is the address for today. It would be nice to pop in, if you care. We are both expected.

Tudor – Go back to your cheesy, syrup-coated dead-poet movies! By the way, I am done with you. I am not coming today.

Adelle – The movie I was watching was the Fox TV production, directed by Julie Taymore. The contemporary 1940s Roman times attempt to capture the history of Titus was bizarre. Not enchanting by any means. I couldn't watch more than 20 minutes of it. The director must have been deranged.

Tudor – You are deranged. It's based on Shakespeare's play, and your rigidity and lack of open-mindedness is equally annoying. What kind of critique is that? I'm just tired of this sham. We are not on the same wavelength by any means.

Adelle – I liked the lines and the cast. But she is one of the worst directors I've ever seen. High-budget waste. She disgraced both history and Shakespeare – he'd roll in his grave if he'd seen his play tarnished that way. Exaggerated and disturbing!

Tudor – You are hopeless.

Adelle – Your excuses are getting … hmm … old.

Adelle – (Many hours later at my friends' house.) The kids are playing Beethoven on the piano so well.

Tudor – Tell them to adopt you.

Adelle – And now Mozart … it's heartbreaking! Really! The kids are only teenagers.

Adelle – (Sends a picture of the family cat.) Say hi to Diego!

Tudor – And goodbye to Adelle!

Adelle – Quit saying goodbye. We are one.

I read the words on the screen, sent them off into cyberspace, and wondered if I still believed them.

Chapter XXX
The Butterfly Holiday Party

My darling love, a butterfly
Your weightless wings deceive
The red and black cover a lie
With pleasure I receive

Your stay in my palm is bliss
The moment's eye to blink
Stay! I want your mortal kiss
My life without it is a crypt

December 12 was right around the corner. I was busy planning my holiday party, an elaborate affair that both excited and worried me since I wasn't sure if Tudor and his family would be there. Butterflies decorated everything, from the invitations to my dress.

December 3, 2009
Adelle – I'm home today, if you'd like to get lunch.
Tudor - Go to work!
Adelle – Luca is licking everything in sight – furniture, windows, mirror … what is wrong with her?
Tudor – That's what she does at my house too.
Adelle – I wonder if she's missing some vitamins.
Tudor – She's missing a brain. Runs in the family.
Tudor – I wouldn't be surprised with the shit you're feeding her.

Adelle – Yeah … that's right.

Adelle – She's getting carrots and cheese. But I'll get her some dog vitamins as well.

Tudor – You're missing vitamins and proteins too, for that matter.

Tudor – Give her some meat. Give yourself some too!

Adelle – Proteins for sure. I do chew on fruits and veggies a lot. Fine … I'll buy some steaks.

Tudor – Whatever. Anorexic city!

Adelle – Do you even know what anorexic is? I weigh 101 pounds now and work out more often. I'm fine. My goal is never to slip below 100 pounds again.

Tudor – OK. Aucschwitz refugee!

Adelle – In fact, I'm getting hungry … wouldn't expect you care much though. Hmm … the first snow.

Tudor – I'm starving. Going with Luke to my bar on Clark. We just finished playing tennis. If you want some chicken wings, that's all I'll offer.

Adelle – That'll do.

I grabbed a cab to Wrigleyville. Tudor and Luke were already at a table in the middle of the bar. Not many people showed up before five on weekdays. The two men stood out just as they had the time when Tudor asked me to join them at Elephant's. I found their vulgar Romanian-English chit-chat as entertaining as ever. A doctor and an artist … one as morally corrupt as the other, one with a wife and a loud mouth but with no hot "action," and the other, a fox without equal, with no "obligations," who used sarcasm and humor to get more action than he could handle.

After we ate, Tudor and I went to his house in Wood Dale.

December 5, 2009

Adelle – Got some fabulous NY steaks from a butcher west of the Loop. We can cook dinner tomorrow. I'll need your expertise on that though.

Tudor – OK.

Tudor – (Several hours later) I can't see you tomorrow, or next weekend at all. Or ever again. I don't feel right about it.

Adelle – I wouldn't expect you would feel good about what you do. It's all fun for a while. Temporary satisfaction is not to be confused with happiness.

Tudor – I won't bug you again. Sorry to make you feel miserable at Christmas, but I'm miserable too.

Adelle – I want to find the secret of making you happy. I suppose I've failed so far.

Tudor – You've tried it all. You cannot blame yourself. We're all doomed to failure from the moment we're born.

Adelle – We are made to find ourselves … the trouble is that, sometimes we find the secret to life too late … not early enough to enjoy a peaceful Christmas or a happy New Year.

Tudor – I can't. I don't feel it, as much as I try.

Adelle – Clear up your phone list of anyone but true friends. Same with Facebook. Once you get a message from a number not on your list, delete it. Try it sometime. Then you'll be free.

Tudor – That's not the answer. I can ignore people I don't like.

Adelle – Well … narrow the list to those women you would not be tempted to do.

Tudor – After you, there's nobody on my list anyway.

Adelle – After 'S' you mean. Funny – I was always one of the last ones to have to stand up in class in Romania because of it. Worked well for me in the end.

Tudor – I'm going to sleep. Fuck it all!

Adelle – Sleep well, love.

December 6, 2009

Adelle – I am really really, hmmmm … reading the whole day only just pushed me over the edge.

Tudor – She doesn't want me. I cannot be with her during the holidays, and I will not be with you as a compromise. Fucking blame God!

Adelle – YOU ONLY THINK YOU ARE IN LOVE WITH HER BECAUSE SHE IS REJECTING YOU! Is that what you want me to do to make you run after me?   It's easier than you imagine.

Tudor – I'm talking to the walls. You keep singing your refrain, as if I have no wishes, but I'm misguided and need your salvation.

Tudor – I only called you when I wanted to have sex, to satisfy my animal instinct.

Adelle – You will find out soon enough who you really love. It will be rough ride through, to say the least. I thought it'd come to this. The gloves are off.

December 7, 2009

Adelle – I want to see you full of life, not having to bring flowers to a grave forty years from now! What are you doing? I adore you, even if you put me through hell! If you push me away now, I'll never come back.

Tudor – I'm working at home.

Tudor – Forty years from now? You're optimistic about both longevities. I hope to die sooner than that. Actually tomorrow would be a good day.

Adelle – I can't contain my tears. I just want … *you* … you sculpting. Everything else will fall into place far easier. The rest is only added bonus.

Tudor – No reason, really.

Gabriela Sbarcea

Adelle – The world is in the center of your palms. All great sculptors were architects as well, I just learned. Your drawings are brilliant.

Tudor – You're the only one who thinks I'm God. I know my value. Zero.

Tudor – (Sends a picture of his plans for his new place above the restaurant.)

Adelle – You can make a palace out of a cottage. (The space where he planned to build was limited.)

Adelle – I love a man who can make something out of anything.

Tudor – What?

Adelle – A home out of earth, water, and wood - a knife out of an old piece of steel, a machine out of a manual thing, an arrow out of a branch.

Tudor – What about all this? (He sends another picture of his building plan.)

Adelle – Your skill and talent is why I adore you, among other things.

December 8, 2009

Tudor – I will not make it to your party, but apparently my aunt and uncle will.

Adelle – I am glad to hear they're coming. I hope your mom will also. They can pick her up and drop her off at home. As for you ... should I pick you up or send a limo?

Tudor – I am not coming. Nor is my mom.

Adelle – This is my Christmas gift for you ... I can't force you. If you do show up, with your mom, it will be a pleasant surprise.

Adelle – (Sends Tudor a picture of the dress she planned to buy for the party.) I am going to need help with zipping it up.

Tudor – I'm only good at *unzipping*.

Adelle – I'll need that too afterwards.

265

Adelle – *Une miserre, quelle une miserre.*

Tudor – My God, please consult a French teacher about grammar and syntax.

Adelle – Hmm … I will. I just don't care much about either. At least misery is spelled right, and it is a feminine substantive, so I thought *quelle* and *une* would be the right pronouns.

Tudor – Syntax is like in Romanian. You say, "*Ce tristețe!*", not "*Ce o tristețe!*" The article becomes understood.

Adelle – Makes sense. *Merci, Monsieur!* I do need to polish that aspect of both my English and French.

Tudor – Stick to what you know, that's all: numbers!

Adelle – Not. A little about a lot.

Tudor – No. That's the wrong philosophy: well-rounded bullshit. That'll translate to mediocrity in all and expertise in none.

Adelle – I agree. But I am curious. One day I just want to write. I see your point though.

Adelle – The proper well-rounded lady is a myth in today's society. It seems there is no room for her.

Tudor – Write? I see your stubbornness has no limits. Do you recognize that you have not mastered English to that level and have simultaneously forgotten the little Romanian you knew? I don't mean to sound harsh, but you have to wake up to reality! You flatter me and my trade the same way, without understanding what an amateur I am.

Tudor – I am going to sleep. I recommend you do the same. Dreams are better left for that part of the day.

Adelle – If I manage to publish a book in the traditional publishing way, and my grammar is pitiful, but I am working on it, then you will have your own gallery as I breathe and exist, for I will not die otherwise. Any reality starts with a dream.

December 9, 2009

Adelle – My life will be so much clearer after this party.

Tudor – I doubt it.

Adelle – It will. It's about time for me to grow up. And this event will do it. I am 31.

Tudor – Sad. But you will survive. You're relentless.

Adelle – Have you ever thought about finishing Demi's sculpture to send it to her for Christmas? (He started but never finished a sculpture based on Demi Moore's *Streaptease* film posters.)

Tudor – Not this Christmas.

Adelle – (Later.) I just watched a Nostradamus documentary on the History Channel. How subjective everything is. His interpretations are so open to debate.

Tudor – Of course. They're vague riddles open to numerous interpretations. What did you expect?

Adelle – You know what? I'll bet there must have been many generations before ours to think the end of the world was almost here. In a way they were right. The end of numerous civilizations. But not the world.

Tudor – True. People always took pleasure in predicting the end. It's like they actually want to see it happen.

December 10, 2009

Adelle – Hot bubble bath! Hot bubble bath!

Tudor – Cold shower! Cold shower!

Adelle – Maybe a cold shower on reality.

Tudor – I think you should try it anyway.

Adelle – You'd suggest anything to get rid of me.

Tudor – And still, nothing would work. My God, you are like Anna from Manole's legend. I'll have to bury you in some wall.

Adelle – Oh well … so be it. I made peace with my fate a long time ago.

Tudor – We all have to do that. You are not alone.

Adelle – Life has a weird way of setting things in their tracks, sooner or later. You will get what or who you want. Bad things and people weed themselves out in time.

Tudor – Same for you.

Adelle – That will be perfect.

Adelle – Unfortunately he wants me "berried" in a wall.

Tudor – You mean buried, not berried.

Adelle – Thanks!

Tudor – I am the next best thing to a dictionary.

Adelle – I know. Every time you point one of those out to me, I never repeat that mistake.

Tudor – It's ok. You seem to have an endless reserve of new ones.

Adelle – You have your hands full in that case.

Tudor – If I wanted to teach English, I'd be doing it. I have my hands full with plenty of other things.

Adelle – Boobs … ass … etc.

Tudor – Among other things.

December 12, 2009

Adelle – Beauty hurts!

Tudor – And I won't be there to witness it all.

Adelle – I need desperate help with zipping the dress! My only option is the maintenance man …

Tudor – Good luck with him then!

Adelle – Stop it. Harra will come to help me.

Tudor – Good.

Adelle b- I still need someone to take me out of it.

True to his word, he didn't show up at my party. Tudor's aunt and uncle were there and their sorrow and regret over their missing nephew was evident. His aunt was as calm and dear natured a woman as his mother.

Gabriela Sbarcea

Naturally, I was humiliated in front of all my guests who kept asking about him. I held up my head bravely, but inside, I was burnt to ashes. His aunt noticed my sadness and took me by the hand. "Please, please forgive him and give him more time. He is a wonderful man."

December 13, 2009

Adelle – (At 2:00 a.m.) Only because someone really special asked me to keep you close, I will not do what I had planned following your last display of utter hate toward me.

Tudor – (At 4:30 am) There is no hate here. Only constant depression.

Tudor – You are a classy woman. I just don't deserve you. I'm attracted to Neanderthals. Find someone you can be proud of.

Adelle – Ten months late into your assessment. The only stupid idiot tonight was me, so far as everyone else was concerned.

Adelle – You can probably draw some parallels, but I was told, without even asking, your ex is seeing someone she is serious about. You've fucked up enough lives! Pick one and make her happy!

Tudor – We are all stupid. You're no exception. I felt like that every time I threw a party.

Tudor – You keep picking on Andrada, but your jealousy is misdirected. I'm not longing for her. You're wrong. She was never good for me. I just didn't want to accept failure. My ideals lie elsewhere, where even your beautiful imagination can't reach. I will not break any more hearts. I'm done.

Adelle – What's that? How could I even fancy you're done? Tonight was not only a party and you know it. I was a pitiful spectacle, but that's my own fault. I believed in you, US, in the end.

Tudor – You were warned.

269

Tudor – (The following day at 5:00 pm) – Still pissed?

Adelle – What am I going to do with you? No. I'm not pissed. Just disappointed.

Tudor – Me too.

Adelle – It's got to be something else. What have I done?

Tudor – You were born.

Adelle – Well ... apparently the feeling is mutual.

Tudor – I didn't ask for it.

Adelle – Me either. I was a mistake, remember?

Tudor – No. You are my punishment.

Adelle – I don't mean to be.

Tudor – And I don't know what I've done to deserve it.

Adelle – I am wondering ...

Tudor – Did my uncle show up for the party? Luke?

Adelle – Both. Luke harassed all my good-looking girlfriends.

Tudor – He's a pig and so am I.

Adelle – You two are not exactly the same ... by no means.

Tudor – I am worse. He's only talk.

Adelle - Maybe. What happens behind closed doors is your own concern.

Tudor – And do you think hypocrisy should be rewarded? I'm a jackass. And I feel really bad for not coming to your party, or for Thanksgiving.

Adelle – No. It shouldn't, because that will only encourage you to do it again and again. But you are *my* jackass ... you tell me what to do to punish you!

Tudor – A good spanking

Adelle – Oh ... it'll be good, alright!

Adelle – You are not in a position to give orders. Today.

Tudor – I'm at my mom's house and going to take a nap now.

Adelle – Get your sleepy and unshowered ass over here later.

Tudor – Don't tempt me!

Adelle – I am!

Tudor – I can meet you for coffee if you want, in the morning.

Adelle – I WORK ON MONDAYS!

Tudor – I'm so tired. The whole last week I slept three hours a night, working on that stupid scale-model building. I'm constantly sleepy.

Tudor – (Later.)I can't make it tonight. I can't stay awake and I just slept an hour at my mom's place.

Adelle – Do you want me to drive to your place in my underwear and a fur coat?

Tudor – You're too much. No. I'll come to you.

Tudor – (Ten minutes later) I can't come. I have to stick to my principles. You are a lovely lady, but I cannot be with you. Not just for sex. I don't need it that desperately. Honestly, I don't even want to do what I'll regret tomorrow. I'll stay in and go to sleep instead.

Adelle – What principles are you talking about? We both know what we want from one another.

Tudor – No. I don't even want that sporadic carnal indulgence and you want love eternal.

Adelle – We have both

Tudor – Very tempting. You know I'm a sucker for your body, but it's wrong. I will send you another nasty message tomorrow after sleeping with you, giving you endless reasons why we cannot be together. Yet at the same time I cannot touch another woman either. You are a witch. You put a curse on me. Remove it!

Adelle - You do realize that's what's called love. It is the same reason why, if the prince of England were to ask for my hand in marriage tomorrow, I would turn him down, because he's not you.

Tudor – You'd be happier with the prince of England. Trust me.

Adelle – I'm not joking. You read it in my palm on our first date.

Tudor – I was only kidding! I can't read palms.

Adelle – Well … you're not the only one who has said that to me.

Tudor – Said what?

Adelle – That I will marry for love only.

Tudor – Yeah, well, you were almost married a year ago. That was for love, too. I wouldn't put too much weight in these oracles.

Adelle – I did not do it because of it! Predictions are whimsical, but it just hits you when they come true.

Tudor – You are not in love with me. I gave you all the reasons to feel the opposite. You are simply ambitious and stubborn and cannot conceive of defeat.

Adelle – If you imagine I'd take a small fraction of the crumbs you feed me sometimes from anyone else, you've committed a great mistake. Only love can explain it.

Tudor – I'll make you tired of the chase soon enough. Andrada got tired of it, too, up to the point of being repulsed by my very presence.

Adelle – Try me. I am my own character.

Adelle – Although some of my friends might start putting a ransom on your head soon.

Tudor – You are your own character? What does *that* mean?

Adelle – I am my own … my character is different from other women's characters, and so is yours from other men's.

Tudor - I couldn't care less about your friends. They obviously don't know you too well … *or* your obsessive behavior. Why is it my fault I'm not in love with you? I can't blame any of the women I'm infatuated with for not feeling the same about me. God's design. Blame *Him*!

Adelle – It's a joke. They figured it's me at this point and not you. And I'm not merely a woman you're infatuated with ... if it were only that, trust me, you would have drowned in hatred by now.

Tudor – You should feel only contempt for a guy who doesn't give a damn about you. Why do I trigger the opposite reaction?

Adelle – Because despite all the crap you dish out to me, I am like a dog – I feel your mind and heart. That's what love does.

Tudor – I feel as if I should reward you for your loyalty.

Adelle – I'm wagging my tail.

Tudor – I'll have a treat for you next time I see you.

Adelle – Unbelievable!

Tudor – Yeah ... can you say that?

Adelle – I agree ... beyond nuts.

Tudor – Nuts. That's all you think about. Nuts and hot dogs.

Chapter XXXI
Year's End

Twelve months gathered in a bag
Snow is gray and sun is sad
All is nothing, one is all
I see endings, beginnings fall

Shakespeare's play, *All's Well That Ends Well,* was a malignant thought. It had to be.

I kneeled before God every night and prayed: "God, give me peace and quiet in my life. Bring the man I would love next to me, so I can make him happy, so he can make me happy in turn. Let us get married and have healthy, happy, intelligent, beautiful children together. Let us live in harmony. Will it be Tudor? God ... Thy will be made."

Maybe we had no future ... but I wished for one more than I wished for a tomorrow.

December 14, 2009
Adelle – This must be a joke.
Tudor - What?
Adelle - My gym is absolutely full!
Tudor – And it will be till Spring
Adelle – Not if I'm not in shape.
Tudor – You are in shape. Stick is a shape.
Adelle – Running usually helps – sex is only an occasional substitute.

Tudor – LOL. Yeah, well, I'm sure you have plenty of offers …

Adelle – Well … they are only as good as the people making them. I have no interest in them.

Tudor – For me too.

Adelle – Doubt that. Unless I turn into you …

Tudor – I think I need help. I've *already* turned into you.

Adelle – We are flippin' hilarious!

Tudor – We are flippin' flipped.

Adelle – Never thought I'd hear that. No … you are you and I am the same. We just started melting into each other and that's causing the confusion. How weird …

Tudor – You'll be fine one day, I promise. You've damaged me forever.

Adelle – T, I adore you. How could I have changed you? All I wish, as I said so many times before, is to make you happy. Your smile is worth the world to me.

Tudor – You are a witch. I tried touching two other women after you and couldn't get an erection. Lift the curse, please, and then I'll be able to smile again.

Adelle – Try more women, you donkey! You now get to understand what true love is. I could have been with other men as well since you started treating me so deplorably. BUT I CAN'T!

Tudor – I think all I need is time. To go out into the world and explore! Yes, tits and ass! Time to break with the past and move on. That's my New Year's resolution.

Tudor – You'll be happy some day. I'm sure. Your prince will come.

Adelle – Get on your damned white horse at once!

Tudor – I'm waiting for January first.

Tudor - My aunt and uncle loved your party. And Luke too, of course.

December 15, 2009

Tudor – Are you stuck at the train crossing?

Adelle – Yes. And is it long!

Tudor – That's what all the girls say!

Adelle – Well … it's also, hmmmmm … damn! Too bad I have to go to work.

Tudor – This coffee is unbearably hot.

Tudor – If you didn't have to work, I'm sure I'd be hobbling around on crutches tomorrow.

Tudor – These train operators are absolutely shameless for doing this in rush hour traffic. Can't wait to move out of this shithole.

Adelle - You'll miss the wildlife.

Tudor – I'm ready to dive into the *human* wildlife of Wrigleyville.

Adelle – A wide variety of specimens.

Tudor – I'll be like a pig in a field of clover.

Adelle – Sure thing.

Tudor – (Later, after I had sent a message to Rita who kept texting Tudor the night before while they were at dinner asking her to stop texting him.) Just got your text to Rita. You do some stupid things sometimes, without thinking that they'll eventually get back to me. Go to work and stop texting to the wrong people, or we'll never talk again.

December 16, 2009

Adelle – My building has a holiday party this evening from six on. If you want, stop by. Drinks, food, live band usually, and lots of my neighbors.

Tudor – I have work to do.

December 17, 2009

Adelle – Look, I hate to do this over texts, as I hated it every time you did it. But I am not going to wait 6 years to get a ring in an envelope after you fucked with me so much I can't even stand looking at you. Sex is fabulous, but it's not worth the emotional jerking around you put me through. Good bye, my love! I love you too much to allow you to damage me.

Tudor – I'm glad you're finally being reasonable and logical about this.

Adelle – When you finally admit your love to me, you'll know what to do.

Tudor – Don't hold your breath …

Adelle – How could I? Had I done that for every time you said you'd be someplace and weren't, I would have been dead by the end of the month. I CAN'T MAKE A BACK-UP plan for EVERY second of my life … just in case you don't show up!

Tudor – OK, then, please carry on with this morning's plan. Seems like a good one. You'll be a nice notch in my belt.

I capitulated … I hid from the world to lick my wounds for some time. He won yet another battle … soon enough the war would be his, and this … his finest victory.

I spent Christmas and New Year's without him that year. It was agonizing. I wanted to live no longer.

Chapter XXXII
Don't Fall In Love With Me!

My heart is bandaged by sweet love
My mind is cropped by madness
My soul is caged with bars of gold
And I succumb to sadness

The first week of January was frigid in more ways than one. I dreaded waking up in the morning, I despised work, and I was repulsed by the very idea of men. My friends lugged me around town for dinner, movies, parties … anything at all to help pull me out of my funk. They hoped I'd meet someone new to get me out of the emotional purgatory where Tudor had abandoned me for the holidays.

I had not heard from him since Christmas Eve when I asked him to check his front door where Santa left a package for him. I sent him the unlocked flip blackberry he said he wanted. He replied that whatever it was, he wouldn't open it. Instead, he would make sure it ended up in the trash.

On January 8, I sent him an email. He called me way past midnight and I kindly asked him if we could reconvene the next day at a more civilized hour. He texted me.

January 9, 2010
Tudor – What are you doing?
Adelle – Watching *Perfect Love.*

Tudor – Keep watching. Only in the movies.

Adelle – Ours is better.

Tudor – Ours is an illusion.

Tudor – I'm falling asleep at my mom's. Worked on plumbing till just now. Moved the laundry room. All works fine. I'll sleep here.

Adelle – Say hi to your mom.

Tudor – I will. Wanna meet for coffee tomorrow?

Adelle – *Oui.*

Tudor – I'll call you in the morning. Good night! - XOX.

Tudor – I just remembered I have to be at my house in the morning. The guy from the bank is coming to serve me the foreclosure notice. Wanna come tonight?

Adelle – In about an hour.

Tudor had tried to sell his house in a short-sale, just to get out from under it, throughout 2009. None of the deals were approved by the bank. Now it was official: he was going to be in foreclosure.

That night I found him in his enormous bathtub in a bathroom that more closely resembled a spa. He had surrounded the tub with candles and opened up a bottle of red wine, aligning a few towels by the tub near two satin robes. When he wanted to, he could make everything perfect. He always remembered what I told him I liked, even if only in passing. He smiled as I sank into the mass of delicate bubbles.

January 11, 2010

Tudor – What's up?

Adelle – Watching *One Tree Hill* and transcribing some of our text messages.

Adelle – How is your back?

Tudor – My back is killing me. My front is longing to probe your insides.

Adelle – Apparently my therapy for your back yesterday was quite ineffective.

Tudor – What therapy?

Adelle – Exactly …

Tudor – Well, it'll be over soon.

Tuesday January 11, 2010

Tudor – Can I see you tonight? I have to go home.

Adelle – *Mais non*! I am busy. Maybe Thursday … or Friday.

Tudor – Thursday then, or skiing over the weekend.

Adelle – Friday is better. We can leave early Saturday and drive up to Wisconsin.

Adelle – There's only one thing on my mind since Sunday.

Tudor – What's that?

Adelle – How splendid your certain "attribute" is.

Tudor – Good answer. Well, I am keeping myself busy with work to distract the "attribute" from taking over my brain.

I'd hired a cleaning service to polish my apartment once a month. I maintained it fairly well most of the time, but the Hispanic man I had hired two years earlier and trusted to clean and do the laundry did a magnificent job. When Tudor learned that my hired help was a man, the snide remarks began falling from his lips like gumdrops from a plastic sack and didn't stop until we'd reached my office.

January 14. 2010

Tudor – Hugs and kisses! Juan.

Adelle – Lick on the nose.

Tudor – I'm jealous.

Adelle – You are funny.

Tudor – Funny looking? You mean like an alien.
Tudor – (Several hours later) I miss you
Adelle – Miss you too!

I packed up Luca and went to Espresso. The horrid Eastern European café was full of smoke as always. I always felt as if I was on display whenever I walked into either Espresso or Elephant's: just another of Tudor's possessions, another trinket that he showed off to the same circle of people, especially the waitresses and the owners of the places he had frequented for years.

The next day we went to breakfast at my favorite Greek diner near his house. I had reminded him frequently that he needed to start sculpting again. But on that particular morning, I was adamant.

January 16, 2010
Tudor – I'm too tired. I'm good for nothing, I'm going to sleep. I slept like crap last night. This morning you destroyed all my motivation to work. What a morale booster you are!

Adelle – I thought you liked old-school motivation techniques.

Tudor – I cannot see you tomorrow. I'll be busy with the work I didn't do today and I should have.

Adelle – *Oui* baby! *Je comprendre tout a fait.*

Tudor – You depressed me to no end today. I was good for nothing. I hope your day is good tomorrow.

Adelle – *Je suis desolee …*

Adelle – Well … pardon me, but what am I to say? I may be a completely uninformed idiot, but I happen to love your work. And I cannot separate you from it. Educate me.

January 20, 2010
Adelle – I just can't see my life without you.

281

Tudor – I'm such an idiot. I'm gambling with your affection.

January 22, 2010
Tudor – I miss you. Can I see you today?
Adelle – Perhaps.
Tudor – OK. If not, let me know when you are free. I have plenty of work to keep me busy.
Adelle – I've committed to accompanying Harra to a Persian event.
Tudor – Fine. Call me after that then.
Tudor – (Sends a picture of the Michael Jackson body he sculpted on commission the summer before, with perfect looking six-pack and muscles.) – me in the real world.
Adelle – If you looked like that, I wouldn't want to see you. There's something weird about it.
Tudor – By the way, forget about tomorrow. You suck.
Adelle – Yes. I have a phone next to me, and not a man!

January 23, 2010
Adelle – Pourquoi tu fais ca ?
Tudor – Because you are crazy.
Adelle – Oui .. je suis un grande idiote parce que je vous aime !
Tudor – OK then. Come see me!

Tudor was tucked in when I tip-towed into his bedroom. Twenty minutes later, he rolled off of me and onto his side. "If we're going to continue this way, I may need to marry you. It doesn't get any better than this." I remained quiet, my heart filled with joy. How I loved those moments, the inner peace, the serenity. It was like meditating, like being in some sort of religious trance. It was as if I had just touched heaven itself with my fingertips.

We went out the next evening and danced until the early hours of the morning. His energy level and enthusiasm far exceeded what I thought a 44-year-old man should possess. I was living in my very own fairy tale - one that existed in real life...

> January 24, 2010
> Tudor – I am so tired.
> Adelle – Are you smiling though? I took another nap.
> Tudor – I hate you!
> Adelle – Baby!
> Tudor – I'm at Elephant's again. I need caffeine!
> Adelle – It's nearly 10! Sleep is better. I'm watching Emma on channel 11. British old-school manners are extreme, but they're so respectful and elegant.
> Tudor – I have it at home on tape. Unfortunately British movies only show the intrigue in high society, people with no daily worries other than creating drama where there should be none.
> Adelle – It's part of human nature. Drama refines a character, regardless of his station in life.
> Tudor – Right. And women thrive on drama.
> Adelle – Not necessarily. Not after a certain point in life.
> Tudor – Going home. I'm so down; I don't even wanna go home. I wonder what would happen if one day I'd just disappear.
> Adelle – Why are you down? You are the light of my life, the hope for some and the salvation for others.
> Tudor – And the darkness for myself. I wish I had died already!

January 27, 2010

Adelle – Work is crazy today. I've literally been buried in numbers for the past two days.

Tudor – Take a break and relax. I have to work on my mom's basement.

Adelle – The year-end financial report is just making me sick. My deadline is tomorrow at noon.

Tudor – Don't waste time texting. I want to work too.

January 28, 2010

Tudor – Wanna go with me to Cozumel for our birthdays?

Adelle – That would be perfect.

Tudor – Let's look up tickets tomorrow.

Adelle – Super. There are some great deals this season.

Tudor – Any plans this Saturday?

Adelle – Do you remember the gangsters' theme party I mentioned the other day?

Tudor – I had another birthday party to go to. Wanted to invite you. I guess I'll have to blow her off after I said yes. A friend I used to work with.

Adelle – This party is only until 1. Then we can go to your girl's party if you want.

Tudor – Alright.

Tudor – Do you have a hat for me? A gangster-type thing? I can't afford a new suit now. I'll sew the torn pants on my brand new pinstripe suit.

Adelle – I have a hat. Don't worry about the suit. Wear the suspenders, and we'll need a cigar.

Tudor – I have a cigar and suspenders.

Adelle – Perfect. It'll be a blast.

January 29, 2010

Tudor – At what time am I seeing you tomorrow?

Adelle – If dinner starts at 8, how does 7:30 sound?

Adelle – Still missing a couple of pieces from my costume.

Tudor – What?

Adelle – A handbag, and a pearl necklace.

Tudor – The country is burning and the old lady is brushing her hair.

Adelle – Exactly.

Tudor – (Many hours later, on Friday night around 11.) Where are you?

Adelle – Home. Watching a French movie.

Tudor – Come to Piece Bar on North Avenue.

Adelle – Give me 20 min.

Tudor – Time's up.

Adelle – So many cops on North.

Tudor – There's more in here.

We were able to make both parties, just as we'd planned. Mark was an eccentric kid, or so I liked to think of him. I met him at a bar in Chicago when he walked up to me and gave me his number on a napkin. That was when I was on a break with Tudor. I never called him. But I did text him ... he was simply charming.

I had turned down a few dates before he invited me and my friends to his birthday party. It was a costume party he was throwing at a new hip club in Chi-Town. Before long, Tudor, Olivia, Harra and Claudiu arrived. Tudor asked me, "So how do you know this guy?"

I hesitated for a moment before replying. "We used to work together."

We danced and drank and made several new friends. Mark shook Tudor's hand at one point and said, "You're a lucky man, I hope you know that." Tudor told me what he'd said on our way to his house just before sunrise.

February 1, 2010

Adelle – Easier to bathe a Tasmanian devil than Luca.

Tudor – Oh, Adelle, I am drunk and I call things by their true name as a result. I couldn't care less about your stupid dog! As a matter of fact, I couldn't care less about its master. I'm just a hypocritical good Samaritan. But I've had enough. I feel better by myself, as if I just escaped Alcatraz. Find a guy to suit your needs.

Adelle – Mark is not someone I used to work with, but someone who courted me and I turned him down because I decided to go back with you, to give you another chance. You are a joke.

Tudor – Well, now is your chance to redeem yourself. You are on your own.

Adelle – You hurt me! I saw you talking with him at the party. I don't know what he said to you. But that's pointless now.

Adelle – I was always on my own. I had NEVER expected you to be there for any help, or anything else, for that matter. Except for fucking. But, as I said, I am the fool, and I hold my head up high, because I loved you, even if you are a notorious player.

Chapter XXXIII
February Cold

My feelings nestle frozen love
I willed to warm it up
The flame died off on icy shore
The hope's forever shut

My dad became ill and went into chemo in early February. I asked Tudor if he could take care of Luca while I went home for two weeks. His answer was a blunt "No." That trip home was one of the most difficult ones of my life for several reasons, not the least of which was my dad's serious illness, my parents' harsh judgment of my situation with Tudor, my second Valentine's day spent alone thinking of him, and not a single word from the man I spent the past thirteen months of my life trying to please and make happy. I sent him an email now and then. They all got lost in the abyss of Tudor's cold indifference.

I fought to redeem a man who refused to redeem himself from his own weakness and vice. My heart was shattered once again. I felt physically ill and found myself living in my doctor's office. My doctor thought I had a crush on him.

When I returned to the states, I was not surprised to find Tudor still missing in action. Sometime in early March, I gave in to my friends' advice and accepted an invitation to a party being thrown by an attractive man who lived in my building. I'd been avoiding him for months, ever since the last holiday party, which of course Tudor hadn't attended, saying only, "I'm sorry. I have work to do. "

I kept busy publishing a series of articles in my home town newspapers. It was a *feuilleton*, a biweekly gossip column, on cultural differences, interwoven with my life experiences as an immigrant in the U.S. Although I wrote only positive things about him, I did label him a "Casanova" in one story. Even at that, I used only a nickname for him in my articles. I emailed him the links to the pieces. He responded by posting some brutally nasty comments about them. He refused to respond to any of the inquiries I sent him via email. The pain I felt in that first month back only helped me immerse myself into my writing even deeper than before.

I called him on his birthday. He hung-up as soon as he heard my voice. He still had a set of my condo keys. He had crushed my heart … but he no longer owned it, nor did he deserve to hold the keys to either any longer.

I e-mailed him one last time on March 17, 2010.

Adelle

Listen … it was rude enough the way things ended YET AGAIN … and WHEN. But regardless, I am doing better than you think, and everything is fabulous.

I wanted to ask you if you would either mail or drop off the keys to my condo sometime. I don't feel like spending another couple of hundred dollars changing the locks.

Happy birthday by the way.

I gave you over a month to get it together, and you failed. I started seeing someone else this weekend. He is an American, a professional boxer, and I'm very happy with him. I don't ever want to see you again for as long as I exist. It would be best if you would mail my keys. You know my address.

A

Tudor

I will make it simple for you: there is nothing of yours that I possess, not keys, nor any other articles you may think you left behind. I have disposed of everything in connection with you.

Unlike your fantasies, I truly am involved with someone and am finally happy! You brought this onto yourself, through your own delusions of "talented penmanship." I think that in doing so, you have sealed your own fate in the community you tried so hard to impress.

Carry on with your life in circles outside the ones in which you have already embarrassed yourself!

Adelle

Ah, yes, writing. The articles. I'm not talented and never claimed to be. It is something I want to do, as you know well. You encouraged me early on.

And I am happy for your happiness.

As for my embarrassment in the community, you know better. I could care less of what others think of me and the fact that a Casanova proved out to be just that. You had that reputation long before I met you. You simply had to prove it to me as well ... despite all my efforts, my affection, and patience with you and your tawdry sexual escapades. I hope you learned something from what you've done to me, to Andrada and the rest. Hopefully this time you will keep it straight and make yourself TRULY happy.

As I said, I never lacked ANYTHING. When I felt things weren't right, I moved on. I stayed with you for more than a year because I am not one to give up easily in the face of a challenge. I wanted to believe in you. WHAT A JOKE that proved to be. A funny one, I must admit.

But I do need to thank you for putting an end to that nonsense. I NOW know what it is to be with a man, and not a Casanova. You made me physically ill to the point where I needed medication.

YOU WERE WORTHLESS. Every time I humiliated myself, I did so to get a reaction out of you. Pure and simple. Not even that worked. You are as cold and heartless as the stone with which you work.

I'm finally happy and no longer stare at my phone, as if my life depended on it. He is a man ... a true man ... in every sense of the word. I'll just leave it at that.

Have fun, my talented artist!

Adelle

Olivia called me that evening, telling me to make sure I sat down to hear what she had to tell me. Tudor called asking her for my address to mail me the keys he had found while cleaning his place. She informed him she would text him the address the following day.

At midnight, a phone call from my doorman woke me up. "Miss, a gentleman left an envelope for you at the front desk." I went down to get it a few minutes later. It was signed "Casanova" for Adelle.

I opened the envelope and, beside the keys, there was a note on a pre-printed sheet of paper with his name and address at the top and a cute little kitten, belly up, playing with a teddy bear, on the bottom. It read, " It's too bad your thoughtlessness and self-infatuation got the best of you. You really have burned the last bridge. Good luck with Mr. Boxer guy! (The real man)."

Epilogue

It had come down to a choice: I no longer had the strength or the will to keep fighting for my butterfly. I released him from our dance. His colorful, august, and delicate wings weighed too heavily under our perfect love. A butterfly needs sunshine, infinite space, and many different flowers where he can rest for a while his gracious and fragile body to prepare for life anew. He may linger in your palm a bit longer ... but beware, my darling reader, the flower next to you, whether smaller, less distinguished, or even perfectly dull, to him, it will be more alluring and dazzling than anything else in the world.

Do not despair: A butterfly belongs in the reddish horizon of a sunset, where the evening sky flows into the real world, where our hidden passions and unspoken desires take form, become substance, and dissipate our daily routine. His mere presence morphs a physical existence into a fairy tale, a fantasy, until you find yourself wondering if he was ever really there at all. Possibly not. Possibly so. If so, he was a chimera, changing who you are and what you think until you emerge only a mere shell of who you were before.

Perhaps I chose to allow him to lure me into his dance, abandoning all before him, recognizing him as the king of it all, the God to whom I submitted voluntarily, regardless of the moral values with which I was raised. Maybe this was my ultimate act of rebellion against the rigid upbringing and unbending values my parents had imposed upon me, simply for having been born. Did it matter to them

291

that I was unique, my own person, an individual of complex moral integrity? I'm not so sure.

Did I fear commitment, myself, and had Tudor been my subconscious rationalization of that fact? Was it my chasing the butterfly that made me feel safe?

Or was it the fact that he was Romanian, just as I am, and we had a common denominator in our values and culture? I missed home; since I wasn't ready to move back, I looked for someone who could bring me closer to it, despite the physical distance. Had I yearned to rediscover my lost national identity in the hands of a stanchly Romanian man, one of my own kind? Could that have blindfolded me into this disjointed union?

In the end, he was my darling butterfly, my guiding and inspiring light out of the dark of my life, the secret fantasy I had held deep within my bosom since high-school when I buried myself in my romantic novels. He was my rough, unpolished, and most precious diamond whose sharp edges nearly drove me to agony. I had glided through Paradise and Purgatory with him, swaying to the sweet music of our pure and insane passion.

Who knows what lay before Tudor and I for the remaining days of our lives? Was Tudor the reflection of his own sculpture, the man undressing his own skin? Were we only means to each other's ends?

I don't know the answers to these questions. I am no longer seeking them. In time, they may be unraveled before me, one by one.

CPSIA information can be obtained at www.ICGtesting.com
Printed in the USA
BVOW04s0234131213

339051BV00003B/18/P